PRAISE FOR

*The*

# COAST

'Lyrically written, *The Coast* is at once brooding and hopeful, a compelling story of loss and liberty and the capacity of the human mind to transcend boundaries.' **Meg Keneally, author of *Fled***

'Both riveting and heart-wrenching, *The Coast* is a fascinating story of love and endurance. Through Alice, Clea, Jack and Will, we are shown the importance of those fleeting moments of human connection and belonging. I always love Eleanor Limprecht's writing and what she chooses to write about.' **Mirandi Riwoe, author of *The Burnished Sun***

'Eleanor Limprecht is the most beautiful writer. With delicate precision and deep empathy, she brings to life the secret world of the lazaret at Little Bay and those who once lived within its confines. Few books have touched me so deeply.' **Suzanne Leal, author of *The Deceptions***

Eleanor Limprecht was born in Washington DC and grew up in the United States, Germany and Pakistan before moving to Australia in 2002. She is the author of *The Passengers* (Allen & Unwin, 2018), *Long Bay* (Sleepers Publishing, 2015) and *What Was Left* (Sleepers Publishing, 2013, shortlisted for the ALS Gold Medal). Her short fiction and essays have been published in various places including *Best Australian Stories, Sydney Noir, Griffith Review, Kill Your Darlings* and *The Big Issue*. She's been the recipient of various residencies, scholarships and grants including from the Australia Council, Copyright Agency and the Australian Society of Authors. Eleanor works as a lecturer in Creative Writing at UTS.

# *The* COAST

## ELEANOR LIMPRECHT

ALLEN&UNWIN
SYDNEY·MELBOURNE·AUCKLAND·LONDON

First published in 2022

asa AUSTRALIAN SOCIETY
OF AUTHORS

Allen & Unwin
83 Alexander Street
Crows Nest NSW 2065
Australia
Phone: (61 2) 8425 0100
Email:   info@allenandunwin.com
Web:     www.allenandunwin.com

NATIONAL
LIBRARY
OF AUSTRALIA
A catalogue record for this
book is available from the
National Library of Australia

ISBN 978 1 76087 940 2

Set in 13/17.6 pt Adobe Garamond Pro by Bookhouse, Sydney
Printed and bound in Australia by Griffin Press, part of Ovato

10 9 8 7 6 5 4 3 2 1

MIX
Paper from
responsible sources
FSC
www.fsc.org
FSC® C009448

The paper in this book is FSC® certified.
FSC® promotes environmentally responsible,
socially beneficial and economically viable
management of the world's forests.

*For Eliza and Sam*

. . . between grief and nothing I will take grief.

WILLIAM FAULKNER, *THE WILD PALMS*


Being a highly civilised community, and under strict and advanced sanitary legislation, with a high standard of personal and civic hygiene, this British dominion constitutes a community where leprosy should not be spread, and one where, should it occur, the source of infection—were it a matter of contagion—should be readily traced.

CECIL COOK, *THE EPIDEMIOLOGY OF LEPROSY IN AUSTRALIA*


And the leper in whom the plague is, his clothes shall be rent, and his head bare, and he shall put a covering upon his upper lip, and shall cry, Unclean, unclean.

LEVITICUS, 13:45

# Prologue

*Alice*

## 1926

Sixteen years captive. But this last year I have hardly felt it, the sky has opened instead of pressing down. When they take me out of doors I am floating. The air of the sickroom is thick and yellow, but out here the ceiling is blue, and beyond the palings is the sea. Sometimes I can still smell the ocean—salt and a fishy tang—seaweed at the back of my throat. I can imagine myself back in the clinker hull, waves spilling over the gunnels.

Three times a day they clean and dress my skin. First the scabs are washed with Eusol, then covered with cod-liver ointment and wrapped in a long ribbon of white bandage. Most places are numb. Some still make me flinch. I am vile but they are used to it: the scabs and sores, the fawnish skin. Each week Dr Stenger comes and touches me with his bare hand. He does not ask the questions he used to but speaks gently to me. I imagine the wrinkles on his forehead creasing. I want to touch his shoulder, to reassure him, but I am long used to not touching. You only need to see that look once to learn. To see how they back away. He scratches in his books, muttering to himself. *Buccal cavities and fauces, normal. Enlargements of glands in the neck. Slight, soft swelling of the right axillary glands. Butterfly swelling on face.*

How pretty it sounds. How deceiving. I remember the year I turned eleven, reading as he wrote: *She has grown three inches over the year.* I was proud of my height, for it made me seem like a normal girl. I thought of the branches I might reach now in the gum tree behind the house at Jiggi, how much quicker I'd climb. My sisters and brothers would be surprised when they saw me. *How you've grown*, Gran would say, when I returned home. *Three inches*, I'd reply.

•

I dreamed the other night that I was back at Jiggi. Looking after Annie, George, Hunter and Irene on the banks of the creek. Charlie was chopping wood in the low paddock. The rolling green hills and the basin of valley, the damp grassy smell. I dreamed that George, the baby, was splashing in the creek and went under, that when I pulled him out his skin was blue. I screamed and Charlie came running with his axe, his sun-flayed face furious and his arm swinging, and I held Annie in front of me for protection. He would not hurt one of his own. When I woke my nightdress was wet. Mama was saying my name. She touched my face—I knew from the sound rather than the sight or feel of it. The sound of her rough skin brushing my own.

'Are you hurting?' she asked.

'I was looking after Sid—only he was George still—and I let him drown.'

'It was just a dream of home. Hush, now.'

She did not remind me that he was gone—dead. Her blurred face hovered above me in the moonlight. I no longer saw the skin. The mottled and the bronzed, the thickening of the earlobes and nostrils.

I heard her climb back into her bed.

'Sleep, Alice. Morning is not far off.'

Let me stay asleep, then. Let me drown, too.

•

'Home' is a strange word for a place I have been away from nearly all my life. For Mama, Jiggi is home—the place where she was born, and her two babies. But for me this is home. This walled prison between the hospital and the sea; our cottages; the stony sandy soil from which we have eked a garden. The flowering coral tree; the melon patch; my oleander bushes and arum lilies; our wisteria, which breaks into pale blossom for a few weeks in spring. The ocean wind kills a delicate flower. We have learned to grow the hardiest breed.

Jiggi is so much bigger—in my memory, at least. There is the house where the seven of us slept, five children in a bed.

The outdoor kitchen; the dragoon birds and carpet snakes; the muddy creek where we bathed and swam and fetched our water, washed our clothes. The creek was a puddle in the dry and flooded high and brown in the wet, banks slippery with mud which stuck to everything. The rushing sound when it was high drowned all noise, even the scream of the sulphur-crested cockatoos. In dry spells I sat on the flat stones warmed by sun and the sound was only a trickle, like water poured from a jug.

It was this creek I crossed to go to the Jiggi school. The first day of school, Gran and the little ones waved to me once I reached the opposite side, Hunter's face scrunched from crying because he was two years behind me and he wanted to go to school too. That feeling of happiness, despite my stiff frock and my dirty feet and the drying creek water and tightening mud on my legs. I nearly ran the whole way. To be off on my own, to be free.

That feeling faded as soon as I entered the schoolyard. There I learned that my family name marked me. Two pink-scrubbed boys—the Faber twins—came up on either side of me and each yanked the end of a plait, then screamed that their hands would fall off. They were boys who rode ponies to school, who had shoes. No one would sit next to me when we took a seat at the wooden desks, with their smooth tops and inkwells, their hard benches with names carved in them. We learned reading, writing, arithmetic, history, geography and scripture. The books, at least, did not despise me. In the yard, the boys played marbles and the girls hopscotch, except for me. I had no older brothers to fight for me. I fought for myself, coming home with hair missing from my scalp, long red scratches on my legs and arms. *You only need one friend,* Gran said, kneeling by the woodstove, blowing on tinder till it caught. The mystery was how to find one.

Walking home, I went deeper into the bush, for silence. Under a canopy of trees sounds are different, more distinct. The slither in leaves which might be a snake. The wet fall of rain dislodged from upturned leaves. Silence is its own solace—one can be lonely surrounded by people.

•

This last year I have rarely left the bed. Sue reads to me. We have a radio, now, and in the Arts Cottage a gramophone, so there is always some distraction. I no longer seek silence, I seek sound to distract me from my thoughts, from the darkness that pools in my centre.

I feel as though I am shrinking sometimes inside my skin, like I might disappear altogether one day. I am that other Alice, *shutting up like a telescope.* My dreams are strange and vivid. Mama asks what she can do to ease my pain. I would like her to read to me, but I would never say as much. She was not there on the creek bank the day I left for school. She never learned to read or write.

The days bleed into each other. Breakfast is porridge at seven, then toast and tea. The porridge is no longer hot by the time it reaches us from the hospital kitchens. We are on the fringe of the grounds, the furthest away besides the men. I have little appetite anyway. I nibble the bread like a mouse, crumb by crumb. The bread, they say, comes from Long Bay Gaol, and I like to imagine the prisoners—men in their striped prison uniforms—forming the soft dough, stoking the ovens, baking the loaves in their tins. Knocking gently on the bottoms of the baked bread for the hollow sound. Mama says the prisoners are women too, but I want my bread from the rough-knuckled, flour-dusted fingers of men.

There are other moments to mark my day. A full sponge at nine, which is done by either Sue or Mama. Soup at eleven—a thin broth of wrinkled carrots, soft potatoes and bones from the meat—followed by lunch at noon: chicken or brains or tripe with vegetables and gravy, sometimes roast beef or mutton. I give most of mine to Mama, and she gives me her steamed pudding, baked custard, jelly and custard or stewed fruit. The sweetness is all I have a taste for now.

At tea there is bread and milk, which comes from the hospital's own herd. Dr Stenger insisted on it when dairies around Sydney became infected with tuberculosis. The milk is creamy and thick, with a lick of salt from the sea. At seven there is cocoa and more milk. In my mind I am back at Jiggi, cutting through a paddock of black-and-white cows on my way to school. The sound of the paspalum grass as they rip mouthfuls from the soil. I tried it myself one day, but the grass was bitter and foul, and I spat it out. The cows turned to look. My stomach was always hollow then, but at the hospital we are never hungry.

I would trade all of the cocoa in the world, though, to lie down on the cold, muddy bottom of Jiggi Creek. To feel the smooth stones, the fresh water running over me, calming me to the bone. To hear Gran's voice, sharp and clear, calling me for tea. Perhaps we long most for the things we can no longer have. The places we can never return, because they only exist in our memories.

# 1

## Jack

### 1905

When the camp dogs started up their barking, he ran to the Narran. Wade into the muddy water, swim to the other side, scoop into the Gidgee scrub. Before he learned to swim the bigger boys would carry him on their backs. *Hurry, hurry! Shhh.* He could feel his own heartbeat against the slipperiness of wet skin. Once they hid in the woolpack instead; afterwards Jack itched for days.

Down the Narran was where they played: rounders, drop the hanky. Where they caught fish in the weir: catfish, yellabellies. Some days Jack went yabbying with a chunk of meat on a string. The older boys at Angledool collected river water to fill the tanks, water for the Chinese gardens. Jack and the other younger ones gathered wood for cooking. They collected bottles and sold them back to the cordial factory, then spent the profit on jam drops at Granny Walden's bakery.

Jack grew up in the laps of women: his mother, aunty, granny—warm arms always pulling him in. He slept on more bosoms than pillows. Jack's granny had white hair and a wrinkled-apple face, long bony fingers and loose skin. He sat with her in the shade on hot days and her singing was a current of cool water. It always put him to sleep.

Then there was the day Jack woke up curled against his mother's back, the sound of the heat already cracking the tin roof, her breath in and out, soft and steady. She smelled like gum leaves and honey. He lay there and watched the light come in through the curtain, the day bring shape to the room. But a cramp came to make him moan and shift: bellyache. She woke, the crease between her eyes when she worried about him. She led him out to the dunny, made him tea to calm his belly, then took him to Aunty Rita. Rita was fixing a net and let him lie on her bed with a paper fan she kept on a high shelf, printed with pictures of dressed-up ladies.

She worked and he dozed, but when he woke she was shaking him, whispering. He heard the voices outside. She ushered him into the corner, covered him with an empty flour bag and told him not to move or make a sound.

'Haven't got any little children,' he heard her say. 'They're all grown up. It's just me and my man.'

'You don't mind if we come inside?' That was a stranger woman's voice, high and sharp.

He could be as still as a goanna, frozen on a tree trunk. He could be a stone in the Narran, water flowing around him. Before, his mother had smeared charcoal mixed with porcupine fat into his skin, but he learned to squirm away from the foul smell, and she stopped trying to hide his difference.

The flour bag was stuffy and dust crept up his nostrils, into his eyes. Hard as he tried to repress it, the wet noise came. He heard Aunty Rita pretend to sneeze, but the voices came near.

'What was that?'

Hands pulled the bag aside. He kept his eyes squeezed shut.

'What have we here?'

Jack opened his eyes. The woman studied him, her eyes pale, skin so white in the dark room she glowed. A man stood behind her, with a moustache that curled up at the edges.

'This one's half-caste,' she said.

'You're sure it's not the flour?' the man replied.

She licked her thumb and pressed it to Jack's forehead. 'See?'

Jack took off out the door and across the camp, followed by the sound of their shouts, the woman's spit still wet on his skin.

Mother was there at the Narran, washing clothes, hanging them on the branches of the tree. He slipped down the bank, hiding behind her long thin legs. The mud sucked his feet. Even the river wanted to keep him.

'This one'—the woman came down the path, holding her skirts high, gesturing towards Jack and speaking in a slow, loud voice—'has to come to the school with us. Learn English. Train to work and make money.'

The galahs screamed, beating the air with their wings. The woman did not realise Mother understood her; she had worked at Angledool Station, before.

The man pulled a folded piece of paper from his jacket pocket.

'This says you must give him to us.' He pointed to Jack with a tobacco-stained finger.

Mother lifted him into her arms—he was still small enough—and he hid his face in her shoulder. 'My boy,' she whispered, 'I'll come for you.'

•

The man had a pistol attached to his leather belt. They doubled Jack on a chestnut horse behind the woman, instructing him to hold her leather belt. She did not sit side-saddle but had a split skirt. Mother followed on foot, until the horse cantered and dust swallowed her whole. He heard her wail and he shrunk into himself. He would have jumped. He should have jumped. But it was so far away, the ground, and there was the man's pistol. He shut his eyes against the print of the muslin dress in front of him, smelling the woman's sour sweat, feeling the hard leather of her belt against the soft folds of her waist. If only he could see Mother in his mind she might reappear. If he could hear the clear voice he could pick out in the dark among many voices, he might be in her arms again. But when he opened his eyes, there were just tiny purple flowers on a brown stretch of fabric. The stranger woman's back. Empty trail and jolting, hoofbeat sky.

When they stopped after hours of riding, the woman pulled a long length of chain from her saddlebag. He thought it was for the horse, but she motioned for him to follow her into a copse of trees. There she put the chain around the tree's base and made a belt with it around his waist.

'Soon we won't need this, as we'll be too far away for you to run home,' she said, as she slid a padlock through the links, clicking it into place. The metal lay heavy against his belly, which now ached only from hunger. Other riders had joined them with other children whom Jack did not recognise; children with red-rimmed eyes. They too were brought into the copse of trees and tied with lengths of chain and rope. They did not speak or look at each other long; he was afraid to see his own fear in their faces. After some time had passed, the woman gave each child a pannikin of stew, but Jack was loath to eat it, in case it was poison (Aunty Rita had told him stories). Soon, though, the smell and sounds of the others eating became too much, and he ate fast, listening to the woman's high sharp voice at the fire.

'They'll be brought up properly, trained to be serviceable boys and girls, away from the degradation of camp life,' she said.

The man with the moustache just grunted, spooning stew into his gob. The man dropped the bowl so the spoon rattled, and stood, scratching his head where his hat had left a red mark.

'We'd best get going. Plenty of distance to cover before the sun goes down.'

•

Jack lost count of how many days they were on the track. They were dusty, thirsty and saddle-sore when they pulled up at a well and were told to scrub their faces. The woman said this was because they were about to arrive at what she called 'the Home'.

'Bugger that. Not my home,' an older boy—Guy—whispered.

'What did you say?' the woman asked.

Guy shook his head. 'No English.'

'You'll speak English soon. That's why you are here: to be educated.'

Jack looked at Guy. He was taller than the rest of them, with wide-set eyes that rarely blinked, and square shoulders held back rather than hunched forward. If Guy felt fear, he had figured out how to keep it hidden. Jack rubbed the cold well water on his face. His mother was coming for him, her arms would pull him close. He washed away the dust and crusted tracks of tears.

# 2

## Alice

### 1910

I was nine the first time I saw the ocean. A day's ride to Lismore, then along the Richmond River on the *Brundah*, a coastal steamer of the North Coast Steam Navigation Company. We had a shared cabin in second class, with small perfect bunks and electric lights; I could not imagine anything finer. First, we chugged along the wide, brown river. By afternoon we were through Ballina Heads and the ship rocked on the rough green sea. The waves were fierce. I was used to water which trickled and flowed. This foamed and roared, crashed and bubbled around us, sucking and swirling away.

I was silent not from shyness but from the desire to remember it all: to press it in my memory like a flower between the pages of a heavy book. In the second-class dining saloon we were given the choice between corned beef and carrots or boiled mutton with caper sauce. The boat rocked and I felt like Gran looked, slightly green. I had a bite of boiled potato, some peas, a spoonful of something called blancmange. It jiggled as the ship moved. The texture was unlike anything I had eaten. Firm and soft, sweet and creamy, smooth as the white of a boiled egg on my tongue. It came up later, in the chamber-pot, studded with peas.

I marvelled at the worn velvet nap of the seats in the second-class lounge, timber tables that folded cleverly away. The chug of the steam engine deep beneath us. The fragrant crackling smoke of a man's cigar, his black-striped suit and shining watch chain, his waxed moustache. A lady across from us in a dress the colour of a violet, that same wild, deep purple. Gran's eyes were wet when she looked at me, like when you stare too long at the sun.

She was taking me on that ship, just the two of us, to visit Mama in Sydney. I had two dresses and my underclothes, a necklace Mama left for me when she went away and a copy of Charles Dickens' *Oliver Twist* which I had been given as a prize for coming first in my class at school. I had yet to read it, though I lied to Gran that I had. I did not want to admit that I found some words difficult. I had a paste brooch that Grandad gave to Gran, which she gave to me.

Weeks before, Dr Moffat came to Jiggi Creek with his leather bag of shining metal instruments and glass vials and his small round spectacles made of silver wire. The most extraordinary thing about him was his motor car, blood-red with iron tyres. It made a noise so loud it scared the birds and spooked the cows in the neighbouring paddocks. He told us it was the first car in the district. If he expected praise, I could have told him he was bound to be disappointed. When I showed Gran the Dickens I won, she frowned. 'Don't let your head get too big—it'll break your neck.'

Dr Moffat was coming to make sure we were all over the flu. We had been sick before Christmas, fevers and chills, too weak to even walk. First the children, then Gran fell ill as we recovered. On unsteady legs, I made her sugared tea and gave her cold cloths, cleaned up the mess. Hunter helped look after the littlest. For a week all we ate were soda biscuits with tea.

I was not brave enough to ask Dr Moffat why he came now, rather than when we were feverish. Asking questions of adults was insolence. Wearing white cotton gloves, he scraped our skin with a little razor and placed it in a tiny lidded dish. He examined me all over, lifting my shift so I had gooseflesh along my arms, and he touched me with many things. A needle, a coin, a thread, the point of a pencil. I was instructed to close my eyes and say what each was, and how much I felt it. Sometimes I said I felt something when I did not, because I was certain that was what he wanted to hear. I had a place on my inner thigh where the skin was pink and shiny, raised. He paid special attention to this.

'What was that?' he asked.

'What was what?'

'Did you feel a prick?'

'Yes,' I said.

He pursed his mouth. 'That was the needle.'

I was tough. The others had cried just at the thought of the needle; I had not flinched. When he put his small razor into the flesh above my eyebrow I did flinch a little.

He laid coins out on the tabletop: a threepenny, sixpence, shilling and penny. He watched me pick them up. It seemed a waste of time. What was the use of picking up a coin if I did not get to keep it? I wanted to ask, but Charlie would have thrashed me into next week.

Gran shooed us out to play when Dr Moffat came back in his mud-spattered motor car weeks later. Glad to get away from his razor and needle, his coins we could not keep, we ran down to the creek. The heat made the grass shimmer. I pressed the pink spot on my thigh myself, under water, and wondered at the absence of feeling there. It was strange; like touching someone else. A funny floating lack.

Dr Moffat was gone when we got back to the house for tea and Gran was sharp-tempered. She sent me to fill the kero tin with water from the creek, though it was Hunter's chore and told me to sleep on the floor that night, with a dusty blanket from the shed which smelled of rat piss and hay.

'Why?' I asked. I wondered if she knew I had lied to the doctor.

Gran just shook her head. 'You're old enough now to sleep on your own.'

'You ask too many questions,' Charlie said. I had not seen him in the doorway, or I would not have spoken at all. He slept with Gran in the side room. Sometimes he thumped about like a possum caught in the roof, and we had to stuff the quilt in our mouths to keep from giggling. Whatever you did, you did not want to make him cross.

I woke in the morning with Hunter's arm across my belly. He slept with his thumb in his mouth, like a baby, though he was already seven. We had slept beside each other every night since he was born.

That morning, instead of school, Gran said we were going to pack our things to visit Mama, just she and I. Mama was in a hospital in Sydney and she was very sick. The others wailed. Annie and Irene because Gran was their mama and she was taking me, but Hunter because I was going to see our mama and he was not coming. George wailed because he was the baby. He always cried.

Charlie said he would look after everyone, but Gran muttered something about teats on a bull and telegrammed Charlie's mother, Eunice, to come quick smart from Brisbane. Eunice was sharper than Gran even. She would come with her cat's-arse mouth and her Bible tucked beneath a wing, and I felt sorry for the rest of them, even for Charlie.

One of the things I would ask Mama when we visited was who my papa was, for I knew it was not Charlie. Whenever I asked Gran, she shook her head and turned her back to me, and Charlie threatened to belt me. But Mama must know. If I knew, I would feel different. The sense of lack would disappear.

•

After a rough night of sleep on the ship, the day dawned calm and bright. I sat in a deckchair which swallowed me. I shaded my eyes with both hands and watched the distant lighthouses and other ships we passed, the smaller craft, the leaping fish. Another day passed at sea. The next afternoon the ship entered what the captain called the Heads, though they looked nothing like heads, and brought us into Circular Quay, where ferries and steamers and smaller fishing boats vied for space. The water churned and boiled as the engine strained, and steam poured from the funnel. The sounds of other horns were loud and low. The sun bounced off the ruffled water of the harbour and burned the forearms of men on the wharf, as with fast fingers and fat rope they tied the boats in place. When it came our turn, we followed the rest of the passengers down the gangway. Gran gave some coins to a porter to help with the trunk. People spilled from the footpath, elbows knocking, and the air itself smelled new. Men shouted, birds screamed and there were so many strange faces. They weren't all sun- and wind-whipped like the faces back home. There were women as pale as a pillowslip and men with fancy whiskers. I stared at every face I could before Gran grabbed my arm.

'Don't just stand with your mouth open like a bloody cow. We're not there yet.'

I wanted to tell her that cows didn't stand with their mouths open, they chewed, but I didn't dare. Gran wore her best frock, the garnet green with black lace trim, and the black felt hat with feathers that Hunter put on the dog once to make me laugh. Charlie whipped him so hard with his belt Hunter had stripes on his bottom for weeks.

'We'll take a cab to the hospital at Little Bay. I can't think how we'll manage the trunk on the tram.'

The porter heaved it onto his shoulder as though it weighed nothing, but he was twice Gran's size and four times mine. We followed him past the ticket booths and the cafe, the paperboys and fruit carts, to the street. The crowds had thinned but there was traffic now: spring-carts and buggies and trams, more horses and transom cabs and bicycles than I had ever seen. The sun beat down on all of it, steamy because it had rained not long before, and the air was still damp. I wrinkled my nose at the stink.

A horse passed just an inch from my face, a rough white tail flicking me aside. A man in a blue uniform sat astride, looking straight ahead, not down or left or right. Gran snatched me back from the kerb. 'Watch you don't get run over now.' We had to cross the road to get to the place where the cabs stood waiting for a fare. Gran led the way, and we dodged steaming piles of horse droppings and puddles of muddy water.

'Coast Hospital,' Gran said to the man holding the reins. She leaned forward, chin jutting, while they argued over the fare. He said it was at least an hour and a quarter. The trunk was on board, the porter gone, the horses tonguing their bits. There were two horses—one brown and the other as black as coal, with white markings on his neck. I wanted to put my palm beneath their lips and feel the hot blow of their breath. Their skin rippled, twitching away flies. Gran pulled me into the cab. The driver sat back and jiggled the reins. The horses started, the wheels jolted, and we were on our way.

There was so much to see: buildings taller than trees, trams and carts and handcarts sharing wide streets, everything busy and buzzing with noise.

Gran patted me on the thigh. 'Excited to see yer ma?'

I nodded.

Gran's face was sun-freckled and deeply lined. Her eyes were plain brown and her hair streaked with coarse greys that kinked out from the scalp despite her attempts to tame them in a bun. She was not tall, but to me she was. She was unyielding. Her hand on my leg was bump-knuckled and coarse from what seemed to me a hundred years of washing, digging, scrubbing.

'She might look different,' Gran said, 'but remember your manners and do not stare.'

'Yes, Gran,' I murmured. I reached for her hand as I had not done for years. She jerked away as though I had scalded her and turned towards the window of the cab.

'What is it?' I asked.

'Pins and needles,' she said in a muffled voice, shaking her hand above her lap.

●

The next hour rattled past, and the cobblestone gave way to rutted road. We passed brick cottages with wide lawns and clay-tiled roofs, sandstone churches with windows of coloured glass, streets lined with fig trees. Corner pubs and shops, dunny carts, cats on fence posts and dogs snuffling among rubbish in gutters. Further out we rode, to low-lying scrub and simple shacks, sand dunes in the distance, a long winding boulevard along the sea. The air smelled like a tin whistle tastes, sharp and half sweet.

Trams rattled past on rails, and the driver shouted into the cab occasionally as the roads grew emptier.

'That's where they've built a new gaol,' he said, pointing to a site where men pushed wheelbarrows among timber scaffold and piles of stone. 'A women's gaol first, now a men's.'

I stared and stared. A high wall was being built.

'Too many wicked women,' the driver said, and cackled. Gran's mouth grew small and tight. He was about to say something else but just then the sky opened, a shower of summer rain.

•

We came to two sandstone pillars on either side of a wide road, a footpath running parallel, and a cottage grown over with ivy except around the words in large letters: COAST HOSPITAL. The driver turned into the wide road and pulled up in front of the cottage, which sat beneath tall spiky trees. I had never seen a thing like them. I thought of how I might shinny up the trunks if I were tall enough, how the straight branches were perfect for climbing. Compared to the city, it was peaceful. Long stretches of rolling green lawn, low white buildings with red-tiled roofs and the wide ocean beyond. There were flowers in front of the buildings and banksia trees with their rubbly shade.

'Wait here,' Gran said.

She clambered down from the cab and walked into the cottage with her head high. The driver was buckling leather feedbags behind the horses' ears, whistling as he moved around. A fairy wren landed in the road, pecking at an insect which I couldn't see, twitching its tail side to side. I leaned my chin on the doorsill. The rain had come and gone. I was hungry and travel-weary. I wanted to eat and lie down for a long sleep. A cool breeze blew in from the ocean and I closed my eyes.

A deep voice woke me. 'And you must be Hilda.'

I sat up and rubbed my cheek. It was ridged from the doorframe.

'It's been a long day,' Gran said.

'I'm certain. Let's get you settled for the evening and we can do the examination in the morning.' The man was narrow-faced, red-haired with small gold spectacles.

'This is Dr Stenger,' Gran said.

'Pleased to meet you,' I mumbled. I was determined to hate doctors after Dr Moffat and his nonsense with coins and pinpricks. This man looked like one of the older boys at school dressing up to be a doctor, except for the Adam's apple that bobbed when he spoke.

'The pleasure is all mine,' the doctor said. 'Your mother is in a cottage in the female section, which we will take you to now. It is not the usual procedure, but we've made up two extra beds in there and you can both stay with her—if that suits you, Mrs Davies?'

'Certainly,' Gran said. She was counting out coins for the cab driver.

'I'll call a man to help with your trunk. Probably best we walk from here.'

I followed them in a daze, confused by where we were and what the doctor had said. What procedure? What examination tomorrow?

We walked along a curving path and the doctor gestured to the buildings we passed. 'Administration block, staff cottages, ordinary wards, infectious wards.'

Nurses in long dresses with stiff aprons, collars and strange white caps walked briskly between buildings. There were iron-framed beds on the verandahs of some of the buildings, occupied by gaunt-faced men. Their heads turned to follow our path.

'That's TB, venereal, surgical and the locked ward,' the doctor said as he walked. 'Sea air does our patients a world of good.'

I only understood about half of the words which came out of his mouth.

'That path goes towards the nurses' beach. There's a boat at the north beach for lazaret patients. The male patients are in the gully just above it. Plenty of the men take the boat out to catch fish.'

'Is it true eating fish causes . . .?' Gran's words trailed off.

'We don't think so. We don't know exactly what the cause is, but we presume it is transmitted through prolonged close contact. It's clear that it can lay dormant for many years. But it seems to have nothing to do with diet.'

'I was about to say, we don't eat fish a'tall.'

We arrived at an area that was surrounded by a high timber fence. There was a sign painted with the words: ISOLATION: NO ADMITTANCE WITHOUT PERMISSION. The door had a narrow, high slot you might peer out of. I half expected to see Mama looking out. I could not have reached it without standing on a chair. A box on an iron post was beside the door. Beyond this enclosure, the doctor said, were the stables and workshops, and beyond that the men's cottages and the sea.

The doctor slid the bolt and the door creaked as we entered a different world. There were four identical cottages inside, a little vegie garden, trellised flowerbeds and tended trees and bushes.

'Your mother is in the first on the right,' Dr Stenger said.

We walked to the cottage, weatherboard with a corrugated-iron roof and a verandah with white timber posts. There were vines growing on the posts, tangled skeins of green. A woman sat in a chair beside the door. 'Hilda?'

I blinked, my eyes adjusting to the shade.

'Look at your blonde hair, love. And how tall you are.' Her voice was froggy.

She rose and walked down the steps to greet us, a dark skirt falling to the toes of her boots, her black hair swept up in a high, loose bun. She looked somewhat like Gran, with the same square chin and fleshy cheeks, but there were small flaky scabs around her mouth and eyebrows, and her earlobes were puffy and swollen. She put her hands on my shoulders gingerly, as though she were afraid to touch me. Her fingers were stubby, scurfy.

I was frightened, but I did not step away. Despite my fear, I was tempted to put my head on her stomach, to feel the warmth of it through the white cotton blouse. Would she smell like Gran, like smoke and sweat and baking bread? From arm's length, she smelled of tobacco and liniment.

'I'm sorry,' Mama said. 'You must blame me.'

The doctor and Gran stood either side of us.

Gran said, 'You look well.'

'So do you.'

'Hilda, you wait here a moment. We're just going to talk inside,' Gran said.

They went into the cottage, shutting the door in my face. I stomped on a bull ant that was trailing along the verandah. His parts were still moving when I took my boot away. My toes were pinched. The boots were too small. I would give them to Hunter when we returned to Jiggi, and he would be pleased. I put my ear against the door, but the voices sounded faint.

At the far end of the verandah was a window that was open at the bottom to let in the breeze. Peering through I saw a bedroom, with two neatly made beds. I pushed the window and it slid up, squeaking just a little. I pulled up my skirt and, ducking my head, I put one leg over the sill and climbed in. If Charlie were here I would get the belt, but he was not and I could not picture Dr Stenger thrashing me.

The door of the bedroom was open, and I heard voices from down a narrow corridor. I tiptoed along it, pausing on creaky floorboards. At the far end was what looked to be a kitchen. There was a hatstand with a coat on it near the door. I flattened myself behind the black folds.

'We haven't told her yet,' Gran was saying. 'I thought she would refuse to come. Got your stubbornness. I just told her we were coming to visit you.'

'So when will you tell her?'

'I thought you might.'

'Of course you did. So she will despise me.'

'She'll not despise—'

'I left her, and now the first time she sees me in seven years . . .'

'Now, now. Let's calm down.' That was the voice of the doctor. 'If you like, I can tell her.'

Mama and Gran were quiet. Tell me what? I was sick of their secrets.

I came out from behind the hatstand then, nearly knocking over Mama as I ran into her stomach. 'Oof,' she said.

'Tell me what?' I demanded.

Gran grabbed my arm like she would whack me. 'I *told* you to stay outside, child.'

'Tell me what?'

Mama put her arms around me; her body was soft. I had a feeling then, as much a feeling as a memory, of her arms around me when I was little. Sitting on her lap, playing with her hands. The mole inside her elbow, running my fingers over the fleshy bump of it.

I could not remember her leaving—I was too little—but her absence was a hollow inside of me.

'I have something called leprosy. It means I need to be kept away from other people. And when the doctor came up to Jiggi Creek and did some tests, he found it in you. You're like me, love. You've got the leprosy too.'

I pushed Mama away and glared at Gran. 'You're leaving me here?'

'I didn't want to, child. But this is where lepers must stay. Dr Moffat said . . .'

I ran from the room, down the verandah steps and out of the cottage, through the gates, past the stables and another high-walled enclosure, down the sandy path lined with bushes that scratched my arms to the beach. The ocean was there—stretching as far as I could see—meeting the sky in the middle in a hard unbroken line. I sat on the sand and took off the pinching boots that I'd worn for three straight days. My toes were numb inside them. My mind was numb too. Mama was a leper, I was a leper and I would stay here—far away from Gran and my brothers and sisters and school and Jiggi. I did not even know what 'leper' meant, only that it was something terrible—something truly awful—the worst thing. I had heard it all my life and fought those who said it, like the children at school who teased because of Grandad, but now the worst had come to pass. They were right. It was true. I hated Gran with her pretending and the way she looked at me on the ship, knowing, not saying. How she jumped from my touch: *pins and needles*. I hated Charlie. I hated Hunter, Annie, Irene and George for not being lepers too.

What I knew was Grandad—the shame of him. Now Mama was like him, and so was I. Would they burn the house at Jiggi? I wished they would. If I could not live there, none of them ought to.

I stumbled through the soft sand to where it was wet and hard. The cool water lapped at my bare feet, stinging the blisters. The endless brightness of sky and water made my eyes ache.

So I would live with Mama. I may be sick, but none of them would have her and I would—all to myself. It all felt so jumbled, what I wanted and did not.

The sea was funny, close up. It rolled away and back again, away and back again, like a marble in a bowl. I did not feel any more queer than I had before. I looked at my toes and thought of them falling off. My skin folding and bubbling like porridge. Popping pus-filled sores. I would never be beautiful.

Somehow this was the worst of all things, and I fell in a heap at the tidemark, among cracked seashells and seaweed strands, fragments of coral, the water lapping and rolling, teasing me. It soaked my dress and my skin. It was salty, sticky, and Gran would scold me when she found me, my dress ruined. I did not care. I lay where the sand changed from stippled to smooth and let the sea water come and go. I stood, finally, my dress as heavy as my chest felt, my skin and clothes stuck all over with clumps of yellow, pebbled sand, and turned towards the path I had come down. Mama and the doctor were standing there. How long had they watched me?

'Come and we'll run you a bath,' Mama said, taking my hand in her own. She did not chide me for my dress being sandy and wet.

'I am staying then?'

Mama nodded, and looked off down the beach, shading her eyes. 'It's not so bad here,' she said. 'Three square meals and never a dish to wash yerself.'

Dr Stenger laughed. 'I'm sure the nurses will find you work if you're feeling idle.'

'That was not a complaint!' Mama said.

I tried to walk but my dress dragged in the sand and made for slow, heavy going. Dr Stenger lifted me in his arms. Mama tutted. 'You'll be all wet too.'

'I can duck to my cottage and change,' he replied.

I shut my eyes in case we saw anyone, and I let myself be brought back through the gate, carried like an infant instead of the big girl I was. It was a bumpier ride than the ship but less so than the cab. The doctor lowered me gently onto the verandah of Mama's cottage.

'I'm due in the infectious ward,' Dr Stenger said, giving a stiff little bow. 'Farewell.'

'Thank you, Doctor,' Mama said.

I kept my eyes closed, too embarrassed to watch him go.

'You might be happy here, love,' she said to me. 'They have music sometimes, and at Christmas a party. There's a clothes allowance, a boat. Sewing and gardening. I'll teach you to play cards. And there is lots to catch up on—you can tell me all the news of Jiggi. It breaks my heart you are here, but I am glad, too, to have my girl again.'

A flock of birds overhead called in strange screeches. It was like the sky caught their cry and bent it. I opened my eyes, looked up and they were black, with wings that flapped slowly. 'Yellow-tailed black cockatoos,' Mama said.

'Where's Gran?' I asked.

A woman was watching me from the verandah of another cottage. She wore a straw hat with a wide, floppy brim.

'Didn't want to make a fuss,' Mama said. 'She's gone.'

•

Mama put me in the galvanised tub for a hot bath in the kitchen, washing away the sand and grime from travel. Baths in Jiggi were never hot, so I did not mind the scrubbing as much as I enjoyed the warmth. When Dr Stenger and Matron Wilson came to visit the next day they scraped, measured and weighed me. They poked me again with needles, cut my skin with a scalpel and even took some blood from my finger. The matron was short and wide with auburn hair. She had a little dog named Judy, who jumped up and put her paws on me in order to lick my face when I sat beside her. Her paws smelled like the grass beside the creek at Jiggi, sun-warmed and damp, at once musty and clean. Judy ran about with her tail straight up in the air, triangle ears and a bucketload of confidence. She thought herself bigger than she was.

'What would you like your new name to be?' Mama asked.

I frowned. 'My name is Hilda.'

'Not any longer. It causes trouble for Gran and Charlie and your brothers and sisters for people to know we are here. It's better that no one can find us. I changed my name to Clea, though I am still Mama to you. Hilda will be gone, but you can be somebody new. What have you always *wished* you were called?'

Mama smiled, and Matron fiddled with her veil. Dr Stenger took a sip of his tea. I thought. I did not like my name, it was true; it was too heavy and muddy, like a man's brown boot. I wanted a light name. I thought of my teacher at school, the new young one who had come just before I left. We called her Miss Miller, but her first name was Alice. She was the one who presented me with the prize, the book, which I had not yet shown Mama.

'Alice,' I said.

Dr Stenger smiled. 'Have you read *Alice's Adventures in Wonderland*?'

I shook my head.

'We shall remedy that.'

The matron wrote in her book. She had Mama make a mark beside my admission to show that she agreed to have me kept in the hospital under the *Leprosy Act of 1890*.

'What's that?' I asked.

'It means they can keep us prisoner,' Mama said, but she still made her mark on the paper. When they left, Judy's tail jigging in the air, Mama put her arm tight around my shoulders.

'I'll have to get used to Alice,' she said, 'but it's a pretty name. Do you want to know why I chose Clea?'

'Why?'

'Makes me think of Cleopatra. She was the Queen of Egypt a long time ago. A man I knew once said she was the prettiest woman alive.'

'It suits you, Mama.'

Was Hilda really gone now? I felt the same, but I was called something different. Would Alice be better—a girl who did not pick her nose, lie to her Gran or go behind the dunny to wee because it smelled better?

I imagined digging a hole for Hilda and seeing her dead at the bottom. I would not cry for her.

Alice was not the kind of girl who cried.

# 3

*Nellie*

1892

Grasshoppers, bark, raw flour licked from a dirty palm. A hungry child will eat all manner of things.

Nellie spent much of the time empty-bellied. Every day, her first and last thought was of food. They had a cow her father got as payment for work done. The milk was separated, churned to butter and sold. But sometimes Nellie crept beneath the cow after Ma had milked and put her mouth over one of the leathery teats. There were always a few drops left. The cow's skin was rough and sour in Nellie's mouth. The cow might have kicked the girl, but she stood there, patiently, while Nellie drank what she could.

Nellie's father had red cracked hands, horny-heeled feet in the dirt. His belt held a tin matchbox and a clasp knife. She felt the scratch of his whiskers when he put his face to her hair; it smelled of hay and sunshine, he said. He smelled of tobacco, rum and the sharp ointment he put on his skin.

He took her sometimes to hunt wallaby and she felt the jolt of his rifle, how it nearly knocked him over when he fired. He almost always missed, but still he had a smile for his girl. He took her clearing, hacking stumps and setting fires which would burn the scrub and make it grow back greener. After, when he washed his arms and face in the creek and rolled up his sleeves, she touched the pink shiny spots. They felt so smooth, like new skin.

'What are they, Pa?'

'My own bad luck,' he said, moving her hand away.

'Next time you go away for work,' Nellie asked, 'can I come? I promise I'll help.'

His strong hands lifted her to his shoulders to cross the creek, his wild hair beneath her chin.

'Ma needs your help at home,' he said, setting Nellie down after flying her high through the air so she squealed.

At night, he gathered her in his lap in front of the fire. How safe she felt there.

Her father was a teamster, logger, girder-squarer. He told Nellie stories of the cedar they sometimes found, of the rigger who climbed the very tallest trees with only spurs on his boots and a rope round his waist, his saw and axe dangling from his belt. It might take him two hours to shinny to the top. Once there, he took out his saw and cut off the tree's crown. Then he would shinny down again, making more cuts as he moved down the trunk.

'Shame you were too frightened of heights to be a rigger,' Ma interrupted. 'We might have had enough money to survive on.'

He pretended not to hear. Instead he told Nellie how the valley was called Jiggi for the call of the catbird. He told her about sleeper-cutting: how, once a tree was felled, they first had to strip the bark and cut it into billets. The billets were put on skids, and two lines marked with a string covered in black ash; these were the straight lines to cut with the squaring axe. Then they would turn it over to do the other side. Every sleeper was nine inches by four and a half, which meant anything that didn't fit went to waste. The railway passer would inspect the sleepers—blueing the rejects with his chalk—and he'd only pay for the ones which passed.

Her father was gone for hungry stretches, weeks and months. 'What work he can do he takes,' Ma said, 'like any half-decent man.' But while logging he cut his hand with the crosscut saw and did not notice until someone else pointed out the blood spilling in the dirt. He returned home ragged and worn, the cut festering and black. His feet were swollen too. His face had changed. He no longer played with Nellie or put her on his shoulders. Ma looked after him, with her short temper, but there were the two littlest ones and Nellie. Finding a way to feed them all: damper and pumpkins and corn. Corned mutton if they were lucky. Spring and summer they picked passionfruit from the vines that grew wild, and raspberries, minding the thorns.

Ma took in laundry and churned the butter. The only time Nellie saw her still was when she woke in the middle of the night and Ma was asleep. In the morning, Ma scraped her black hair into a bun so tight she almost smiled. Nellie watched Elma and Avery while Ma chopped wood, boiled the copper, stirred the steaming tub. Nellie helped her with the mangle. Many were the ways Ma said she did things wrong. One day Mrs Frame came riding side-saddle on her mare to pick up her laundry, carrying a parasol to keep the sun off her face. She saw Pa, sitting in the sun, smoking. She was the one who reported him, Ma said. Thinking her clothes would be *contaminated* somehow. Horrified that they sold their butter, too.

When the men from the Board of Health came, Pa called them rotten effing buggers.

Ma turned to Nellie, hovering in the doorway watching, and said, 'Take the little ones and wait by the creek.'

Nellie carried Elma in her arms and showed Avery how to make boats from twigs and gum leaves. Elma cried because she was thirsty, but Nellie's paps were flat. She thought of the cow.

The hut was quiet when they walked past to the cow tied to her post at the back. The grass around her was chewed to nubs. She must have been hungry too. Nellie put Avery in the wheelbarrow and told him *wait*. She lay flat on her back beneath the cow and sat Elma on her belly. She put a teat in Elma's mouth and tried to show her what to do. There was shouting from the front of the house. The cow got a fright, kicked her legs and reared back. Elma tumbled and Nellie scrambled away, frightened. She ran behind the woodpile, not even thinking of snakes. She could hear Ma screaming. But where was Elma? And Avery? Nellie ran back to the cow and saw Elma face down in mud, her small body still. Avery wailed in the wheelbarrow. Nellie lifted her sister up but something was not right, her head was the wrong shape. Ma found Nellie in the mud, shaking Elma, willing her to wake.

Then it was just Avery, Ma and Nellie. Men came to burn the hut, and the neighbours packed their cart and moved away. People stood nearby just to watch the flames lick the sky. They said it would get rid of the leper taint. Nellie clung to Ma's skirts as a man walked past with a sunburnt nose, grey whiskers.

'Best if they burn the lot of them in there,' he said, and Ma turned towards him, her eyes fierce.

'Pardon me?'

He ducked his head and walked away.

Ma did not blink when the kero was lit, when the crackle became a roar. It started at the woodpile and moved in, the walls slower to catch with the mud between logs. Nellie watched for snakes, but none came. Black smoke stained the sky. Afterwards, Ma went through the charcoal, taking the smudged pots and pans. Later, when she spoke of what they took from her, she made it grander every time, more than it really was.

'Do you remember the teapot and cups I had? Blue Willow china? Not a chip in sight.'

'I never drank from anything but tin,' Nellie would reply.

'You've never had a mind for much.'

They did not speak of Elma. Ma never said outright that Nellie was to blame, but she did not leave Avery in her eldest daughter's care again. She did not let her son out of her sight.

No one paid Ma to wash their clothes any longer, and there was no butter, for the cow had been sold to buy an old nag.

Two years they lived in a patched canvas tent while Ma wrote letters to the government asking for money. People were scared of them, scared to come near, scared to take their money in the shop, but there were kindnesses too. A priest who came to Jiggi church all the way from Nimbin every Sunday would come to pray with Ma after the service, so that even though she had not prayed before she decided it was a worthwhile thing. He brought food: a slab of salt pork, a basket of withered apples, once a rabbit stew.

One day Nellie came upon Ma sitting beside the fire with the billy boiling over and spitting in the flames. She had a piece of paper in her hands.

'What does it say?' Nellie asked. Her own mother had taught Ma to read and she tried with Nellie but soon gave up, saying the girl was too stupid to learn. After lifting the billy off the rack with a hook, Nellie threw in a handful of tea-leaves and left it to steep.

'They've given us a bank cheque for a hundred pounds,' Ma said.

'Who?'

'The government. To build a new house. For lost wages, too.'

'We'll have a house?'

Ma nodded, watching the flames bite the wood with wet eyes.

'Are you glad?'

Ma continued nodding slowly, but her face looked sadder than Nellie had ever seen it. Her hand shook as she folded the paper and stuck it in the bosom of her dress.

'We're going to ride to Lismore to the bank, first thing,' Ma said. 'We'll wash in the creek tonight.'

•

Nellie was thirteen then and skinny as a post. She had breasts, though, small like the teacups Ma seemed to recall having. When she washed in the creek she told Avery to stay away and crouched in the knee-deep water, looking down at her strange, changing body. There was hair in places it had not been, and tenderness in her new breasts. If she had friends in the same circumstances, it might have seemed normal, or if she had a mother who spoke to her about anything except her troubles. But Nellie did not go to school, and people kept their distance. Used to be she would do anything for her ma, to try to make her happy, but Nellie cared less now. She lay in the tent longer in the morning. She put the dishes away still damp. She disappeared for hours down the creek, watching the trees shiver in the breeze and the mad, zigzag path of an ant. Across the creek there was an old shack where neighbours used to live—now the walls slowly rotted and the tin roof grew holes. Nellie climbed through the ruins, imagining it her own. She lay on an old pallet, staring through the rusted gaps at the sky. She thought of her father, wished for his return. It was there Nellie first saw the blood.

When she saw the stains in Nellie's bloomers, Ma gave her cloths and told her not to let a man near if she wanted anything besides sorrow.

•

It took a long time to find builders. Ma was not going to part with the money easily. Various men came and sat around their fire. Ma laid out her conditions, what she desired and when she would pay, and the men stood up and left, refusing her tea, spitting as they climbed back on their horses. Avery was ten then and sat always at Ma's side; her shadow. She sent him to spy on Nellie when she walked in the bush, to the deserted shack, up Billygoat Mountain, Muckleewee. He was scared of everything, so he never got far before running home.

They all had black hair, but Avery's eyes were green while Ma's and Nellie's were ordinary brown. Lighter colours show more of what the person is thinking. Avery sometimes looked at Nellie with his clear green eyes and she could tell he was thinking of Elma, how Nellie killed her, though he was hardly big enough to remember. Nellie scared him, and so he stayed beneath Ma's wing. Nellie felt sorry for him, because she knew Ma would only use him to get what she needed.

Nellie was returning from one of her walks when she saw a different horse tied beside the tent. A palomino mare, well kept, with a saddle so polished it glinted as Nellie edged closer. By the fire, a man sat with her ma drinking tea; another builder. Nellie touched the horse's mane, at once coarse and smooth.

The mare eyed her through thick white lashes. Her tail flicked and her flank quivered.

'Careful, she don't like strangers much.'

'Come here, Nellie,' Ma said. Her voice was wound tight.

Nellie went and sat on the log beside her.

'This is Ned. This here's my daughter, Nellie.'

'Pleased to meet you.'

He was looking at her and she returned the gaze. He was not weather-beaten with wild whiskers like the others who had come. He was young, clean-shaven, with pale-blond hair and eyes the colour of his shirt, blue. He wore moleskin trousers which had once been white.

'About the payments,' Ma said. 'I'll give ten per cent before, plus materials, another ten halfway through, and the rest when the house is done.'

'You drive a hard bargain,' Ned said.

'Ma, tell him what yer rules are,' Avery said.

'No drinking, no swearing, no pissing in the creek and no leaving your tools laying about.'

'Sounds—'

'Oh, and no talking to my daughter.'

'Ma!' Nellie said, out of embarrassment.

She stood and disappeared into the tent. She would not listen to Ma carrying on for another moment. But when Ned got up to leave, she watched him through the gap in the tent flap. It would be the last she would see of him anyway. His shoulders strained the back of his shirt, which was damp down the spine from sweat. Large hands with square-tipped fingers, golden hair on his arms which carried light. He pulled his spurs from his pocket and buckled them over his boots. Ned spoke softly to the horse as he untied her, and Nellie wished she could swap places. The mare could stay here with Ma and Avery.

•

Ned agreed to build the house. Things must have been slow. He came with horse-drawn carts of supplies, tents for him and six others, and a skinny black dog which followed him everywhere he went. Ma had agreed to cook for them if they brought food, and there was salt beef and pork, white beans and flour, tea and sugar, even eggs. One of them had a rifle and he shot wallabies and skinned and gutted them. The dog ate the guts and Nellie felt sick, watching it gorge on entrails. Ma cooked the strips of red flesh on the fire. They were not to touch the men's food except to cook and serve it, Ma said, and Nellie watched her fry the eggs in the morning, her belly making noises she was certain the men could hear. Ma made Nellie help cook and clean for them, clearing plates, washing dishes and pouring tea.

Ned obeyed Ma's rules and did not speak more than the obligatory 'please' and 'thank you', but Nellie felt his eyes on her by the fire in the evenings and coming from the tent in the mornings. Moving back and forth from the creek when she washed dishes or fetched water, or bathed, she knew she could look up and catch him. It seemed to be what she wanted, because when he was not watching her she felt empty, like a billy boiled dry.

# 4

*Jack*

First they washed him in sheep dip and cut his hair so short it almost wasn't there. Then they gave him a number, 122, which he would use instead of his name. He was shown to a bed in a room with a long row of them, given an enamel cup and a bar of soap. There were pyjamas to sleep in, and clothes to wear during the day. He hated the coarse cotton on his skin. *It's time to forget that life and do things our way*, they said. But they did not say how it was Jack was meant to forget.

At Angledool he was Jack, but now he was 122 and *half-caste*. The children were mostly like him, also half-caste, though some were *quarter-caste* or even *octoroon*. They said they'd taken him away to breed the colour out of him, and Jack imagined it like dye in water, floating away, and wondered what he would be left with. Whether, when she came, his mother would even recognise him.

Before dawn Jack was woken to wash at the basin, then scrub dishes and floors, peel potatoes, chop wood, weed gardens, sweep paths. He was given castor oil and eye drops from a blue bottle. Between the hours of nine and noon they were taught the three r's and how to speak and sit and eat like a whitefella. Brother Jeffrey put the lightest shades in the front of the classroom. His favourite was an octoroon, number 97. He could pass easily, Brother used to say. Brother Jeffrey walked in front of their desks, mopping the sweat from in front of his ears with a handkerchief. *You must forget your language, your culture and all of that. Stop acting like an uncivilised Aborigine.* The hot wind of Brother's breath when he looked over your shoulder made Jack want to gag. Guy said Brother Jeffrey might promise sweets and whatnot but never to follow him to his room. Jack had taken to following Guy. Standing behind him in the queue for porridge, kneeling beside him in chapel.

'You're awful scrawny to be my shadow,' Guy said. Jack just ducked his head and shrugged; he didn't want to be told to get lost. He needn't have worried: Guy saved his harsh words for the brothers. Jack and Guy were together whenever they could be, and Guy had some words of advice. 'Do your best to be average,' he said to Jack. 'You're little, but don't call attention to yourself. You don't want to be noticed.' Guy sometimes did not take his own advice. His temper was known throughout the Home, and the brothers were quick to blame him when something went awry.

The afternoons were farm labour until prayers and lights out. Every night in bed Jack thought of the Narran River, jumping in and the cool water closing over his ears. He thought of his mother, the smell of gum leaves and honey, and her voice when she sang, high and clear. Her breathing at night beside him on gubba blankets, soft and steady, the sound of her fingernails when she scratched his scalp. What it felt like to rest his head on her chest, or against the softness of his aunty and granny. He was scared of forgetting how, when it was hot and still at home, they slept under the stars, and his mother told him stories. Sometimes he could feel her hands brushing his cheeks, dry and rough. He covered his mouth with the pillow when he cried. The building they slept in creaked and rattled at the smallest breeze, the frogs outside croaked. Sometimes the keening was human. He wasn't alone.

At the Home they told them prayer and work would save their souls. Try to run away and you were beaten with a stock-whip. Fail to clean the stalls properly or sweep the paths clean and you went to bed without tea. Jack had his mouth washed out with Velvet soap once. *Only English*, they said. He did not speak Yuwaalaraay again. He stopped waiting for his mother to come. If a boy was locked in the shed for talking back, forgetting to wash behind his ears or taking a second helping at dinner, the others would bring him food pocketed from their own meals. One boy, Owen, 129, spent three days there once for trying to run away. For weeks afterwards he complained at how the light hurt his eyes.

When Guy was in the shed, Jack rolled a withered apple under the door. Guy whinnied like a horse. He could always make you laugh.

•

At eleven Jack was chosen to work in the stables. His uncle was a boundary rider at Angledool; he had been around horses. Jack never dropped a sack of grain or let the hay in a stall grow stale. Guy worked in the stables as well, and taught Jack to polish saddles and keep the harnesses untangled, the difference between a girth and a surcingle. It was the nearest thing he felt to contentment, being with Guy and around horses. You did not show fear to a horse, but you could be gentle. You could be wild and trustworthy; careful and free.

Sundays they were woken early for church, but afterwards they were allowed an afternoon off, and Jack ran down to the creek with Guy and several other boys. It was nothing like the Narran, but they set yabby traps with old chicken wire. The first time he saw a trapped yabby, Jack swallowed a lump like a stone in his throat.

Sometimes on Sundays they played cricket in the paddock beside the cemetery, if it had been mown. Jack had heard the story of 63, a skinny twelve-year-old boy who died two years before from a black snake bite while playing cricket in the long grass on a Sunday. No one played in the paddock now if it had not been mown. They tried to stretch Sunday into the week by keeping small jokes between them, reasons to laugh when no one was watching. They called each other by name, in secret, and had names for the brothers too—the Goanna, Stone Face, Fat Chook.

They did not speak of their families.

•

At thirteen, Jack was sometimes allowed to ride a horse to take messages or mail. He did not understand why he was trusted to do this; perhaps because he was quiet. Or it might be because of his work in the stables. There was a younger boy working with him in the stables now, because Guy had left the Home when he turned fifteen.

It was a dizzying feeling to let the horse go beneath an open sky, to have a beast large enough to kill him under his control. His movement was how he spoke to the horse. The ridge of stirrup leathers pressed into his legs, the hot leather of the reins. You could be hard and soft at the same time. It was the best feeling he knew. On these errands he learned not to hurry. He learned that there were some things he might keep to himself.

# 5

*Will*

## 1910

Will woke before the sun was up and picked his way down to the bay. The path was stony but he knew it well enough to discern it in the predawn light. A creek trickled alongside, its banks soft with maidenhair ferns and wild violets. The ocean was glassy; lines of breakers rolled in at the entrance to the bay, but the bay itself was calm. The incoming tide lapped the shell-strewn sand. The sandstone went right up to the water in places, flat shelves of rock with platforms and seats, naturally carved fingerholds and grooves in the blond stone. It rose behind the beach into cliffs with small pockets and shelters. He left his dressing-gown on a high shelf and walked in despite the chill, the sea water at his ankles, knees, hips, until it was too much and he ducked beneath the glass-green. The water took his breath away. When he surfaced, the sky was apricot-hued, and the cries of the seabirds echoed across the bay. He watched a gannet drop into the water then emerge, flapping towards the clouds. Will floated on his back, skin tingling, the dome of coloured sky above. It was his favourite part of the day, this moment of peace. Before all the madness the day might bring.

There was a swimming costume in his room which his mother had bought him, but he saw no purpose in donning it for an empty beach. He would shake himself afterwards, like the dogs used to do after swimming in the dam, water droplets flying. He tied the sash on his dressing-gown and walked back to the cottage, salt-sticky but refreshed. If he could, he would bathe before work, but sometimes there was no time and through the day the salt on his skin and his scalp would tighten as it dried. If he touched his tongue to the corners of his mouth he would taste the ocean. Far better than the smells which overwhelmed the wards. Gangrenous flesh, suppurating sores. Sometimes death.

Will's home was along the avenue of Norfolk pines—their distinct branches filtered sunlight into his weatherboard cottage. There were four doctors, each with his own small cottage, but the other three had families; Will was the only bachelor. The other cottages were for lay staff and were constructed entirely of corrugated iron. When it rained they would sound as the sheds at the farm did, as though you were inside a tin drum. The ward buildings were made of sandstone, with wide verandahs where patients sometimes slept. Beside the wards were the nurses' living quarters, and behind those were quarters for the bob-a-day men. Further back still, right on the edge of the hospital grounds, were the male and female lazarets.

As Will dressed he looked out into the bush which surrounded them: the spindly wattle, banksia and low scrub of coastal heath. There was still dew on the grey-green leaves of the wattle, but soon the sun would burn it off. He heard the sounds of chickens laying in the fowl yard, the carts being wheeled to the wards from the kitchen and a distant horse complaining at being harnessed. He stood in front of the small, spotted looking glass and combed his hair. It was tangled and stiff from the sea.

'Doctor.' There was a shout followed by a knock at the door.

'Yes, coming,' he called, and opened the door.

A probationer nurse stood in her neat uniform, her chin tucked so it nearly sat upon her collar.

'Dr Whitbourne's requested you in surgical, sir.'

'I'll be right there.'

He reached for his hat on the hook beside the door.

•

The surgical ward was closest to the entrance gates, easiest to reach from an ambulance. As he drew near, he heard the screams from inside. He pressed down his dread and entered.

'The patient?' he asked the closest nurse.

'Botched abortion. Septic. D and C but may be too late.'

He put on a gown, scrubbed his hands in the sink and tied a mask behind his head.

Dr Whitbourne nodded at him. 'Transfusion,' he said. 'We've lost a great deal of blood.'

Will saw it pooling beneath the woman. The screams had stopped; she was etherised now, her face as white as the sheet pulled up to her chin.

'Any family?'

'No—just fetch someone!' Dr Whitbourne ordered.

Will hurried outside. A bob-a-day man was snipping back honey myrtle in the garden.

'You, fellow,' Will called.

The man looked up. His face was creased from sun. 'Willing to do a transfusion?'

Sometimes it worked, other times it did not. That it worked sometimes was enough to use it as a last resort. The man came in and Will watched him scrub his hands at the sink. Another bed was set up beside the patient's. There was the sterile tubing, needles and dressings. Will found the vein in the crook of the man's arm, a strong beating blue. The blood came and they got a clear line, no air. He raised his bed higher than hers. He kept his focus on the man. It would do no good to take too much blood.

•

Later, he scrubbed the blood from his arms at the sink. He sat with Dr Whitbourne on the verandah, and the probationer nurse brought them tea on a tin tray, the cups and saucers rattling.

'Bad luck, old fellow,' Will said.

'Wrong type of blood.'

'Did you see the bob-a-day man's tears?'

'I told him to take the rest of the day off. We should send over a lager.'

'I hate to think where that poor young lady went.'

'I don't gather she was much of a lady.'

Will stood and replaced his hat. Dr Whitbourne sighed.

'Oh, don't take it personally, Stenger. You know the type. We get dozens.'

'Let's not speak ill of the dead. I'd best get down to the lazarets. See you at tea.'

Will tipped his hat to Dr Whitbourne and took his leave.

•

Will visited the lazarets several times a week, though he was only required to report once. The matron was also drawn there. There were always things the patients needed from the outside world, small reassurances. A handkerchief, a box of China tea, sheet music for the piano, some tincture from the chemist they'd read about in the newspaper. Isolation shrinks a life. If the world is small, little wonder that it is taken over with an obsession over small things. Will was working to educate the rest of the hospital, but so many were still petrified of these patients. Only the previous year a probationer nurse was fired because she refused to treat a leprosy patient who came into the general ward with a life-threatening injury. They had all of their laundry and washing-up kept separate—not because it needed to be, but because of the fear of contagion.

He told anyone who would listen it took prolonged exposure to infection combined with a genetic predisposition to the disease, but his words made little apparent difference. Even those with medical training seemed to forget science and logic when confronted with that five-letter word. *Leper.* The history of prejudice and fear was difficult to overcome.

The men's lazaret was furthest from the rest of the hospital, so Will walked there first. There were nine cottages inside a fenced area in the gully at the northern edge of the beach. A sandstone wall separated the lazaret from the beach, with a door and slip rails for the lepers' boat. The sun disappeared first from this valley, and when it rained the area flooded. There were twelve men: three Chinese, one Javanese, one West Indian and seven of European descent. In the early days the lazaret had been occupied entirely by Chinese patients, but then the disease spread through the rest of the population. Back in 1896, nineteen Chinese lepers were taken from the Coast Hospital to Hong Kong and then Canton to be repatriated.

Will shut the gate behind him, and Ted, who was on duty, stood from where he had been smoking a pipe in the front of the attendants' cottage.

'Dr Stenger.'

'Good afternoon. Any urgent?'

'Billy's been saying his finger's ready. Jim hasn't eaten in a few days.'

'I'll visit them first.'

They knocked on the door of Billy's cottage. He had been there the longest of any patient—coming on fifteen years— which was how he had a cottage of his own. Inside it was dark, dusty, foul-smelling. He could not walk anymore, and so the ulcers and sores from lying in bed required constant attention.

He had a wife who visited him, though, on Fridays and Sundays between two and five in the afternoon, which was more than most of the others had. How she stood the smell of him, Will could not imagine.

'I'll open a window,' Will said, stepping across the room to the curtain-shrouded glass.

'No light,' Billy croaked.

That often happened in the later stages: the light hurt their eyes. Billy's irises had the reddish-brown hue of macular lesions.

'Just for a minute. Otherwise we'll all die of the smell.'

Pulling back the scratchy woollen blanket covering his legs was a worse assault than the smell.

'How often are you changing the dressings?' Will asked Ted.

'Twice a day.'

'Tell me truthfully.'

'Once.'

Will threw the blanket to the floor. 'You must. Clean. And dress. His sores. Twice. Daily.'

Billy's feet were swollen, brown and purple. The tuberosities were red and angry; some the sores from leprosy and some the sores from simply lying in bed. Billy did not have the feeling in his body that told him to move when he had lain in one place too long.

'You'll stay and dress them now, Ted. And every day—twice. Keep the windows open, if you can. We must keep this skin dressed and clean.'

'What of my finger, Doc?'

'Show me.'

Billy held his right hand out. Most of his fingers were stubs only, but what was left of one finger hung limply. The leprosy bacilli thrived in cooler skin, like fingers, toes, earlobes, cheekbones, wrists and knees. Testicles. Will took his forceps from his bag.

'Have you fresh dressings?' he asked the attendant.

Ted nodded.

With the forceps, Will grasped hold of what was left of the finger and twisted it. It came away, and he wrapped it in gauze. It caused Billy no pain, as the bones had all been resorbed—broken down into the circulatory system—and the tissue denervated. The finger would go in the incinerator.

Ted dressed the fresh wound, and Will stepped outside. He needed a smoke. The worst of the day was over, he thought. The wind rattled the fronds in the date palm. When Ted emerged they walked to Jim's cottage.

Will had gone to medical school to spite his father. His father wanted his only son to take over their 2500-acre sheep station near Walgett. As a boy, Will wanted nothing more than to leave. The harsh landscape, the tired stock, the brute violence of sheep-shearing and drafting and every single part, it seemed, of farming life wore on him. He was inured early to blood and death. One of his earliest memories was his father shooting sheep during a drought, the smell of their corpses thrown in an outdoor vat and boiled down.

He would have gladly remained beside the kitchen hearth, the smell of bread baking and the warmth of the fire. Helping his mother cut, measure and shape. But the kitchen was no place for a boy, according to his father.

At nine Will spent four months invalided after a case of pneumonia, and the doctor who came was a different man from any Will had met before. When he opened his bag it was as though another world existed of which Will had known nothing. A world of shining metal instruments, glass vials and bottles, needles, syringes and the smallest scissors Will had ever seen. After several weeks of treating the boy, the doctor acknowledged Will's curiosity and began explaining each of the instruments to him, allowing him to hold them, and giving brief lectures on the various treatments for the most common forms of disease. When Will asked whether he had any books he might leave—Will was desperate for reading—he lent the boy his old copy of *Gray's Anatomy of the Human Body*.

Will's world cracked open like an egg. Here were the skeleton, muscle, tissue and organs which made up the human body. The sections of the human skull: frontal, parietal, temporal, sphenoid, lambdoid, occipital, zygomatic, nasal, lacrimal, ethmoid and maxilla. The way the bones fit together, the way joints cradled them. The shape and valves of a heart. To name these things made sense to him. He had seen them in the animals slaughtered, but to know that inside they were the same calmed him somehow. He wanted to label every single part of his life. To keep it clean and separate as it was in that book. He kept the lamp on far past darkness, lying in his crisp white sheets, reading. When his mother came in during the night to rub Bates' salve into Will's chest—his cough was still green and racking—she took the book away.

'You must rest,' she said, smelling of eucalyptus oil, sour breath, paraffin.

'You will give it back?'

'In the morning,' she said.

Will was sent to King's School in Sydney at the age of ten, and from there he would have been happy never to return. His friends became the family he chose, similar boys with a penchant for learning rather than sport, a love of fact and figures, a practical jokery that stood for affection in their world. The school itself was harsh, but the boys protected one another. Will thought he would miss his mother, but in fact seeing her again made him angry. Angry that she never stood up to his father, that she agreed with every word he spoke, even when it came to the comportment of the daughters she gave birth to after Will.

Will's youngest sister, Cathy, was the boy he was meant to be. She wanted to do the work of the farm, following Father wherever he went, learning the best ways to dip a sheep and dock a tail. If you kept her indoors she would howl, but his father refused to see her as anything but the sex she had been born with. They sent her after her older sister to Kambala, and her spirit was broken—school had the opposite effect on her that it had on her brother. She was not made for piano lessons and French, cooking lessons and myriad ways to fold a linen napkin. She was happiest on horseback, looking for lost stock in the pouring rain. Will wished his father would realise that and let Cathy be the farmer he would never be. But his father was a foolish man. People rarely see what is right before them, Will had learned.

•

After leaving the men's lazaret, he knocked at the cottage Clea now shared with her daughter, Alice. Other doctors just barged in, same as they would on a ward, but the leprosy patients must make this their home, often for the rest of their lives, and he believed the staff ought to respect that.

Clea opened the door. He followed her to the small sitting room. Clea was telling him the symptoms of her neuralgia, but Will was remembering the day he drove to the wharf to fetch her. It was not required—he might have sent a bob-a-day man—but the last patient had been so dehydrated from the journey he nearly died. Clea was covered in filth, her hand was infected and she smelled to high heaven. There was a mad look in her eyes. Compared to now, one would not recognise her, with her pressed collar and carefully plaited hair. An educated eye could still see the symptoms: there was the telltale swelling on her face. Her nostrils, eyes, earlobes and lips were puffy. There was some hard oedema on her cheeks and wrists. But the stigma had done her far more harm than the disease itself.

The sitting room in Clea and Alice's cottage had framed landscapes on the walls, a few books on the shelves and a jug of water with several glasses on the side table. Beside the window was a hairbrush and hand mirror, both silver-plated with flowers engraved on the backs. At first, Will had been surprised that the patients in the lazaret kept mirrors at all. But it was a slow disfigurement. Perhaps they grew used to each change.

Alice entered the room, her eyes red as though she had been crying, and sat beside her mother. Will wished that she had not been lied to, but her method of arrival was far better than her mother's.

'Say good morning to Dr Stenger,' Clea simpered.

It irritated him when people changed their voices for children.

'Good morning, Doctor,' Alice said seriously, fixing him with her grey eyes. She had light hair pulled back from her face and plaited, the end tied with a wide satin ribbon.

'Good morning, Miss,' he said. 'I brought you this.' He pulled a book of fairy tales from his doctor's bag. The doctor in the cottage beside him had two little girls, and Will had asked him if he had any books to lend to a sick child. The man had brought him the book of fairy tales. Will did not mention which patient they were for; his neighbour would burn the book afterwards if he knew.

It was worth the deception to watch the slow smile spread across Alice's face. It was the first time he had seen her smile in the month since she'd arrived. Clea seemed cross, though, and told her sharply to put it in her room.

As she walked past him, Alice looked over and whispered, 'Thank you.' She had that way of some precocious children of seeming grown up in her mannerisms. As though she had skipped childhood entirely and decided to embark upon adult life from the tender age of nine.

'How is she?' Will asked, once she had left.

'Sulking still,' Clea said. 'Does not think much of me.'

'It is the shock. Give her time. She will settle in.'

He watched a moment's grief pass over Clea's face, but when she raised her hand to touch her hair it was gone, as quick as a fish leaping. He knew more than she thought he did.

Clea's mother, Dulcie, had told him how she had become the common-law wife of Clea's husband, less from her own wishes than of circumstance. It should not surprise him but it did. What did he know, Will thought, of what women must do?

Alice returned to the room and he pulled the instruments from his bag as his childhood doctor once did, explaining each one, allowing her to hold them, showing her how they worked. Inside the glass thermometer the mercury which moved. The way the needle, attached to the syringe, draws blood. Will thought of the young woman that morning in the surgery, the wasted life. Alice had already had smears taken, but she watched as he took Clea's. Will explained how the glass slide was air-dried then passed over a flame. Beneath a microscope, the leprosy bacilli appeared brownish and rod-shaped. Alice watched, rapt, as her mother did not wince.

'I will let you in the lab one day and show you the microscopes,' Will said. 'There are things on this slide which are not visible to us, but which one might see under magnification.'

'Like magic?' Alice asked.

'More like science,' he replied. 'Just as miraculous, though.'

Afterwards, Clea boiled the kettle and poured the tea. Will knew he ought to press on with his work, but since he was a boy he had longed for the company of women. Alice snuck her book back into the room and began reading, settling on the sofa beside her mother, her legs tucked up beneath her. He finished his tea and packed the instruments back in their cases. He took his leave, saying he would see them later in the week. Alice looked up from her book long enough to smile at the doctor. Clea seemed dour as she saw him out, and he hoped he had not caused trouble between them.

Will was drawn to that which was still a mystery. He wanted to know why leprosy could lay latent for so long. In Alice's case, it was latent up to nine years, other patients as long as twenty years. The shortest number of years it took to show up was four. To think that a patient might have this bacteria inactive but present for so long. What was it that brought on the symptoms, he wondered. What made it become active?

Alice and Clea came from near Lismore, in northern New South Wales, the centre of a mixed-farming district. The climate was subtropical, warm and humid, and the families were primarily of European heredity. Will had certainly heard of endemic areas in Queensland, but not in the Northern Rivers. There had been others, though, not only Clea's father. If he only had time, Will thought, he would trace the lineages. Ascertain connections. Attempt to find the original source—it must be there.

Perhaps when the condition was better understood, the stigma would lessen. So many of the diseases treated at the Coast were far more contagious—scarlet fever, influenza and tuberculosis, to name a few—but only the leprosy patients were locked away. Everyone was terrified of catching their disfiguring disease. It was because of the biblical references, Will thought, recalling his scripture classes at King's. The Bible had not done the disease any favours. What they referred to as leprosy in Leviticus was probably a generalised term for a terrible and highly contagious disease. Hence the word 'leper': one who is shunned by society, and cast out. In the Bible, leprosy was a form of sin that only the Bible could cure, and therefore whoever had leprosy had brought it upon themselves. It was obscene to think that a child such as Alice had brought this upon herself.

The previous week he had received a letter from a journalist—using the term loosely—from *The Truth*. The man had wanted to come and visit the lazaret, to write a piece about 'those awful outcasts, those unfortunate souls'. He promised anonymity but wrote that regular Sydney folk were curious to know that people with the disease were just on the city's fringe. Will tore up this letter and tossed it in the wastepaper basket. He assumed the man wanted to profit from the suffering of his patients, that he would write some lurid piece that would titillate readers and make them gasp. But afterwards he questioned his hastiness. Perhaps he might enlighten the journalist on the facts of the disease, and combat the damaging fears and rumours that ignorance gave credence to. Perhaps he could clear up some misconceptions, and there would be fewer people in the world who went around thinking that touching a leper would make your fingers drop off.

But no, he decided, they were better off keeping the outside world at bay. Their patients suffered enough without an audience.

•

Will dined alone in his cottage that night, forgoing the doctors' dining room. He planned to catch up on the correspondence he had been falling behind on. After bathing—he always checked for skin patches—he sat in his comfortable chair. By the steady light of his table lamp he read a letter from his mother, who wrote of the drought and Father burning mulga so the young, tender shoots would grow back and the sheep would have something to eat. He'd had to cull some of the flock, she revealed. Will pictured his father with his rifle, making quick work of it. He was conscious of the silent accusation behind every word. *Your father is doing it without you.* Most families, he wanted to tell her, would be happy with a doctor for a son. But he never told them of his work in the lazaret, because he knew they would not understand his desire to work with leprosy patients. They would think there was something deficient about him as a doctor. Will did write to them about the Coast Hospital, and the strange juxtaposition of the beautiful seaside vistas with the wards of the gravely ill, and how it was an extraordinary place for people to rest and recuperate.

His mother replied to that letter saying that she did not know how, surrounded by lovely young nurses, her son had not yet found a wife. He did not respond.

There was also a letter from Dr Donald Cillen, the Government Medical Advisor. The matron could not bear him, and few of the doctors could either. He disliked the Coast immensely, although no one was quite certain why, except perhaps that he resented the time it took to travel there by carriage when he visited, which he was required to do once a month. Dr Cillen was meant to be an expert on leprosy; he made an annual report on the lazaret, and Stenger always found it to be his most trying time of year. Dr Cillen had travelled to Kalaupapa, the leper colony on the Hawaiian island of Moloka'i, two years earlier and studied the legend of Father Damien among the lepers. He would not cease talking, since he returned, about how incredibly orderly and happy the lepers were there. He would be delighted, Will was certain, to ship his patients off to an island and find a mad Catholic priest to tend to them rather than a doctor. It seemed to be the approach up north. Cillen wrote in this most recent letter of how just three years earlier Peel Island near Brisbane had been turned into a leprosarium for those unfortunate souls in Queensland. Will had heard rumours, already, of the lack of medical care on Peel, which was visited by a doctor only once a month. Of the very basic accommodation. Of how the barge which took those leprosy sufferers to the island did not even allow them on board, but towed them behind in a dinghy.

Will put Cillen's letter aside; he would reply when he was less aggrieved. He drank the last sips of his tea, already cold, and placed the tray beside the sink. He stood by the window for a moment, then went to the bookshelves that lined the walls. He ran his hands across the worn leather spines—they gave him comfort—then settled in his armchair for the last letter, the one he had saved. The bone-handled letter opener felt weighty in his palm and he slowed his movements: the soft tear of paper, the evenly folded page. It was from Isaac: he knew the moment he glimpsed the hasty, nearly illegible script on the envelope, the Melbourne postmark. He held the page to his nose. It did not have a distinct scent, only paper and ink, a faint bitterness of glue. He imagined Isaac shoving it in the envelope, dashing to the postbox on his way somewhere in the rain, a long black umbrella in his hand. His lovely, thin fingers, the cuticles translucent like pearls. He was a surgeon and looked after his hands meticulously. They were his living, he told Will once, and Will understood what he meant. That there was no property in Isaac's family, no allowance or connection or money that he would one day inherit. All that he was must come from his own work.

Dear Will,

Your latest missive made me laugh, and frown, and even shed a tear—though I shouldn't admit it. You are too good at describing the people around you, that wild cast of doctors and nurses, and the patients who are sometimes brave and sometimes stupid, and who occasionally insist on dying, despite your best efforts.

Only today I had to perform surgery on a small girl, not more than four years old, whose foot had been crushed by the boot of her own father, and intentionally, I might add: there was very little hint of accident there. The man ought to be in prison, but his wife is terrified to stand up to him in court and the daughter herself is mute with fear. The policemen have too many other cases and there would be no happy ending for this girl in an orphanage, and so she will probably, once her foot is healed, if she can walk again, return to her violent father and her unfortunate home.

I recall how in medical school you confided in me that you were frightened of how you would recover if one of your patients were to die, and you felt that you were to blame. That was the moment I knew we would be friends. To admit this vulnerability in a sea of bravado was a true sign of your character. Do you recall that conversation?

And the many we had down beside the Glebe Island Bridge about our fathers' expectations, which weighed heavily on our minds? I still think of them often, Will, and cherish those memories.

Now Rose is reminding me that it is time to leave for the dinner we are attending and I still have not dressed and she is quite insistent. I shall post this tomorrow, and await your next letter eagerly.

Your dear friend,
Isaac

Will read the letter twice, then folded it and returned it to its envelope. He placed the envelope in the drawer beside his bed, with a stack of others. He imagined Rose's dark eyes flashing at Isaac as she urged him to hurry. Him trying to make her laugh, to be light-hearted. She was the woman his parents chose for him to marry. The daughter of a family friend.

With each letter Will opened he was afraid to read that Rose was pregnant. Even though he had accepted, long ago, that Isaac was hers. Perhaps, he thought, it would be the proof he needed to move on. Isaac was a part of his past; Will knew that. They would never share a future.

# 6

## Alice

On stormy days at Little Bay I thought the sea might spill and spume beneath our door. Cracks of lightning turned the bedroom white and sheets of rain poured from the overflowing gutters. My first week there I lay in bed and felt sorry for myself. Then I began to investigate the women's lazaret. We all shared a dunny, which was kept clean and always had squares of newspaper on a nail. We were brought meals three times a day in our own cottages. I lingered over mine, not ever having known such a quantity of food. I grew used to not having to share it. I grew used to having Mama around. I met the other women, one by one, as they called me into their cottages, curious to see the leper child. I learned that the ones who look the worst do not always suffer. The one in the hat the first day was Agatha; she lived in a cottage with Lillian. The other two women, Iris and Callie, lived in the third cottage. Callie had ugly lumps of growths. She looked monstrous, but she did not get the pain in her nerves that the others had. Iris was seventy and her hands were claws—she could barely lift a cup of tea—but otherwise, to look at her, you would think nothing was wrong. She had a special teacup with a wide handle, and forks, knives and spoons made with oddly shaped handles so she could grip them. I picked them up from beside the sink in her cottage, where they lay drying on a tea towel. I imagined how it might feel to eat with such strange-looking implements.

I had to sit through test after test in which Dr Stenger and others pricked and scraped my skin. Or they would instruct me to close my eyes and then they'd place a strip of blotting paper somewhere on my body and ask if I felt where it was. Dr Stenger was the kind one. Once a month another doctor visited: his name was Dr Cillen and Mama said we had to respect him. The first time I met him he looked at me through his spectacles as though I were smaller than a grain of sand.

But Dr Stenger liked me to ask him questions and he always had answers. One day he was using a knife to cut away an ulcer on Agatha's foot, and I was watching the way he carved away the flesh like butter. There was a particular vile smell to these ulcers, a smell of rot, like a potato which has turned liquid in the bottom of the barrel, or the water in a vase when the flowers have turned brown. We were on Agatha's verandah and Dr Stenger crouched on a stool across from her, with her foot on another stool between them. There was a basin of carbolic and he kept dipping the knife in the basin, washing her foot with a carbolic-soaked rag. That was the other smell that followed me. They washed everything we wore, all of our linens, and mopped our floors with carbolic. That sharp, coal tar smell had settled permanently inside my nostrils, at the back of my throat.

'Why aren't there any Chinawomen in the lazaret, since there are Chinamen?' I asked.

I had seen a newspaper cutting which Agatha had stuck to the back of the dunny door with paste.

Scattered throughout the cities, towns and villages, and remote out-back settlements, aliens may develop and spread the virus of the many strange Eastern diseases which they carry with them in their wanderings. They are permitted to deal in food and wearing apparel; they produce food for consumption; they handle toilet requirements as dealers, and in a hundred other ways they come in close and intimate contact with our European population. From a hygienic point of view, as well as a racial one, the people are dangerous. Leprosy is the legacy of woe which their yellow, black and brown forerunners of the early 'sixties' left to Australia. In every State there is a Lazarette in which European men, women and children are slowly crumbling to death. That is the heritage of woe unutterable left to this generation of white Australians by the hordes of coloured aliens which poured into the country before our fathers awakened to the danger, and barred the door against the incoming tide of human scum from the foetid East.

When I asked Dr Stenger what foetid meant he said, 'smelling extremely unpleasant'. There were three Chinese men in the lazaret then, but the only one I had met was Ah Foo. He kept a garden, and when he heard that I liked strawberries he said he would grow some just for me. We had a melon vine at Jiggi, but I had only once tasted a strawberry. Ah Foo did not smell unpleasant. There was a particular smell which emanated from the men's lazaret when the three Chinamen cooked the fish they had caught, for they rarely ate from the hospital kitchens, but it was not vile, only different. There were many in the lazaret—Agatha included, with her ulcerating feet—who smelled worse.

'Only Chinamen have been allowed into Australia,' Dr Stenger explained. 'They came for the gold rush. Some suppose they brought leprosy, but I think they are just susceptible—as are the Aborigines. The first recorded case of leprosy in New South Wales was a West Indian in Parramatta in 1859.'

'Always watch out for the blacks,' Agatha said.

'Why are there hardly any Aborigines here at the Coast then?' I asked. There were a few back at Jiggi. Once in a long while we saw them, but not often. Gran told us stories of how she used to see them frequently, how they would fetch honey. They would catch a bee, then stick a small white feather to it with sap and let it fly home. Then they could watch it, to find the hive.

'I'd thank me lucky stars for that if I were you, Alice,' Agatha said. 'Still have to deal with all the kanakas and slanty eyes—the Chows. The scourge of the East, leprosy is. Their fault I'm here.'

'They're mostly up north, so they're sent to different leprosaria, Alice. There are three places they go: Peel Island outside of Brisbane, and Friday and Mud islands further north. And there is no factual evidence, Agatha, that the Chinese brought the disease.'

'I heard it was Chinese laundries,' Agatha said. 'I heard a man sent his silk jacket to be washed, and first time he wore it, he gets leprosy. First white man to get it.'

'That's a tall tale, you know you oughtn't spread it. The first white with leprosy was discovered on the South Coast in 1869, ten years after the first case. It comes from a bacteria. Most of the population is not susceptible, but it seems that susceptibility is inherited. So the disease is not passed down through families, but the likelihood that you would catch it if exposed is. Does that make sense?' Dr Stenger asked me.

'So I got it from my mama, even though she left when I was two?' I asked.

'That's the thing: it can sit dormant for many, many years. And then some taxing event can make the symptoms appear. For your mother it was Hunter's birth. For you it was probably when you had the flu.'

'For me it was when I married me husband,' Agatha said, and laughed so hard that Dr Stenger had to hold the knife away and wait for her to stop.

Lillian banged on the wall. She was still sleeping, even though it was ten in the morning. We settled down. Mama called Agatha 'the Mick', because she was vehemently Catholic. She loved to talk about what a crook her husband was. But she never turned him away when he visited. Quite the opposite, Mama would say.

•

It was months before I agreed to let Mama take me out in the boat. Summer had turned to autumn by then—that time of year when the sun does not have such heat and the wind can make you shiver. We went late in the day, when the beach was empty. The sea was dark green and foamy. We met up with Fred, Mama's friend from the men's lazaret. His face was pitted with scars and his ears mangled.

'This is my daughter, Alice,' Mama said.

He took my hand in his, and I tried not to stare at the stumps of his fingers. They still had fingernails. Mama had seen me counting my fingers and toes each morning—I had been worrying I would lose one while I slept—and explained that they did not drop off. She said that they were bumped and burned from loss of feeling. The nerves shrunk back on themselves. *Resorbed*, Dr Stenger said. Another of his fancy words.

Fred looked closely at my face. 'She has your eyes, only lighter. More grey,' he said to Mama, and I saw then that his were pale blue, kind, crinkled at the edges. His nose was thickened and spread. He cracked jokes while the three of us dragged the clinker hull down the beach on slip rails. He rowed us out in the small waves, the sound of the oars thumping in their oarlocks, the water slapping wood. The spray from the wind made me shiver. Once we were far from land, Fred threaded the hook of a handline with a small, slimy piece of fish and tossed it out into the waves. He scattered burley, which stank, but it smelled good to the fish, he said. When the season was right, he said he would go diving for mutton-fish.

'Ever tasted 'em?'

I shook my head.

He grinned. 'They're beautiful.'

Mama pointed out places along the coast: Long Bay, Maroubra, Cóogee—the words all unfamiliar. The hospital looked so small from out at sea, a low-slung collection of buildings which hugged the coastline. I could not see the cottages of the women's lazaret, just the wall of the men's. But there was the green of the golf course and the specks of cattle in their paddock.

'Where's Jiggi?' I asked Mama.

She laughed. 'Thataway.' She pointed up the coast. 'Not nearly close enough to see.'

Fred spun the reel and brought a pink-and-orange fish in. He ripped the hook from its fleshy mouth. It was the size of my arm. It gasped and flopped on the bottom of the boat. I stared at it, transfixed. 'Snapper,' Fred said. I hoped it would not snap me.

Rowing back to shore was the best part. The boat caught a wave and flew, nearly toppling before sliding up the sand with a *husssh* sound. We were weightless for a moment. Like dropping from the branch of a tree, that moment before hitting the dirt. I had marks in my palms from where I had clutched the gunnels.

We pulled the boat up the rails and into the men's lazaret then gathered wood while the sky caught fire, all pink and red. There were little shallow caves in the sandstone cliff where you could sit, hidden from the rest of the beach, and Ma and Fred lit a fire in one, protected from the wind. Fred had a bottle that they drank from—rum, like Charlie drank at Jiggi Creek. I listened to their talk, huddling close to the flickering flame for warmth. Fred told Mama of a Chinaman in America named Mock Sen. Mock Sen was studying there and about to go home when he became ill. When the local officials found out he had leprosy, they put him in a sealed freight car and pushed him over the state line. The state he was rolled into pushed him back. Back and forth Mock Sen went, pushed from state to state until, after nine days, he died. Mama saw my expression and widened her eyes at him. It was a sign adults used. *She's listening—be careful what you say.*

I wrapped my arms tight across my chest and moved nearer to the fire.

When the fish was cooked, we picked at the white flesh, pulling it from the charred skin, and I plucked scales from my tongue, translucent and fingernail-shaped. Mama pulled me down from the cave to the sand to dance in the firelight. She was wobbly on her feet, smelling of char and sea and skin. It was all so unfamiliar, I felt like that gasping fish.

A lantern came towards us along the beach. The breeze carried a high, sharp bark. It was Matron Wilson, swathed in white, Judy at her heels. 'Come with me,' she said, and took my hand in her rough one.

Judy followed us back to the lazaret. Matron helped me change out of my sandy clothes, ran a hot bath and once I was bathed, dried and in my nightdress she tucked me into bed.

I think Mama stayed on the beach that night. The next morning, I listened through the open bedroom window as Matron had words with her on the verandah.

'You have to set a good example for Alice,' Matron was saying.

Mama was crying, as she sometimes did after a night on the grog.

'I'll never be good enough,' Mama said.

•

She was still asleep that afternoon and I walked down to the beach on my own. In the cave in the cliff there was the charcoal of our burnt-out fire and the bones of the fish, picked by the gulls. Down in the sand was the flutter of a torn white handkerchief trapped in the sand and I tucked it in my pocket; Mama could mend it. I was squinting out to sea—there had been a flash of shining movement, a shift within the water— and did not notice the other person until she spoke beside me.

'Dolphins,' she said.

I jumped.

A girl in a white frock with a shawl wrapped around her shoulders stood beside me. She was tall with gaunt cheeks and deep-set eyes. Her hair fell around her cheeks in brown ringlets. 'Sorry,' she said, 'did I give you a fright?'

'Yes,' I said. 'Are those really dolphins?'

'They are.' She pulled the shawl tight and covered her mouth as she coughed.

'I've only read about them in books,' I said.

'I see them in Coogee sometimes, where I live.' Then, lowering her voice, she said, 'I ran away from my ward—don't tell anyone.'

'I won't,' I said. Her white dress must be a hospital gown, I thought. 'What ward are you in?'

'Tuberculosis. I'm improving, though. What about—oh, look!'

A dolphin leaped from the water, its silvery skin glistening in the light. She clapped her hands together, then clutched my arm.

'Will you walk back with me? What's your name? I'm so rude!'

'Alice.'

'I'm Greta. There are no other girls where I am. What about you?'

'Not a one.'

We walked up the path that skirted the stables and the fowl yard. 'Have you fed the horses?' Greta asked.

'No, we're not meant to go there.'

Greta tossed her head. 'So many silly rules. Meet me here tomorrow, after tea. I know where to get apples.'

She reached out to grab my hand. I drew back from habit.

'See you tomorrow,' I said, but the voice was not mine at all.

I ran all the way back to the lazaret, my heart pounding in my ears.

# 7

*Nellie*

## 1900

In the tent, Avery and Ma slept on the kapok mattress and Nellie on the ground wrapped in a rug. Ma said Avery bruised too easily to sleep on the bare earth. She taught Avery how to read and write but still refused to teach Nellie, insisting she was too slow to learn. Avery did not wash or clean, but worked on his letters, numbers and read aloud to Ma by candlelight while wax dripped onto a metal tray. He never took off into the bush. If she had not killed Elma, Nellie wondered, would she have been Ma's favourite? Would she have been allowed the space beside her?

One day after lunch, Nellie finished hanging out the washing in the heat of the day while Ma was resting. Avery sat beside the tent, whittling with the clasp knife he teased Nellie with, knowing how much she would like one of her own.

'Knives aren't for girls,' he often said.

Nellie did not say where she was going but walked down the path and past the site where the builders were resting in the shade. Some of them slept and others smoked pipes and drank tea. There was a skeleton of a house now, and the sound of hammering peppered their days. She had hours before she was due to help Ma put on another meal. Ignoring the men but feeling their eyes on her, Nellie ducked down a wallaby trail which led to the creek. It was a steep slope to the banks through wattle and scrub but then a shallow crossing. The rain had been sparse that summer, and she needed only lift her skirt to her knees to walk to the other side, stepping gingerly to avoid the sharpest rocks on the callused soles of her feet. The rocks were slippery, but she was nimble and soon stood on the far bank, dropping her skirt again. She was climbing up, holding roots and slipping on leaf litter, when she heard him.

'Nellie.'

Ned stood on the opposite bank, back bent as he took his boots off, one leg folded up like a bird.

'Can I join ya?'

She didn't say anything but waited, halfway up the bank, leaning against a rock which jutted from the hill.

He left his boots and rolled up his moleskin trousers. His legs were pale compared to his brown arms, and his feet must have been softer than Nellie's, since he grimaced at the sharp creek stones. When he was nearly across his foot slipped and he lost his balance, falling backwards into the water. The look of surprise on his smooth face! When he came up, shaking the water from his ears, Nellie was laughing.

'The water's fine,' he called. 'You'll have a swim too?'

She scrambled up the bank, grabbing roots to steady her. He followed. When Nellie glanced back she saw his wet shirt and trousers stuck to him. She turned again, face hot.

'Slow down! Where you goin'?'

'There's a spot—I'll show you.'

'Alright. Better not be far. Haven't got long.'

She ducked beneath branches and let them snap back across him. She leaped over fallen logs soft with moss. She considered showing him the old shack but decided not to. She would keep that for herself. His breath was heavy behind her and she heard the flap, flap of wet fabric. Nellie led him into the clearing. Here the grass was soft and short; there were wild violets and lady's slippers among green. She sat, knees to her chest, and he stretched out in the sun, grasping his shirt in a fist and wringing the drops from it.

'Why don't the trees grow here?' he asked.

'The pademelons come and graze.'

'I heard places like this are where the fairies live.'

'You believe in fairies then?'

Ned snorted, plucking a blade of grass. He cupped it between his thumbs and blew so it made a high, sharp whistle.

'Yer Ma will fire me if she hears I'm talking to you.'

'So why are you?'

He shrugged. 'Not scared.'

'What about the rumours?'

'Your father was a leper?'

She nodded.

He shrugged. 'Is it true?'

'They took him away.'

'And you?'

'Do I look like a leper?'

'Can't say you do.'

She brought her knees down then and studied his face as he gazed across the clearing. The sun was drying his wet clothes, and where he shaved the stubble on his cheeks was coming in gold.

'Where's your family?' she asked.

'Lismore way.'

He shut his eyes for a minute, nearly. She did the same, wanting to see what he was seeing, the same patterns behind her eyelids, pink and black and green.

She opened her eyes when she felt the shadow. He stood above her, blocking the sun, holding out his hand.

'I'd best be getting back. They'll wonder where I've got to.'

Nellie looked at his hand too long, hanging there in the air.

'I'll help you up,' he said.

She put out her hand. He grasped, hard, and pulled her to her feet so quick she stumbled forward, then caught her to his chest. He smelled of fresh-cut timber and pitch. Nellie stepped back. He grinned.

'Sorry—you're light as a feather, though. Here . . .' Ned touched her waist. 'You've got grass on your skirt.'

She looked over her shoulder, brushing it away.

'You've got a spider in your hair,' she said, and laughed when he madly raked his hands over his scalp. She ran towards the creek, springing across the ground so fast he had no chance of catching up.

•

It became a habit, during the sleepy time after the midday meal, when the dishes were washed but the men still rested in the shade. Nellie would head one way into the bush, Ned would go the other, and they doubled back after crossing the creek and met at the clearing. He asked about the shack one day, having seen it through the trees, and she said they ought not go there: it was haunted.

'What happened to the people who lived there?' he asked.

'I was a child when they moved away. Ma says the woman died in there.'

She grew bolder, sometimes grabbing the sleeve of his shirt. He tickled her bare feet with a blade of grass, then his rough wide fingers.

'So small,' he said, touching the bony tops of her feet.

One day he told her why he'd left Lismore, where there was plenty of work. Why he took their job, even though Ma offered paltry pay.

Last summer, he had been out in the bush behind their acreage with his two brothers, shooting wallabies. His father had bought the land only the year before and, with his sons, built a small house. There were plans to cultivate the soil and plant mangoes, once they cleared the land and cut out the galvanised burr. It was late in the day, and the light was fading. The three of them chose different directions and took off with their rifles slung over their shoulders. Ned had fired

74

at three wallabies already and missed. He knew his brother James would rib him. James always claimed he was a better shot, simply on account of being older. Ned decided to have one more go before heading home, where he knew there was meat on the stove. Just then, he saw movement in the long grass beside a distant tree. It was something, no doubt, and he took aim and pulled the trigger.

'That's when I heard my brother scream,' he said. 'The worst sound I ever heard. I ran over and found I'd hit him in the chest. I tried to stop the bleeding, but it was no use. He died before I could carry him home. I could not hit a wallaby, but I killed my brother.'

He was pale, all the colour gone from his face. Nellie put her arms around his neck and tried to comfort him. He pulled her onto his lap to hold her close. What were the chances? she wondered. Someone who lived with the same sin as hers.

When she told him about Elma he said it weren't her fault. He said she was too small to know. He put two fingers beneath her chin to lift her face to his, and with lips rough and windburned he kissed her. It was her first kiss, Nellie said, and he looked at her through white lashes.

'First of many.'

•

The house came along every day. They clad the sides, hung windows and doors, brought in the sheets of corrugated iron which would become the roof. The floor was dirt, but they would sprinkle it with ashes from the fireplace and sweep it with a wattle broom until it became hard.

Ned and Nellie never spoke in front of the others, but she could not help turning her eyes to him. You would have been blind not to notice.

In the meadow, in the soft green with hard small stones beneath, they had done what Ma had warned her against, and he whispered words that no one had said to Nellie before. She was pretty as a picture, he said. He would take her away from here. Ants bit her bared skin, and he kissed the angry lumps. He rolled away then, and they each dressed quickly, backs to one another. The words he'd said before did not come after.

The day the last coat of paint went on they were loading their supplies into the carts. Ma had gone to town to draw the money from the bank. She asked Nellie to go with her, but Nellie feigned a stomach-ache. 'Take Avery,' she said. Ma frowned but was quiet, except for instructions on what to prepare for dinner.

When her mother and brother were out of sight, she combed her hair back in the tent and put on the faded blue dress which stopped above her ankles but was still her nicest thing. She walked to the house and admired the glass windows, the way they gleamed in the sun, and the white paint which had gone on in strokes and stripes and was now so pleasing and even. The men were loading their tools and timber, and she watched from the house. Ned would surely walk over when he saw her.

She waited until the cart was packed, and the cloth on top secured with ropes, tied with knots. The horses stood twitching at flies. The skinny black dog circled, worrying he would be left behind. Finally, she walked over to the cart. Ned was crouched beside a wheel.

Nellie coughed, and he looked up.

The others all stopped what they were doing and watched as well.

'Could we have a word?' she asked, her voice more querulous than she intended.

'Be right with you,' Ned said.

Nellie waited beside the banked fire. Without even looking she could sense the men's smirks, their eyes. She crouched by the ashes. There were potatoes to peel and she started the work, to keep herself looking busy. She used Avery's knife.

'Your ma needs you,' he said when at last he came to stand beside her.

The knife slipped and cut her finger. She cried out.

'Careful, now.'

Nellie stuck her finger in her mouth, the taste of blood like nails.

'I have houses to build, Nellie. You see how rough these men are. It's no place for a girl. I will come back when I have saved enough. When I can build you a house of your own.'

Perhaps it was the blood that made her angry. Or the way the words came so smoothly from his mouth, like water-worn stones.

'You lied,' she said, pinching the whitened skin on her finger.

'I did not,' he said.

'Liar.'

The men were all silent by the carts, no doubt straining their ears.

She would make it easy for them.

Nellie stood and threw the knife, missing his boot by an inch. He jumped and picked it up, holding it out of her reach.

'I hate you.' She swung at him with her fist. 'I hope you die.'

The men were laughing now, and one hooted. Nellie could not bear it any longer. She ran into the tent and buried her face in the blankets.

When she came out, later, Ma and Avery had returned. Avery's knife was on a log, clasped shut, and Ned was gone.

# 8

## Alice

I dreamed of marrying Dr Stenger. He brought me books and explained things to me in a quiet, calm way. I watched his long-fingered, clean hands as he prepared a needle or tested my skin. The way his reddish hair was thin at the temples, and the way he pushed his gold spectacles up the bridge of his nose when looking down at a page while writing his notes. He even had freckles on the lobes of his ears. I thought that he knew everything, that he was capable of anything, and that one day, if I listened and followed his instructions to the letter, he would cure me. That was never what he said, mind you, but it was what I thought. Why would he spend so much time on us if he knew we were only going to die?

Of course I was aware I was a child, and a leprous one at that, and that he would never choose to marry me, but I was content simply to be in his proximity. To have him touch me now and again without cringing, to hear his deep voice explaining things to me, to ask him questions and hear his careful reply. He was always rushing from place to place, always late and doing a dozen things, but in spite of this he took the time to speak with us. I had never known such a kind man.

He was the opposite of Charlie, with his dark whiskers and hard face, his loud voice and rough hand. When I was very small, no more than four, I banged into the table when running across the room, playing, and spilled Charlie's tea and scalded him.

'Since you can't learn to sit quietly, you will sit all night here,' he said. 'And if you move, you'll be in greater trouble.'

That night I was not allowed to lie down to sleep.

Each time I put my head down on the table he would box my ears. My head was heavy as lead, my ears rang, and still my eyes couldn't help but shut of their own accord. Gran wanted him to at least let me lie beneath the table, but he refused until he was too tired himself to continue and finally went to bed. My head could barely reach the table, that's how small I was, but I rested it on the edge to sleep. In the grey hours of dawn Gran pulled me from the chair and pointed me towards bed. I felt as though my limbs were stone. When I woke, the sun was high in the sky and Charlie was off at work. I had a crease on my forehead from the edge of the table which remained there the rest of the day.

•

Greta and I continued to meet. She was twelve and loved to talk, which was lucky, as I loved to listen. We made plans to meet each day around the hospital—at the pond beside the nurses' dormitories, the edge of the golf course, down on the beach. I told Mama I was running errands for Matron. I did not think twice about my lie. Greta made no mention of my swollen ears or the raised patches of shiny pink skin on my arms. She did not ask what was wrong with me, which made me think perhaps she knew. She was being kind—she was that sort; she did not allow one horse to gobble up the carrots and apples, she made them share, and she always said hello to those we passed on our outings.

'Will we not get in trouble?' I whispered, more than once.

'You'll only draw attention if you act guilty,' she said.

I thought of Greta before I fell asleep at night and first thing when I woke in the morning. As I touched every inch of myself to see if any of my skin had changed, I thought of her skin, how smooth and unblemished it was. It was her insides which were faulty. She had coughing fits, and there were times when she was too tired to keep walking. I pretended that nothing was wrong. I made dandelion chains while I waited for her to be ready to continue, necklaces and crowns for both of us. The flowers bled white sap onto my fingertips when I snapped their stems.

Greta and Dr Stenger were not the only people who were kind to me. The attendant, Olive, gave me ribbons for my long thick hair. Matron Wilson gave me sweets, and then beads when she learned that I liked to make necklaces from them.

I was not allowed to attend school, but each of them taught me what they could. The doctor with his books and his medicine and big words, and Mama to sew and iron, to plait hair. Olive taught me to cook simple dishes, and Matron Wilson gave me lessons in language and elocution. I heard her speak strictly to the nurses and probationers, and even some of the grown patients, but she was kind to me. Her sharpest words were when she corrected the way people spoke. She could not bear slang, and the day she heard Fred refer to himself as a leppo I thought steam would shoot from her ears.

'You will not speak that way in *my* hospital,' she said. 'I will not hear that kind of language.'

Fred had to apologise, though he still called himself a leppo, as all the men did, just not in her hearing. I knew that desire: to criticise yourself before someone else did.

We had to have a particular reason to visit the men's lazaret, and they were not allowed into ours, but there were special concessions, like concerts. Matron Wilson thought culture had as much place inside a lazaret as outside. She would survey her nurses, find any with a fraction of musical talent, and get them to perform for us. Sometimes she roped in the doctors as well. It cut through the tedium—there was a doctor who played the violin and a few nurses who could play piano, and there were always those who could sing. Dr Stenger said he didn't have a single talent besides being a doctor. The day of a concert, Mama and I would spend hours getting dressed, ironing our nicest clothes, starching our white blouses, curling my hair so it fell in ringlets around my face. Those days I had to make up excuses why I could not meet Greta.

My first concert at the hospital was also the first time I entered the men's lazaret. It was larger than ours. They were in a gully on the north end of the bay, closest to the leper beach. They had nine cottages inside their fence, and the same kind of door with a narrow high opening and the sign which read, ISOLATION: NO ADMITTANCE WITHOUT PERMISSION. But one of the men had scratched out some of the letters, so that instead of PERMISSION it read P ISS . No admittance without piss. I jabbed my elbow into Mama and read it out to her. She grinned. 'Bunch of smartarses.'

Inside they had a special cottage—called the Arts Cottage— set aside for the men to gather in and do their woodwork or painting, play music or cards. Mama said they played a lot of cards, and they gambled things like their liquor ration or their tobacco ration, since hardly any of them had money.

'Not fair they have a cottage just for extra,' I said, but Mama hushed me. We were inside their compound, which had a tall date palm in the furthest corner, and a group of men were coming over to greet Mama. They all embraced and kissed her and made a big fuss of me, even the ones I hadn't met yet. There was Fred and Red, Billy, Ah Foo and Java Jim. Some were a mess of sores and missing fingers, squashed and swollen noses, but others looked like any man you might see out on the street. I saw how Mama was around them and it made me comfortable too.

Inside the Arts Cottage, the chairs had been arranged along three sides of the main room, and there was a piano and a music stand against the remaining wall. Off the main room was a smaller room with floor-to-ceiling bookshelves.

I longed to explore them further. Matron stood over in the corner beside a tea trolley on which were biscuits and pots of tea. The male attendant, Ted, was pouring tea and offering around the biscuits.

'Ya should've worn yer apron,' Mama said to Ted, and his ears turned red.

'Where's the grog? I'm no teetotaller,' Fred said, when he was offered a cuppa, and Matron gave him a sharp look. Mama elbowed him in the ribs and he shrieked, diving to the floor. 'She's knocked me nipple off, nurse! Help find me nipple!'

Matron stood in the centre of the room until it was dead quiet, and we scurried to find chairs.

'Good evening, ladies and gentlemen,' she boomed. 'Tonight's entertainment is straight from the considerable talent pool of the West End of hospitals, the Coast. First, I would like everyone to put their hands together to welcome Miss . . . Ivy . . . Rogers.'

A nurse with black hair and dark red lipstick glided into the room. She wore a floor-length red dress with a fur fox stole around her neck, and her hair spilled loose over her shoulders. It gleamed in the lamplight. This was glamorous enough, but I still wasn't prepared for what happened when she opened her mouth and sang, without any accompaniment, not even the piano. It was a language I did not know, it was a song I had never heard, but oh! I could have listened forever. I cannot even remember what came next. There was piano playing, I'm sure, perhaps a skit? But I just kept Ivy Rogers' voice in my head, that high, clear way she hit those notes, that lovely, aching sound.

Matron told me later it was called opera, and that the nurse had sung in Italian. For weeks afterwards I tried to make those noises myself when I thought I was alone, in a little cubby beneath the verandah I had made nice with all of my shells and an old blanket to sit on. Sometimes Judy came to visit me there and I fed her the broken biscuits I saved and crusts of bread. I would learn to sing like Ivy, and show Greta, and I imagined how impressed she would be. *Your voice is so beautiful*, she would say.

Mama pounded on the floorboards of the verandah above, where she was sitting darning stockings and smoking.

'When will you stop that bloody racket? You sound like a dying cat!' she shouted.

Judy licked my tears. I shouldn't have cared but I did. I knew I would never *be* beautiful, but I had thought perhaps I might sound that way.

•

Christmas at Jiggi was lying in the creek trying to stay cool and Gran dragging us all to church by lantern light for midnight mass on Christmas Eve, the stars glimmers of light in the sky, the crunch of horse hooves in the dark, the rush of the creek and the cart bumping on the familiar ruts of Jiggi Road. After mass we slept a few hours but were up early and lighting the fire in the outdoor kitchen and cooking a lunch Gran had been scrounging together for months. I would be put to work plucking the chicken or wild duck—when we had one—scrubbing potatoes or carrots, stirring the gravy. After we ate we played rounders in the paddock, and Charlie rode the horse back from Nimbin pub late afternoon with his pockets full of lemon drops and cherry lozenges. We split them—even the baby got two—until Gran realised what we'd done and sent us outside as George coughed and choked and Charlie swore. Turned out you were not meant to give a baby lollies.

Christmas at the Coast was something else altogether. The nurses and attendants spent weeks tying branches of greenery to the windows and doorways, putting up trees in the wards and practising their carols. We practised a song, too—'Deck the Halls', which sounded alright with Lillian's soprano. Most of the women's voices were hoarse. I learned that leprosy makes your voice funny too.

Christmas morning I woke at dawn with a pillowslip at the end of my bed filled with presents. I asked Mama where they were from, and she grinned from her bed on the other side of the room.

'Father Christmas!'

'Why don't you have any?'

'He only visits children.'

'Why's he never given me presents before, then?'

'I dunno. He probably couldn't get to Jiggi. Are you going to keep asking questions or are you going to open the bloody things?'

I pulled out the parcels and carefully unwrapped each one. There was a tortoiseshell comb, two books, a porcelain doll with real hair and a soft body, and three new ribbons for my hair. I showed Mama everything and she bit her lip.

'Will you read one of your books aloud?' she asked.

She had never wanted to hear me read before. I worried I would stumble over my words. I had already missed nearly a whole year of school. I sat the doll beside me in bed and, with the curtains flung open for light and air, I began to read the first book, which had my name in it: *Alice's Adventures in Wonderland*. I remembered how Dr Stenger said he would give me a copy and I wondered if Father Christmas was really him.

> Alice was beginning to get very tired of sitting by her sister on the bank, and of having nothing to do: once or twice she had peeped into the book her sister was reading, but it had no pictures or conversations in it, 'and what is the use of a book,' thought Alice, 'without pictures or conversation?'

Mama didn't chide me when I lost my place or stumbled over a word. We sat there for nearly an hour, until there was a knock on the door. Still in her nightdress, Mama went to open it.

'Alice, come see,' she called, and I came, cradling my new doll in my arms.

There, standing in the grass, was a group of sisters, at least twenty of them, all in their veils and uniforms and wearing holly pinned to their chests. It was still early enough that the fog sat in the lower parts of the garden, and they looked like angels, the mist around their feet, the light still that soft yellow of morning.

They had knocked on all the doors in the women's lazaret. We stood on our verandahs and listened as they sang Christmas carols: 'Silent Night', 'Jingle Bells', 'The First Noel'. I sang along to the ones I knew and after each song I clapped together the hands of my new doll. Most of the nurses had never before been in the lazaret, and they looked around wide-eyed as they sang, their eyes often landing on me. I was the poor leper child, but I had, for the first time in my life, a real Christmas, so I didn't mind if they were sorry for me. I had books and a doll and ribbons all my own. I had my first friend, too, and that afternoon we had plans to meet at the beach.

After their songs we gathered together on the path—Agatha and Lillian, Iris, Callie, Mama and me—and sang our version of 'Deck the Halls'. I forgot some words, and those high notes sounded shrill, but the nurses all clapped and smiled. They left us with calls of 'Merry Christmas', and went to the men's lazaret to repeat their performance. The fog had burned off and the grass looked parched as the sun rose higher in the sky.

'Callie and I are going to the Catholic service,' Agatha said, narrowing her eyes at our nightdresses.

'We've been reading in bed,' I said.

'Will you join us?'

Mama shook her head, drawing a shawl tight around her shoulders. 'Go if you like, Alice. I'm going back to bed.'

'I'll stay with Mama,' I said. The only thing I liked about church in Jiggi was the middle-of-the-nightness of it; otherwise my collar always itched and Gran would glare and pinch if we did not sit still.

'There's a Church of England service after,' Agatha called out.

I followed Mama inside and curled up again with my book. I read until Olive peeked her head in, by which stage Mama had fallen back asleep. I put my finger over my lips and tiptoed out to the table in the kitchen. Olive had brought porridge and toast. She had white hair and a daughter who was grown and lived up north. Her husband had died with all kinds of debts, Mama said, so poor Olive had to work even through Christmas and we ought to be nice to her.

She gave me a dish of beads of all colours—pinks and greens, blues and reds. I gave her a pair of socks I had knitted with Mama's help. I took my Easton's syrup with cod-liver oil and malt, ate my porridge and Mama's, and saved her all the toast because it was better cold. Later, Olive said, we would have a special Christmas lunch.

'Have you ever had roast chicken?' she asked.

I shook my head, even though I had, because I saw that Olive liked when I hadn't.

'Christmas pudding?'

I shook my head again.

'Well, you are in for a treat.'

I wished that I could save some for Hunter, Annie, George and Irene. I would even let them play with my doll. I would not let them touch my book, though; they would probably ruin it.

•

I had made a necklace of blue and green beads for Greta because I knew they were her favourite colours, and I wrapped it in the leftover paper from one of my parcels, brown paper stamped with holly leaves and berries, and tied it with red satin ribbon. After lunch, when everyone seemed to be sleeping, I snuck down to the leper beach on my own and waited for my friend.

I squinted in the hot sun, rubbing my fingers against the rough-textured sandstone. My brow felt damp from perspiration. We *had* made plans to meet on Christmas afternoon. Where was she? There were distant figures on the nurses' beach, a cluster of them swimming in their rock pool. Once or twice before Greta had not shown up at our meetings, but there were always profuse apologies the next day and excellent excuses (the nurses were on to her, the doctor sedated her in order to force some rest). I had given up and stood to leave when I saw her at the top of the steep path, and waved with both arms. I could tell there was something amiss from the way she only lifted a hand. Two figures appeared behind her, wavering in the heat.

It was worse to wait where I was, on the sandstone, so I walked up the path to meet them halfway.

I guessed they were her parents. Greta's father wore a bowler hat and pince-nez, and her mother was in a starched-stiff black dress. Between them, Greta looked frail and unwell, and for the first time I wondered if people survived tuberculosis. Perhaps she had not been the only incurious one.

'Happy Christmas,' I mumbled, holding out the wrapped parcel.

We stood on that sandy path facing one another, but Greta did not move to take it. I lowered my arm. Her lip trembled, and I saw her eyes were rubbed raw. 'You didn't tell me,' she said in a small voice. 'You're a leper.'

Her mother recoiled at the word.

'I thought you knew,' I said. 'We met on the leper beach. The lazarets are just there.'

I pointed and her parents turned to look, as though they might see festering lepers with faces eaten by vermin.

'My parents said we're not to meet again,' Greta said, her voice becoming clearer. She had on a new dress. I wondered if she was going home. She stifled a cough in her sleeve. 'We cannot be friends.'

'That's fine,' I said, blinking fast. Hilda was dead, Alice did not cry. 'I've got lots of other friends, besides.'

'Good day to you, then,' Greta's father said.

I turned before they could and ran down onto the beach, my feet sinking in the scalding sand. I thought I heard Greta call, 'Goodbye,' but it could have been a gull, or her crying at the sand stinging her face from the wind that had picked up.

I ran straight to the water's edge and hurled her parcel, as hard as I could, into the sea. I hoped she was watching.

The parcel bobbed on the water, threatening to wash back in. Slowly, then all at once, it grew heavy. Slowly, then all at once, it drowned.

# 9

*Jack*

## 1914

The day Jack turned fifteen, the brothers gave him five pounds,
a set of second-hand clothes, new boots and a letter which
recommended him for employment. He took his enamel
drinking cup but left the scratchy pyjamas behind. He was
still a ward of the state until he was eighteen, and all of his
wages would go to the Board for the Protection of Aborigines,
so instead of knocking on doors looking for work, he spent three
days travelling back to Angledool. First up top a stage coach and
then in the back of a farmer's cart from Walgett. The Narran
was barely running, a trickle on claypan. He walked through
town past the Chinese gardens, Granny Walden's bakery, the
cordial factory where he had earned his coins, the Old Bark

Pub, Hatfield's General Store. The post office, police station and lock-up. At the mission there was a sign now: ANGLEDOOL ABORIGINAL RESERVE.

The sun beat down as he blinked away flies. The camp looked empty, the only sound his footsteps, his feet kicking up small clouds of dust. He stood in the doorway of his old home, the walls of flattened kero tins and lime-washed hessian bags shabbier than he remembered. No one was there. Heat so oppressive the sweat evaporated from his skin as soon as it appeared. He had a drink from the water drum outside and went to Aunty Rita's. She was asleep, an occasional snore rumbling the air. As he watched, her eyes popped open; she must have felt him staring.

Rita clutched her chest, sitting straight up.

'It's me, Aunty Rita. Sorry to give you a fright.'

'Jack?'

She scooted off the bed and came over to feel that he was solid, not a ghost.

It took her a moment, but her face crumpled like paper in a flame, as much crying as laughing at the sight of him. Shouting loud enough to wake anyone else having their midday sleep: 'Our boy Jack is back home.' She had grown fat, with dark circles beneath her eyes. She said his mother was working as a domestic at Angledool Station again; she would return that evening.

•

His mother came at dusk, out of breath from running; she'd heard the news that he was home. She pulled him in close, then held him out at arm's length. Her chapped hands felt the bones of his cheeks. 'I tried to come get you, but they wouldn't let me.'

'I'm sorry.'

'Shh. Look at you. Handsome. Come eat. Have you had something?'

'What,' Aunty Rita said, 'd'you think I didn't offer him food?'

The two sisters laughed and he felt warm with the sound.

His mother was skinny to Aunty Rita's fat, hair threaded with silver, wrung through and worn. She watched him eat Aunty Rita's johnny cakes and stew like it was going into her own belly. He did not know how else to comfort them, so he ate until his stomach ached. The billy boiling over the fire was a seven-pound treacle tin.

'Where's Granny?' Jack asked, when he could not fit in another bite of food.

The looks on their faces told him.

•

After dinner, Jack walked down to the Narran to wash, but there was hardly enough water to bathe in. He splashed it on his face, under his arms: even the water smelled like dust. The stars were spread thick across the night sky and he could not help but think, what if he could take back the last ten years? To grow up here, to come home every day to this, his family, instead of strangers. To be with his granny again, and hear her voice like a blanket, putting him to sleep.

He slept that night in the same bed he had slept in as a boy, beside his mother. She slept sitting up in a chair, said it was better for her back. He wanted to tell his mother how much he'd missed her, how every night since he had been taken he went to sleep thinking of her, but he couldn't find the words.

•

Ten years don't disappear because of everything that happened in between. He had a sister, Daisy. She had been hiding the day before, scared of this brother she had never met. She was knobble-kneed with eyes that saw right through him. She was clever as. He couldn't help but feel jealous of her. She grew up swimming in the Narran, fishing at the weir, hunting emu eggs, yabbying. She leaned against their mother with an easy familiarity—the kind that comes with never having been denied something. Jack felt the stiffness of his own affection, like the pyjamas he had left behind.

Daisy went to school—there was a school now just for the reserve, which started with an early bell and finished before lunch.

'What do you learn?' Jack asked.

'Gardening, sewing, raffia,' Daisy listed on her fingers. 'Cooking, mending. Boys learn boot mending and boat repair, carpentry.'

'What about reading and arithmetic?'

Daisy shrugged. 'Little bit.'

With Daisy in the big bed, he slept now in the sleepout, under the bough shed. Jack kept dreaming he was falling. He'd wake with a start, grabbing the blankets like they would somehow catch him. After nights of broken sleep, he slept so late he was woken by the rattle of the fruit cart, Old Donoghue come to sell his fruit before it went off. It took some getting used to, the knowledge that he did not have anywhere he was meant to be.

•

Jack had been home two weeks when he got a letter from Guy.

Dear Jack. I hear you're free! Good for you. Working as a boundary rider, musterer, can see if there's anything around if you're looking. Never too much for an ugly friend.

Got myself a beautiful woman and a sweet baby now to look after so I'm always working, but I hope we catch up soon. For old time's sake,

Guy

Jack wrote back saying yes to the work if Guy heard of any, and congratulations on the wife and little one. He wondered if having his own family would make him feel settled, like he had something solid. Or if it was just more to worry about. More to lose.

Having spent the last ten years surrounded only by boys, Jack did not know how to speak to any of the girls. They said 'hello' sometimes, walking past, but his reply was too soft. 'Why's he so stuck up?' he heard Daisy asking his mother once as they were washing up, when they didn't know he was home.

'He's not—just shy. You be nice to him, hear? He was a long time away.'

•

There was the School of the Arts in Angledool, a hall made of ant bed, and Friday nights were dances or pantomimes. Aunty Rita played the concertina and Jack stood with the other young men from the reserve outside, watching the girls glide in through the big open doors. He watched the dancing pairs, marvelling at how they knew to move in the same direction. The music filled his chest, the sweetness of it.

The mission manager, a thin-lipped man who carried his black record book everywhere, told Jack he ought to learn shearing and crutching in the shearing shed with the other boys. Jack preferred horses to sheep, but he learned to use the blade shear and, with the sheep between his knees, make long confident blows. The click of the shear blades punctuated his days as Jack learned to skirt and roll the fleece. He grew stronger, the muscles in his arms and back visible beneath the skin. But he missed the stables. When he got a letter from Guy saying he'd asked around and heard there was fencing work at Llanillo, he went. When there was work closer to home, he told his mother, he would come back to Angledool.

•

At Llanillo, Jack was in a bunkhouse with a dozen other men, he ate at the designated time and slept hard every night from exhaustion. He would do a hundred fence posts a day; he dreamed of braces and bits, crowbars and shovels. The dreams of falling stopped. He had one day off a month, and he spent most of it riding home and back. At Llanillo, Jack still thought of his mother every night before sleep, but it was easier to miss her, the idea of her, from far away. It was harder up close.

The distance was what he knew.

# 10

*Alice*

## 1915

At fourteen I hated the Coast.

Fury woke me in the morning, my jaw already clenched with it. I had gone to bed with a cloth, and it felt bulky between my legs, already stiff with dried blood.

I had begun to bleed. Mama showed me what to wear and how to soak it after, where to wash and hang it secretly, so the others did not see. She told me it would happen every month now, I would grow used to it. As I picked the stitches from a dress I was letting down the hem on, she said, 'What not to do is let a man stick his thing in you now, because it will make a baby. And the last thing you want is one of them.'

'Mama!'

'No one told me the way it was. I'm doing you a favour,' she said.

'Am I the last thing you wanted, then?'

'That's not what I meant. I meant you are too young for a bub of your own. And who wants to give someone this, what I've given you?'

'No one will ever want me anyway,' I said, turning away from her. 'I wish I was never born.'

She worked in silence, then, and I did too. I wanted to chew this life up and spit it out, so it was as mangled as my skin. I would not rest until the world was torn apart around me.

'It's no place to grow up,' Mama said to Matron as an excuse, when I spat out my vile-tasting chaulmoogra capsules or refused to let Olive dress my sores.

'You should see the other leper colonies,' Matron said.

'One's plenty,' Mama replied.

'Well, you are lucky to be here. Imagine being one of our young men, sent to war.'

'I would rather fight the Germans,' I said. 'Imagine how many would flee if I told them I was a leper. You should send us all to war.'

'Fine lot of good that would do,' Matron said.

Some days, instead of fury, I succumbed to weariness. I would stay in bed longer than I should, watching the square of daylight from the window shift across the bedroom. I read all of the books Dr Stenger brought me, all of the books I could borrow, but it was not the same as school. There were no teachers to please with my progress. No other pupils to compete with. When he had time, Dr Stenger would discuss the books with me, but he had so much to do, he was often called away. For him there was never enough time. For me there was far too much. It slowed and pooled around me, viscous and sticky. I played cards with the old women, sewed, gardened and walked on the beach. I spent hours on the rock shelves, peering for sea creatures in the pock holes brimming with brackish water. I saw limpets and pennywinkles, starfish, anemones and spiky sea urchins. I poked at swift-footed crabs and they scuttled out of sight. I draped strands of Neptune's necklace around my throat, pretending they were pearls. Sometimes I waded in and felt the salt water sting my legs. I wondered what it would be like to surrender to the power of it, to be swept away. Sometimes I still expected to see Greta's parcel, waterlogged and faded in the sand. The nurses were rarely on their beach then, many had signed up as nursing sisters for the Australian Army and those who were left were busier than ever. Dr Stenger still swam early every morning. What was it like for him to swim? I had seen him, naked, entering the sea at dawn. Hiding behind sandstone, surprised at the glaring whiteness of his skin. It felt wrong to watch him; afterwards I wished I had never seen.

Back at the lazaret, I read to others who were losing their sight. At nine, it might have been enough. At fourteen, it was not. When I touched each part of my skin now before sleep there were more patches of numbness, but there were other changes. Softness around my belly and hips. Tenderness in my breasts.

I took to walking at night. I walked until my feet were raw and bleeding. Dr Stenger said leprosy made us hurt our feet more, because we could not feel the pain that tells us to change the way we walk. That heel is tired, your foot will say. Walk more on your toes. 'My feet don't speak,' I said to him. He sighed. 'You know what I mean.' He said he had once amputated a woman's foot because she stepped on a nail and did not realise it for a week. So I wore clunky black shoes with buckles at the ankle that were too large and stuffed with gauze inside. They made me graceless, heavy on my feet.

Still, even with the clomping, it was too dark for them to find me, and I walked across the cliffs and rocks, finding paths through the golf course and out past the bay. Mama knew I escaped, but she couldn't say much because I learned how from her. I knew where she went, over by the men's lazaret in the northern corner of the bay. I went in the other direction, south.

Those night walks prepared me for losing my sight. The world was sounds, shapes and smells then. The waves crashing on rocks beneath meant I was close to the edge of a cliff. The outline of lighter grey against dark. The sap smell of cut grass meant I was on the cemetery or the golf course. I listened for the soft whoosh of an owl in the grove of Norfolk pines. On a clear night the moon would make a shining path across the dark ocean. The branches of the pines sieved the moonlight. I heard the rustle of cats out hunting, saw their eyes glinting green through bushes. The sounds in the bushes could be a lizard or a red-bellied black snake. What was there to be scared of? My life could not be worse. There was nothing to look forward to, only the same dull existence every day until my body failed me and I died. I walked to feel alive.

Past our settlement there were goat tracks through the bush, fox trails. The smell sometimes of a rotting fish told me I was near the fishing spot, and the *croa croa* of frogs meant I was near the reservoir. One windy night I walked for miles along the coast, to some huts at a beach where vagrants camped. Sheets of corrugated tin and hessian bags were cobbled together for shelter. For a while I stayed beyond the firelight and watched men and women drinking, heard the sounds of babies waking as bottles smashed against rocks and settling again. And then, overcome by some reckless impulse, I stood and went over to the edge of the fire, calling, 'Hello.'

'Who's this?' a man replied, poking a stick at the coals so they let off red sparks in the wind. 'A young lady. Where'd you come from?'

'An evening ramble.'

'You're not from the camp, are ya?' A woman with tangled hair squinted at me.

'We came today,' I said. 'I'm Alice.'

'Welcome, Alice,' said a younger man with a beard. 'I'm Bobby. Come sit beside me. Watch out for them old fellas.'

I sat beside him on a log, on the darker side, further from the firelight. He had smooth skin; I did not want him to see mine.

He held out his bottle and I took a swig, coughing after.

'Have you got any food?' he asked.

'No.'

'Stone me, I'm starving. What I'd do for a johnny cake. Sometimes drink kills the hunger. Some nights makes it worse.'

I made a small sound that was meant to be agreement.

He turned towards me. 'Move closer, Alice. I can't see ya. You're not very big. How old—'

'Eighteen,' I said.

'If you're eighteen, I'm King of England.'

'Sixteen.'

'Huh.' He reached out and put a hand on my leg. I shifted away. He raised his hands. 'Sorry.'

'I've got to go. My mother will be looking for me.'

'See you around then, Alice?'

I did not reply, but ducked off into the brush behind the fire and found the trail I had followed, my eyes adjusting again to the night. How daft I was! What if he had noticed, or someone else had? They would have thrown me into the fire. Or the sea. I clasped one hand around my wrist; I was hardly bigger than a child, but I was still the worst thing imaginable: a leper. Still, my heart was beating twice as fast, and I was feeling what I secretly sought now—fear. The best reminder that you are still alive.

I never went back to that beach.

I never went back and showed my face, that is. I hid and watched them in the firelight. I watched Bobby, and I watched the women who sat on his lap or beside him. I watched them laugh and drink and sometimes fight, blood noses and bruised faces, grazed fists.

One night I watched a woman who was passed out get dragged into the bushes by two men, and I wanted to call out but cared more about myself, about them not discovering me. She woke screaming and others came. The men stumbled away, buttoning their trousers, mumbling excuses.

'Where do you go?' Mama asked, when I came back into our room through the window.

'Where do you?' I replied.

'You know full—'

'Yes.'

'And you?'

'Not there.'

'I worry,' Mama said, her voice muffled by sheets. She slept with them over her face, so she looked like a corpse. She said it was so she could sleep later. So the light didn't wake her. 'Life was easier when you weren't here.'

'Thanks, Mama.'

'Just, I worry now. I have you as well as me to worry about.'

'I don't need your worry.'

'I can't help it,' she said. 'One day you'll . . .' Her voice faded. One day I wouldn't. What was the point, then?

I swallowed the lump in my throat and rolled over. My hands smelled like smoke from the fires. I pretended they were Bobby's, not mine, and before long it was morning.

•

Everything changed the day that George arrived. It was the last thing any of us expected.

Dr Stenger brought him from the gatehouse; later we learned that Charlie had dropped him off there, refusing to come inside.

'I'll bet he was terrified of what would happen if I saw him,' Clea said. 'What I might say or do.' I suspect she was right.

George was seven years old, two years younger than I had been when I arrived at the Coast. His face had several open lesions. I think they must have known, Gran and Charlie, but they did not want to believe it could happen again. George was already worse off than I had ever been.

He stood looking at the ground when Dr Stenger brought him into the women's lazaret. I knelt down outside our cottage and put my hand out. He had the same blue eyes and dark hair as Charlie. Mama was sitting on the verandah, and I could see how torn she was between feeling sorry for the child and hating him merely for existing. He was proof of betrayal—her mother's and Charlie's. I wondered what George knew of his condition and what Charlie told him, how much he understood.

'You won't remember me,' I said, 'but I used to look after you when you were a bub. You had the loudest cry.'

George's arms and legs were marked with bruises, and besides the sores on his face there was a crust; no one had shown him how to wash, evidently. His eyes were large. I remembered my own arrival, the terror I felt at what I did not know.

'You must miss Jiggi. Do you still have that ginger cat around? Have you ever seen a carpet snake?'

George blinked. His grubby fist rubbed an eye.

'Were you in school before you left? Is Miss Miller still there?'

He shook his head. I wondered whether Gran had been scared to send him to school.

'It's not as bad as you think here. You have me and Mama. We'll look after you. All the tucker you can dream of. A whole bed to yourself, can you imagine?'

George looked at me for the first time and I felt the clutch of his fear.

Dr Stenger cleared his throat. 'We can ease restrictions on visiting, but I'm afraid George will need to stay in the men's cottages.'

'That's ridiculous. The boy's too little. He can stay 'ere with us.' Mama's voice was so loud all of us jumped.

'I've tried to convince others of that,' Dr Stenger said, 'but even though you are blood relations, neither is the parent. He will be perfectly well looked after in the men's lazaret. I'll put him in the cottage with Fred, and he can spend much of the day here, if he likes. He will be free to come and go between the two lazarets.'

George was squatting now; he had some marbles out of his pocket and was rolling them together in the dust. I put my hand out to him. 'Would you like to see our beach?'

He considered this for a moment. Then, slipping his marbles back in his pocket, he put his hand in mine. It was a clammy, sticky little hand. Had I ever been so small?

Dr Stenger was watching us, eyebrows raised. I gave a little shake of my head. He could wait for his examination. The doctor nodded, and George and I walked out of the gate of the women's lazaret and towards the sea.

There was so much to show him.

•

George chose to be called Sid. I took him walking when he was up to it. We sat on the beach, digging for pipis, or picked our way across the rock pools, looking for strange creatures. I wanted to be his teacher, to show him how to read and write, but he had little interest.

I grew fond of Fred because of how he was with Sid—he took him out in the boat when the sea was calm and they spent more time fishing than anything. I asked him once what they spoke of out there, and Fred shrugged. 'Not much of one for words, that boy. I tell him stories. Show 'im how to read the currents.'

And I felt relieved, because Sid hardly spoke to me either. He did seek me out, though, and I was pleased by his silent company. He would put his hand in mine often. Sometimes, on a stifling afternoon, he came to our cottage and curled up beside me to rest on my bed. Mama would say, 'What nonsense,' but she was alone in her bed on the other side of the room. I had forgotten—though I spent my first nine years knowing—what it is to be touched. To have other skin against mine. It reminded me of how Hunter used to sleep curled against me. Sid filled a space I had not known was empty.

•

As months passed, Sid showed us more of himself. He would go to any extent to make me laugh. He could change his small, frail boy's body into anyone's he chose. He would mimic perfectly the heavy, wide-hipped walk of Matron, the unsteady stumble and grin of Fred, Mama's quick tiny steps and her sharp stare. He had Gran's squint sorted and Charlie's broad-armed, chest-thumping yawn conjured him so clearly my heart jumped with fright.

'Do me,' I said, and he shook his head and flushed, staring at the ground.

'Go on, I can take it.'

We were in the kitchen. I was making tea, and Mama was still asleep from a late night on the grog. Sid looked away for a moment. When he looked back his eyes were narrower, and his fingers fluttered across his cheeks. He glanced at the mirror on the wall and away. He folded his arms tightly across his chest, pulled the sleeves of an imaginary dress over his fingers. I saw myself for what I was: self-conscious, deeply flawed. He stopped, and threw himself at my stomach, his head against my ribs.

'Sorry, Alice,' he said to my blouse.

'That was splendid,' I said. 'You're a funny one.' But I'm certain he heard my voice crack.

# 11

*Nellie*

## 1901

When her courses stopped, Ma brewed Nellie a tea to make them come again. Then she gave her sulphur and treacle, to burn it off her insides. Ma was angry first, saying that Nellie was stupid, and if for once she had listened they would not be in this mess.

Nellie spit the tea and spit the sulphur because it was bitter and so was she. Ned had left her and now she would be stuck too. Just like Ma. Babies clinging while she scraped the bottoms of blackened pots and pretended she'd once had something fine.

Ma softened when Nellie's belly grew, when she could put her hand on it and even see the baby move, all knee and elbow. Ma started knitting a blanket then, told Nellie things she did not want to hear about where it would come out of and how much it would hurt. How it would drink milk from her little paps and she would have to eat enough to make the milk. She gave Nellie mutton tallow to rub into her tight skin and said it was so she did not get ugly marks later, when her belly disappeared. She told her of her own pregnancies, and how Nellie had kicked the hardest. About how they had just moved north from a timber-getter's camp in Coffs and her father had gone looking for a place, and how they found Jiggi because of her, because Ma had said they needed a home. Nellie shut her eyes and pretended these stories were for her and not the baby.

'What was he like then?' Nellie asked.

A rare smile crossed Ma's lips, gone as soon as Nellie saw it.

'Full of himself. Nothing to look at, but he could spin a good yarn. He was convincing.'

Some old memory flickered under Ma's skin. Did he love her? Nellie wondered. Did Ma long for him?

'He's gone now, dead and buried,' Ma said.

'Why didn't you say?' Nellie wrapped her arms around her belly. She felt a lump in her throat, but swallowed, knowing Ma would not approve.

'I thought I told you,' Ma said, turning away.

'When?'

'When I got the money, to build the house.'

Later, Nellie walked the familiar paths through the bush, thinking she might cry. But her father seemed distant now. It was Ned she longed for. Everything changed so fast.

When she returned, Avery sulked at the table. Nellie slept in a room with Ma now, where the baby would sleep too when it came. Avery slept out on the verandah. He claimed it was because he slept better out of doors, but he was sore because he did not like this baby, and he did not like that Ma was keen on it.

•

They were slowly filling the house. Once Nellie rode all day to Lismore and back with Ma in the wagonette to buy things they needed—swaddling cloths, a new galvanised tub. By that stage her belly stuck far out in front of her stick arms and legs, and there was no hiding it. There were pointed looks and women talking behind their hands at the dry goods store, but Nellie followed Ma's lead in pretending they did not exist.

'Pay them no mind,' Ma said. 'If it's not one thing it's another. We will never be good enough anyway, so what is the use in trying?'

She was right, of course, but still it smarted. Nellie had hardly known what it meant to be a woman before she was saddled with the worst parts. And she was the only one carrying the blame.

Would she take Ned back if he came for her? She imagined it all the time. Every time she heard the sound of a horse's hooves on the track beside their place. He would have to plead first, she decided. Knees in the mud, telling her how truly wrong he had been. But then Nellie would take his hand and climb on the back of his horse in a hurry. She never saw herself pregnant in those imaginings. Somehow all that was gone, and it was just her and him again, riding hell for leather into the distance.

•

Instead, Nellie ended up cursing the world, pacing the house in the worst pain she had ever known. Avery got sick of her screaming and said he was going to town. It would hit, a thrust of agony, and she would be on her knees. Then on the bed, somehow, surrounded by mess and blood, screaming as she was split in two. Ma cut the blue pulsing cord with her sewing shears and told Nellie she had a little girl.

Once the muck was washed off in the galvanised tub, Ma put the strange, squalling creature in Nellie's arms. The baby's face was red and squashed, her head like a cone and her navel a knot of blistered blood.

'What'll you call her?' Ma asked, after dragging off the basin, the bloody sheets.

How could she act as though this were all normal? Nellie could not even speak from the shock.

'What about Hilda? That was your father's mother who died when he was born.'

It came to her then that this was how she paid her Ma back for killing Elma. She let her have this child.

The thing was still squalling, and Ma shoved her head up towards Nellie's breast. 'She wants a feed—see if you can get her to suck. Go on, Hilda. Have a little drink.'

To their surprise, Hilda had a powerful mouth; like a leech she grabbed on, and she weren't about to let go. It hurt, too, Nellie found, but not as much as before. Not as much as when the baby split her open between the legs. Ma handed Nellie a cloth to clean down there, and it came away bright with blood. That much was gone, she figured. Any chance of Ned again.

•

It did not take long for Nellie to start fighting with Ma once more, Ma always telling her how to look after Hilda. *Don't go to her every time she's crying, you'll spoil her*, but then, when she left her, *How can you listen to her cry like that? Be a decent mother and go see what she needs.* Nellie wanted to go on walks again across the creek, but she could not leave Hilda. She wanted to go to the old shack and see how much of the roof had fallen in, but Ma said she must stay with the baby. She was always there, that baby. She wrapped her little fist around Nellie's hair tight and would not let go.

Avery complained about her screaming and how he couldn't sleep because of it, and he decided to go out and look for work the way their father once did, though he wasn't nearly as capable or strong. There was no more cedar left to cut; the timber-getters had carted it all away. He went to the coast to find work fishing and he didn't come back for a while, so they figured he must have had some luck. Ma pined for him the way Nellie knew she would. Nellie had never seen her pray except when the priest used to come, but every night Avery was gone she prayed on her knees beside the bed with her head bent for God to keep him safe and protect him and bring him home soon.

Ma's praying worked, because when Hilda was starting to sit up and eat something Avery came home, taller and brown, with a fluffy excuse for whiskers on his chin and a man with him called Charlie.

Ma was suspicious of strangers; they all were, for good reason. But she was not about to ruin her happiness at Avery being home, and so they cooked up all the tucker in the house and she put out the grog she saved for toothaches. They had a proper celebration. Avery and Charlie told of catching striped marlin and jewfish and tailor, and of the captain of the fishing boat who was a right arse, and before long they had all warmed to Charlie. He was easygoing and seemed to be just the mate that Avery needed. Charlie was headed north to look for work in the cane fields, and Avery planned to go with him.

'Harder work than fishing,' Ma said.

But Charlie shrugged. 'I get seasick,' he confided, winking at Nellie with his deep-set blue eyes, and just then Hilda started crying.

'What're you doing, Nellie? Go see what she needs,' Ma said, and Nellie heard Charlie saying as she left the room, 'She seems awful young to have a baby.'

Nellie picked Hilda up and sat on the edge of the bed, opening the buttons on her dress, her fingers tingling; they were hard to manage. Hilda's hair was turning blonde, and when she saw Nellie she made happy, gurgly sounds which made the milk flow in Nellie's paps whether she wanted it to or not. She was glad that she could see some of Ned in Hilda; it made the child less maddening.

Nellie strained to hear what they were talking of in the other room. Ma was probably criticising her, she thought, telling

Charlie what an awful daughter she was, Avery chiming in. When Hilda was finished Nellie put her on her shoulder and grinned when the child burped loud in her ear. Nellie changed her cloth and straightened her nightdress and brought Hilda with her when she returned to the table.

'Well, who's this beautiful bub?' Charlie asked, and held out his arms. Nellie put Hilda in them. He dandled the baby on his knee and seemed easy with her, confident. He was the kind of fella who was ageless, his face lined and dark hair flecked with grey but there was a lightness to him—a jesting. Ma watched with her lips tight for a minute before she snapped, 'Put her back to bed, Nellie. It's too late for her to be up.'

If Charlie had not been there, Nellie would have snapped right back: *Put her yourself, if it's what you want*, or, *Don't be telling me what to do.* But instead she pretended to be the good daughter she was not and waved Hilda's little hand goodbye at them as she took her to bed. Even Avery seemed surprised at how pretty the child was.

Nellie kissed Hilda and lay down beside her in the big bed, singing a lullaby in a soft voice. The grog must've gone to Nellie's head, because that's where she woke in the morning, Hilda chortling on one side, Ma farting and snoring on the other.

•

Charlie decided to stay a few more days before heading north and Nellie found herself watching him. Pouring his tea without being asked, finding reasons to sit beside him at the table, bringing Hilda for him to admire. Avery and him drank day and night, but that was what her father had done when he finished a job so it didn't seem unusual. They did not get too rowdy, just laughed a lot and stumbled around the place, never making it to the dunny when they had to piss but standing at least with their backs to the house. Ma drank with them sometimes, but Nellie did not want to miss anything—some meaningful look Charlie might give her or a wink across the table—so she did not have another sip of their grog.

On the third day, Charlie went into town to ask about work further north, and when he was gone Ma said to Avery, 'What's his story?'

Avery said he had left his wife and family in Melbourne because his wife was unfaithful to him, and it was terribly sad because she had money and he didn't, so now he was poor as a church mouse and headed north with a broken heart and empty purse.

'Likely story,' Ma said, chewing the stem of her pipe, but she looked thoughtful as she stirred the tea-leaves in the pot.

'What're you cooking up, Ma?' Avery asked. 'I know that look of yours—you've got some scheme.'

Ma pinched him on the arm.

'Ow!'

'Not a scheme—just, he needs a wife to look after 'im, and Nellie needs a husband so's Hilda's not a bastard.'

'Don't I get a say in this?' Nellie asked, jiggling Hilda on her lap.

'You? Doesn't Charlie get a say in this?' Avery replied, his lip curling in disgust. 'He doesn't want *her*.'

'Both of you shut your mouths. I've seen the way you watch him, Nellie, and maybe he's just looking for a night of company, but he's watching you the same way. I'm just saying he's not a bad sort—we might as well try to hold on to him.'

'Why don't *you* marry him, Ma?' Nellie suggested, dropping into a chair, putting Hilda on her breast.

'Can you not do that in private?' Avery covered his eyes with one hand.

'Maybe *Avery* wants to marry him,' Nellie said, and he took his hand away, looking at his sister through slitted eyes.

'I wish I'd never brought him home,' he said. He got up and stormed out the door.

Ma came and sat beside Nellie.

'I'm not about to marry him, because he doesn't want an old, worn-out bag of bones. You may as well use your youth to your advantage instead of frittering it on useless ne'er-do-wells. Now tell me the truth: do you want a husband?'

Nellie did not look up from Hilda's peaceful face, but she nodded. 'I suppose.'

'Right, then listen to me, and you'll need to do exactly as I say.'

•

That afternoon Nellie washed her hair in the creek and let it dry in the sun, loose over her shoulders. She wore a clean white blouse buttoned to the neck, but Ma undid the top three buttons.

Ma took Hilda for a walk across the creek—something she would never let Nellie do. She had made a stew and said Nellie was to tell Charlie she made it herself. They both knew Avery would be off sulking all day.

When Charlie walked up carrying a sack of bottles, Nellie was in the outdoor kitchen stirring the stew. The light came as it did that time of day all streaming golden. He sat down on a chair beside the stove and took a bottle from his bag. She could tell he had been drinking. Nellie felt a funny twist in the bottom of her stomach then, but he made a joke and told Nellie a story about the crone in the shop who would not post his letter because he wrote the address wrong.

'You must be hungry,' she said, just as Ma had told her, and he nodded and belched.

It was not as sweet as when Hilda did it.

'Where's everyone else?' he asked then, and Nellie told him that Ma was visiting a friend and had taken Hilda to show her off, which was a lie because they had no friends, but she told him the truth when she said she did not know where Avery had got to.

'So's just you and me,' he said. And Nellie told him Ma was not expecting him back so soon.

'She doesn't trust me here alone with you?' he asked.

And Nellie did not know how to answer because Ma had not told her. She smiled and served his stew, which smelled so good it made her stomach rumble, but Ma had told her not to eat. She cut him bread from the day-old loaf and poured the bottle of beer Ma had left.

He patted the chair beside him. 'Come sit and keep me company,' he said.

She sat, not sure what to do with her hands, so she folded them in her lap.

'Your ma likes to tell you what to do,' he said.

Nellie nodded. 'I get weary of it.'

'You must. Pretty girl like you needs a man more than a mother.'

Her face felt hot and she ran her finger over the cracks in the worn timber table. He ate his stew fast and there was some in his beard but she did not dare tell him.

'Would you have more?' she asked, standing to take his bowl, to refill or wash it in the basin.

'I would have you,' he said, pulling her in so his face was against her waist. Nellie knew the stew in his beard would stain her white blouse but she resisted the urge to push him away. 'Would you have me, Nellie?' he asked, looking up, and she took his hand as Ma had told her to and led him inside, shutting the door as instructed and bringing him to the big bed where Nellie slept with Hilda and Ma.

He started moving fast then, tearing the clothes from her like a wild dog, not a man, and Nellie began to pull away as Ma had told her to, and ran to the corner of the room.

'Come, little wren, I didn't mean to scare you,' he said.

And she screamed then, and right on cue Ma came running into the house with Hilda, hollering and carrying the only thing of worth Pa had left them: his Martini-Henry breech-loading rifle.

Charlie pulled his trousers up quick smart and sat on the edge of the bed with his hands in the air.

'I leave for a moment and you have your way with my daughter?' Ma shouted, shaking her head in disbelief.

Nellie wiped her nose on her arm and tried to pull the tatters of her blouse closed.

'Don't hurt him, Ma,' she cried, following Ma's script. 'It was my fault too.'

Charlie looked at Nellie oddly then, still drunk, and clearly muddled by the way things were going. 'Put that down, Dulcie,' he said. 'You'll hurt the bub.'

'I'm not putting anything down,' Ma roared, and hitched Hilda in one arm and the Martini-Henry in the crook of the other. 'You'll not be the second man to shame my daughter. You will marry her or you will know what a bullet to the heart feels like.'

Charlie put his hands to his face, and Nellie thought maybe he was crying, because he was shaking, but when he brought his hands away she saw he laughed.

Oh no, she thought. The game is up.

'I'll marry your daughter, but you will rue the day,' he said. 'Come here, Nellie.' She sat beside him. 'Your ma is a cruel woman,' he said, 'using you like chattel.'

Nellie did not know what he meant. She did not know whether to be frightened or pleased.

Ma left the room then, with Hilda and the Martini-Henry, and Nellie stood to follow her.

'Oh no,' said Charlie. 'Let's have a taste of what it is I've been tricked into marrying.'

She turned away, scared by the look in his eyes, but Ma was in the doorway watching.

'It's what you wanted,' she said, shutting the door in Nellie's face.

•

They married at the Jiggi church, though Nellie did not have a nice dress. Her nicest blouse was only rags now, but Ma helped her take in a dress that she had once worn. It used to be black, but had faded so much it was now grey. Charlie shaved his whiskers and winked at Nellie with those deep-set blue eyes, and she thought perhaps she might bear him.

It was not long until she had a swollen belly again, and Charlie had gone off to the cane fields and Avery with him.

The house was easier to live in when he was gone. There was no drinking and carrying on late into the night—it was just Ma and Hilda and Nellie working and keeping things right.

Sometimes—if Ma would watch Hilda—Nellie even walked across the creek again on her own. She followed the bush trails of pademelons and stood stock-still when she came upon snakes. She lay in the clearing where she had lain once with Ned and imagined him better than he had been. She went back to the shack—so much smaller than she remembered—and poked her finger in the rotting planks. The entire roof had fallen in and there were weeds growing up from the floor. She imagined cleaning it up, and the peace of living there alone. Without Charlie, Ma or Avery. Without Hilda, some days.

•

One day Nellie found a mango tree growing wild, laden with ripe fruit, and she ate until her stomach ached and her teeth were full of strings. Then she filled her apron and brought as many home as she could. Ma said she was witless, for they were filled with worms, and sure enough that night Nellie was in the dunny, her stomach cramping but emptied of all food. Ma shouted over the door that she needed to come and lie down, the baby would come early.

Ma went to fetch the midwife who lived two miles away as Nellie lay moaning, soiling herself on the bedclothes.

When the midwife came she cleaned Nellie up again and gave her a tincture. She had only had a sip when the pain came in earnest, and before Ma could boil the kettle for water Hunter had arrived in the world. Too small and fragile, but still he had a kittenish cry and an even meeker drink before they both fell deep into sleep.

Nellie was sixteen.

•

After her second was born, Nellie noticed a numbness in her right arm. She thought it was that she was always holding Hunter in it. But when she swapped him to her left it did not improve. Charlie returned from the cane fields and met his son for the first time. Hunter had grown larger on Nellie's milk and was a normal size now, though still with a sad little mewl. She was taking off her shift at night with her back turned to Charlie so he would not see the sagging skin where the baby had been.

'What happened to yer back?'

'Nothing.'

'Here, feel it,' he said, and brought Nellie's left hand to the spot where the skin was shiny, he said, and pink. The strange thing was, she felt it in her fingers but not her back. The spot was numb.

'I must've burned it,' she said. She tried to keep her voice calm, to hush the fear that was hurrying her heart.

'You ought to stay out of the sun,' he said. 'Your cheeks and nose are red.'

'You ought to buy me a nice hat then,' Nellie replied. 'Hard to stay out of the sun when there's washing to hang and weeds to pull. Did you see the cockatoo fence needs fixing?'

'You oughtn't be so demanding. Did you miss me?'

Nellie looked at his red, hairy body sitting on the bed. He was struggling to undo the belt which held his trousers up, and strands of hair were plastered to his forehead with sweat. Most of the time it only took a few minutes, but it had been different since Hunter was born. He didn't wait for her reply, but pulled Nellie to lie down beneath him. She shut her eyes, pulling up the image of Ned astride his horse she kept there for these moments. Charlie prised her knees apart with his own.

Nellie felt as though he was lost inside her now; everything was stretched like the clothes she had worn when her belly was huge. Stretched but tender, if it could even be those two things at once, and he grunted for ages, dripping sweat which made slow trails down her skin, some sliding into her ears, some stinging the corner of her eye. Finally he shuddered and fell, crushing the breath from her. He smelled of sweat and the chicken manure they used growing sugar cane. It was the worst manure, with a sharp, foul smell that lingered.

He cleaned himself with Nellie's shift, then tossed it to her to do the same.

'You should have your ma look at that burn on your back,' he said, standing to dress. 'She might have a balm.'

Nellie heard Hunter crying from the other room and hurried to calm him. She took a clean shift. She stung down below, her arm felt asleep and the skin on her face itched and ached. She thought of her father's face before he was taken away. The craters and bumps, the hideous scabs.

When she reached Hunter, Hilda was already shushing him, her tiny blonde head peering over the side of his cradle. Hunter was sucking on two of Hilda's dirty fingers, and she was grinning at his gummy mouth. Nellie lifted him out, sat in a chair, and situated her good arm beneath him. She pulled out her sore, aching pap and fed him, though she would have been happy if no one ever touched her again. Hilda spread her sweaty, grubby fingers on Nellie's knee and she swatted her away.

Hilda ran to sulk in the corner.

Ma came in from the garden. 'Charlie says you have a burn on your back I ought to look at?' She dumped an apronful of chokos on the table.

How did Charlie get to Ma so quickly?

'Not now,' Nellie muttered. 'Can't you see I'm busy?'

'Someone's cranky,' Ma said to Hilda, and passed her the little wattle broom that was a miniature version of her own. 'Who wants to help Gran sweep? What a good girl you are.'

Nellie watched them together, their backs bent, with tears at the corners of her eyes. How did her life end up this way? She imagined herself with Ned in a carriage, riding trains together across the country, ships across the sea. She imagined a necklace which sat in the hollow of her throat, a jewel as big as a possum's eye.

Instead she had babies, a husband she didn't care for, and she was stuck in Jiggi, tied to the lack they had always known, the skin of her father somehow festering inside her, making its way to the surface at last.

Hilda turned and smiled, showing the dimple in the corner of her cheek. At least Ned was in her. At least he'd left Nellie something to remember him by.

# 12

*Jack*

## 1917

Jack stayed around Angledool for three years, working when he could—first fencing, then as a boundary rider at Angledool and Llanillo stations. He was glad when there was work close to home; he would sleep at his mother's and walk to the station with her early, as the sun pinked the edges of clouds. She did not ask him about the Home, but he told her little things, funny stories. How Guy would hide Brother Jeffrey's spectacles, how he got caught mimicking Brother Matthew. He wanted to make her laugh, but all she did was nod and listen.

When there was no work, Jack played dice with Aunty Rita, gambling fish he had yet to catch. When he had money he spent it at the Old Bark Pub, the pine-slab walls and bark roof lit by slush lamps, drinking with other shearers and station workers. They were older, now the war was on. The young whitefellas had gone to fight. The white men could drink until they passed out on the road, but the police fined Jack two pounds if they saw him or any of the reserve boys drunk.

He was there to see the golden wattle and paper daisies in the spring, when the Narran flooded, the water so muddy then his mother said they didn't need milk with their tea. His feet toughened enough to walk barefoot among the cathead burrs. He woke to the mournful cry of a curlew before dawn, watched the whirly wind that piled roly-polies against fences, and smelled the bush oranges. Hot afternoons he slept under the bough shed. He got to know Daisy from the tricks she played on him: a frog in his boot, the leg of his trousers stitched shut. He made her write him notes, so she could practise her letters.

*Buy soop bones and 1 loaf bred in town*, she wrote, and he showed her how to spell soup. The difference between *soup* and *soap* was only a letter, but one was good to eat and the other bitter. The long double-o sound in words like *root, loot, tooth* and *roof*. Then the different double-o sound in words like *spool, tool* and *school*.

'Can you think of any others?'

'Fool,' Daisy said. 'But only because there's one right in front of me.'

He let her laugh. He was going to explain the difference between *bred, breed* and *bread*, but she skipped off. Her legs had grown like saplings, thin and reedy.

•

Twice a week the mail coach came to Angledool from Collarenebri, and when Jack went to town for the soup bones and bread, he stopped in at the post office. There was a letter from Guy. Jack stood outside to tear it open and read that Guy was enlisting up at Mungindi, on the Queensland border. They needed boys who could ride, he said. They'd lifted the colour bar. The war had been going almost three years.

That night, at home, his mother shook her head. Daisy ran outside.

He found her sitting on the riverbank, knees tucked to her chin.

'I wish you'd stay put,' Daisy said. The steady call of frogs filled the night. Something splashed in the Narran: a fish leaping in the dark.

'It's different for me than for you,' Jack said. 'I don't know where I belong.'

'Here with us,' Daisy said.

'I'll come back. I promise.'

•

The only question the officer at Mungindi asked was whether Jack could ride. 'Good-o,' he said, when Jack replied that he could. 'We'll take ya.'

It was easy for Jack to be with Guy again, easier than it was to be anywhere else. They had a silent language between them, always knowing what the other was thinking. Like those pairs Jack had watched on the dancefloor in the School of Arts. They had survived so much together. It was pleasing to be told what to do with all their waking hours again. To be woken at five and spend most of the day learning the only acceptable way to get a thing done.

Guy was right: because they knew horses, they were put in the 12th Regiment of the 4th Light Horse Brigade. To join, Jack had to ride an army horse bareback over a sod wall and a water jump. When he passed, they gave him the jacket of the Australian Imperial Forces, cord riding breeches and leather puttees. He was given a slouch hat with an emu feather and a bandolier that carried ninety rounds of ammunition.

The army sent them by ship, first to Egypt, their horses— Walers—in stalls below. Jack had Jenny, a dappled grey with wide smooth haunches and a deep-barrelled chest. She stood sixteen hands and above her hooves was a fringe of white fur; her tongue was dry and coarse on his palm. Guy had a nimble bay colt, Lucky. They visited their horses in the hold three times a day and cleaned out the stalls daily. They took Jenny and Lucky carrots which the cook traded for their rations of rum. Some of the others brought their horses from home—the army paid sixteen pounds for them. None of the horses had enough space or feed. Several died, and the ship slowed to slide them into the ocean. Jack watched the water swallow them and wondered how long it took for the body to sink. When he imagined the dead horses they were suspended, never quite reaching the bottom.

To pass the time on the ship, Guy taught Jack to play draughts; he had a travel draughts set which folded into a neat timber veneer box that doubled as the board, with the black and white painted pieces inside. They made a joke between them of fighting over who got to play the black pieces. Jack and Guy were the only blackfellas in their section, but there were others in their regiment. Because of the Home they knew how to be. They knew to be friendly but keep some distance—they had each other. They played draughts, smoked, looked after their horses and slept. On the ship it mattered, in the regiment it mattered. Only in battle did no one seem to care about the colour of their skin.

·

In Egypt they were sent on reconnaissance missions to protect the Suez Canal. They woke before four in the morning, stopped for a cup of tea and some bully stew, and then rode again until eight. On burning sandhills the horses sunk to their knees.

After breakfast they rested in their unlined tents as the temperature climbed beyond bearable. The men stripped naked and lay, sweating, when the sun was high in the sky. Those were the hours it was too hot to move. Later, when it cooled, they would polish their saddles. Across the front of Jack's saddle was a rolled greatcoat and a groundsheet. A mess tin, nosebag for Jenny and canvas water bucket were slung from the back. There was a heel rope, neck rope, feed, picket line, and a bag which held two horseshoes and nails. His haversack contained food, eating utensils, spare underpants, soap, a pocketknife, a notebook and bandages. Finally: a saddle blanket, extra ammo, a billy and a metal quart canteen for water. All up, once Jack was mounted, it was more than two hundred and fifty pounds of extra weight for Jenny.

Some days, when the hot winds blew, it was all they could do to water the horses on their lines. Jenny suffered; her coat grew patchy, her dapples faded and her eyes had a dull film. At least the men had the tents, the horses had no shade. Jack felt his lungs scald as he breathed the foul dust. That was the khamsin. No one could consider fighting then.

There were four men in his section—Guy, Jack, Rich and Johnno. They ate, slept, lived and fought together. He knew how they chewed, snored, who needed to piss in the night. He knew his tentmates like he knew the backs of his own teeth. Johnno had a book of Keats' poems he read aloud. Guy had his draughts. Rich had a mouth organ he played. Jack whittled with his pocketknife, but finding wood in the desert was near impossible. He used the same piece again and again, changing the shape until there was nothing left to carve away.

He woke each morning with sand squeaking in his teeth, already thirsty. They said the Australians were prepared for the desert because they were desert dwellers and bushmen, but nothing prepared them for the Sinai. He was no stranger to heat and flies in Angledool, but never to this degree. He lost his appetite. To swallow some food each day took effort.

Jack and Guy did everything together. Guy was a head taller than most of the men, but he never used this to his advantage. He was a better horseman than any. Jack saw Guy pour water from his flask into his hat to share with his horse. They only had one quart of water a day. Guy knew that Jack found it hard to eat rations and would save him the dry biscuits that were more palatable to Jack than bully stew. He knew that Jack had not yet been with a woman. The distance between them was smaller than a hair's breadth.

If they were on watch together the time flowed like sand. They shared cigarettes and spoke in low voices so as not to get in trouble.

'D'ya think that Johnny Turk is so different?' Guy asked one night, the red glow of his cigarette tip the only thing visible to Jack.

'What d'ya mean?' Jack asked.

'I mean, they're the enemy, right? But there's two Turks out there sharing a cigarette and talking about home, about the food they miss, the girls, same as us.'

'I s'pose.'

'But if we see them like that, we can't kill 'em, can we?'

'It's why they have to make us hate them,' Jack said.

'Exactly. Problem is, to hate something you have to at least know it a little. We've come in blind. We don't even know what it is we're meant to hate.'

'Well, we're meant to hate them because they're different. Problem is, we're different too,' Jack said.

'In some ways we're more like them,' Guy said.

'And we know what it's like to be hated.'

•

From Egypt they rode to Palestine, where they tried and failed to take Gaza, the walls of cactus an impenetrable border on horseback. Their regiment was sent to El Arish to rest. They spent days swimming in the flat bright blue of the Mediterranean Sea. It was Jack's first time swimming in the sea, and he was surprised by the saltiness, the buoyancy. Not as soft as the

Narran, it left his skin sticky and tight. The salt stayed on his lips after.

Then they got the orders to ride to Khalasa, across the desert at night. Jack felt like he was disappearing into the dark. He chewed dry biscuits to try to stay awake, eventually succumbing to sleep in the saddle.

At Khalasa, they watered their horses and camped for the last time before the long night march to the outskirts of Beersheba. Capturing Beersheba, the lieutenant said, would give them access to water. The enemies thought they were focused on Gaza. This would take Johnny Turk by surprise.

The attack began with artillery at dawn, and then the infantry was sent in. Jack and Guy's regiment had been there since daybreak, and so the 4th and 12th regiments of the 4th Light Horse Brigade were chosen to ride. The sun was beginning to set, the minarets of the mosque reflecting the pinkish-orange light. Their horses had not been watered for forty-eight hours. Jenny was carrying all the weight. Jack poured the last of his water into his hat for her. If they did not capture Beersheba, they would both perish from thirst. At the command, they trotted, then galloped across a wadi, over rolling brown hills, two miles. The horses smelled the wells. Blinded by the setting sun and the dust of horse hooves, they rode into one thousand Turkish riflemen and nine machine guns. Jack galloped with hundreds of others across the plain, the muscles in Jenny's neck cording, her mane purling in the hot wind. The dust swirled and there was the flash of rifles from the enemy trenches, from the field guns beyond; the anguished screams of horses hit.

Jack pressed himself flat on Jenny's neck as bullets ploughed the ground at her feet. He waved the bayonet, spurring her on. It was impossible to see through the dust and to think amid the noise and chaos. Shells whistled overhead and there were rattling dry bursts of machine-gun fire. The sharp-sweet smell of cordite. Their own shells exploded over the Turks, cratering their crescent-shaped trenches. He was soaring, grasping Jenny's mane as she leaped the two lines of deep trenches. Lead flew from every direction. Men beneath him, death beneath him and gone. Turning Jenny quick, he dismounted. They rode in section—Rich took the horses while the other three fought the Turks hand-to-hand. Jack was mad with fear as he drove his bayonet into the gut of a Turkish soldier, a sick feeling. His hearing muffled, his breath in his belly, trench slick with blood. When he saw Guy stumble towards him, time slowed and stopped. There was blood flowing from Guy's neck like water. Tearing strips from his shirt, Jack fashioned a quick tourniquet and carried Guy to the dressing station, where, as he lay his friend down, he saw Guy's face gone yellow and strained. The place smelled of death.

'Tell Sally I love her,' Guy whispered.

'I'll look after 'em,' Jack promised, and the tears were falling down his neck into his collar. He had not cried since the Home. Since the long nights of stifled tears. Jack sat and held his hand while Guy struggled through his last breaths. The nurse came and checked Guy's pulse. She asked Jack to wait outside while she cleaned him and gathered his personal effects. When she called him back in, she gave him a small bundle of papers, a cigarette tin and the draughts set.

When Jack left the dressing tent, the stretcher where Guy had lain was occupied by another man.

Stillness was death, so he dug graves to bury the fallen. In the heat, they had to work fast. The smell of a dead body was a smell Jack would never forget, alongside the feel of bayoneting another man. He would never forget the sound, either, of injured horses screaming. Those first few nights, none of them could sleep through the cries of wounded horses, wild with terror and pain. Jack helped kill them, for they ran in fear in spite of their injuries, their guts spilled open, broken legs. He spoke softly, came close when others could not. A bullet was the only thing that could stop the terrible sound. At least Jenny and Lucky were safe. The dead men were buried, but the dead horses were left to rot in the sun.

•

Beersheba was a few stone buildings and dusty earth, intermi-nable heat. More goats, chickens and donkeys than men, but there was water for the horses. Just not enough. The Turks had tried to blow up all the wells, but they only managed two. After raiding the stores, Jack's brigade was given orders to continue on, to join the fighting around Khuweilfe, towards Gaza.

He was parched, sunworn, bereft. They were given a new man for their section, Eli, who had lost everyone in his. No one spoke much now, they just lay in the tent at night, tossing in their blankets. With Guy no longer beside him, Jack did not know how to carry on.

Less than a week after losing Guy, they were ordered to charge the trenches at the high point of Tel el Sheria near

Khuweilfe. Jack rode through a field of dead and dying British infantrymen, the fire so intense from the Turks that they were given orders to take cover in a wadi. Dismounting, he took a bullet in the leg, one that would have otherwise hit Jenny. He lay in the wadi while Eli tied a tourniquet around his thigh.

'Look after Jenny,' he said, when the medics came to take him away. There was relief at being on that stretcher. Ceding control. Waking in a dressing tent with nurses hovering, cleaning and feeding him, asking questions, trying to ease his pain. They were Australian women; their voices filled him with homesickness. They spooned broth between his lips and sponged him with cloths. When infection set in he thought he might die. It seemed right, since Guy was gone. Since he had followed him in all things.

The surgeon who cut off Jack's leg gave him ether on a rag. He was half conscious still, just too drugged to scream in time for the pain. He heard the saw cutting his bone. He watched the nurse dressing the stump as though it were someone else's. When his faculties returned in full, it was like being half of what he had been before. Jack had spent his childhood being told only half of him was worthy—the white half—and now he felt like that had been halved again.

•

They sent him to a hospital in Cairo to rehabilitate.

At first he wanted to give up and die there. What was left to live for, besides the message to deliver to Guy's widow? For days he did not even have the strength to open his eyes. He was in his own room, alone. But there was a nurse, Mariam, who cleaned Jack's stump with gentle hands, her lashes a dark blur against her cheek. When her hands strayed upwards he gasped, and she put her finger to her lips to quiet him.

'Enjoy the time we have,' she said. Or that is what Jack imagined she said, because she spoke no English and he spoke no Arabic. She would come to him at night. In the dawn, he would wake with the call of the muezzins in their minarets, their calls echoing each other in the grey dawn. She would be gone.

When she turned to dress in the lamplight once he saw she had marks, lighter pink ones, on her back. Jack didn't ask her about them. He was missing a leg. He knew he could not draw attention to another's disfigurement.

When he had first arrived in Cairo, off the ship, they were warned against the prostitutes. It was legal there, and in the narrow laneways of the Wazzir district they would show you their certificates from the government, the ones that supposedly marked them as clean. The Tommies told them that these women bought the papers, not to trust them. Jack watched the belly dancers with their swinging, pendulous breasts. They groped him in the evil-smelling laneways, but he was not going to part with his money. Mariam was different from those women; she was true.

When Jack got his medical release, Mariam stroked his head in her lap as he wet her smock with tears. The horses were not to be brought back to Australia. They were classed depending on age and health: the higher classes would be sold locally, the lower shot. Those shot were skinned and had their tails and manes removed. It was harder to imagine the cruel life

Jenny would have without him than to imagine her shot and skinned. In a letter, Eli told Jack that many light horsemen took their horses which had been classed high and shot them rather than subject them to the indignity. This was Jenny's fate, he assured Jack. And Lucky. Jack hoped Jenny did not know what was coming. She was not spooked by the sight or sound of a gun.

While Jack cried, Mariam murmured words in Arabic. He imagined she spoke of their life together, if things were different, if he had stayed.

He left on the hospital ship the *Wandilla* the following week. He could walk—with a limp—on his wooden leg. He was slow, but steady. He would miss the mint tea and small dishes of spiced meats which Mariam brought, but he looked forward to the smell of gum trees, the taste of black tea. He knew that he would go home even stranger to his family. But he was alive, with promises to keep.

# 13

*Will*

## 1919

He did not have a moment spare: the war was over but the wards were full, overflowing with victims of the Spanish flu. They came by the tramcar full, more and more of them every day. There were beds on the verandahs and frame to frame in the rooms; beds so close there was no space to walk between them. Will no longer swam in the mornings—he was too tired—and he only visited the lazarets once a week. His dreams were full of blue-skinned patients, men who came back from the war drowning in their own lung fluid. It was nearly always young men. So many lives cut short.

Each morning Will donned his mask and gown and went back into the fray. The skin on his hands peeled from constant washing. Already they had more than two thousand patients, and around two hundred of them had died. Across Sydney, the schools, universities, picture theatres and churches were closed. People wore masks in public and it was second nature now for him to wear one in the wards. Schools and showgrounds were makeshift hospitals. Will knew of three nurses at the Coast who had died, one doctor who had fallen ill. He had been inoculated, but there were those inoculated who still caught the disease. One Sunday—at his mother's urging—he visited an inhalatorium in the city, breathing in a zinc oxide mist, but there was little evidence that it did any good. Most days he was sleepwalking, pushing headfirst against an overwhelming tide of death. He had been numbed to it. He no longer grieved.

•

And then there was Sid. The message came to him in the morning from Ted, the attendant to the men's lazaret. Sid, Ted said, had woken in the night with laboured breathing.

He could not visit until evening, once he had changed from his mask and gown. He did not want to cause a flu outbreak in the lazaret. Those patients were vulnerable enough.

When he entered the sparsely furnished cottage—two iron-framed beds, a table, two chairs—Clea and Alice were there already.

'Dr Stenger, what took you so—'

Alice interrupted her mother. 'You look tired Dr Stenger,' she said. 'When did you last get a proper night's sleep?'

Will shook his head; it didn't matter.

Sid was in bed, his face pale, damp with sweat. He did not require his stethoscope to hear that Sid's breath was a whistle coming in and out. He and Alice had been inseparable since the child arrived four years earlier. There was nothing he would not do to make her laugh. But he was still small and frail; the regular meals hadn't made up for his early malnutrition and his advanced disease. Dr Stenger knew that there were growths on Sid's larynx, so any disease affecting his breathing would be worrisome—and it only took moments to confirm his fear.

Alice stood, holding Sid's hand, and Will patted her shoulder. She was, from a distance, a beautiful young woman. It was only up close you saw the damage the disease had wrought. Her eyes were wet, Sid's hand was limp between both of hers. Dr Stenger saw on the bedside table the copy of *Alice's Adventures in Wonderland* which he had given Alice as a girl. Was it her first Christmas at the Coast?

'Are you going to tell us what's wrong?' Clea seemed jumpy.

'Where's Fred?' Will asked.

'Fishing,' Clea said. 'He finds it too hard to watch the boy suffer.'

'Sid has pneumonia. But we cannot put him with the other patients, because of his advanced leprosy. I'll struggle to convince the hospital to treat him as they would a normal patient. It has been challenging, as you are aware, with the pandemic. Leprosy can cause growths on the larynx, and his breathing will be even more laboured as a result.'

'So the leprosy would make the pneumonia worse?'

'Most certainly it would,' Will said.

He went to order the serum, and returned with a nurse, carrying a tray of syringes. She looked around, scowling, as though daring anyone in the lazaret to touch her.

'This is Sister Smith.'

The nurse set down the tray and turned on her heel, the flyscreen bouncing behind her.

'Well, I was going to ask her to help administer the serum, but I suppose I'll do it myself.'

•

The serum did not help, and Sid's cough grew worse, bringing sputum that stained the sheets and sleeves of his pyjamas. Alice was in his room every time Will came, reading aloud, sleeping in the chair beside the boy. Clea brought her needlework over and sat with them, humming beneath her breath.

Will came at the end of long days. Seeing Alice's and Clea's love for Sid buoyed him. It gave him a pleasant vision before he was overwhelmed by sleep. This changed when he performed a tracheotomy in order to help Sid breathe. Afterwards there was a tube extending from the frail boy's throat. His breathing seemed less laboured, but he could no longer speak. Will increased the pain medication, and Sid hardly opened his eyes. He had shrunk even further in his bed. Will wanted Sid to die peacefully, as much for Alice's sake as his own. He knew that Alice spent the night in the cottage in the men's lazaret and that Clea hid the fact, covering for her daughter so Sid would not die alone.

Alice was there, then, when Sid choked to death in the middle of the night. When word came to Will the next morning

143

he went first thing. The combined effects of the leprosy and the pneumonia had overwhelmed Sid's larynx. Will knew what it would have looked like, and he wished he could have spared Alice the sight. The boy was cold when Will arrived, and Fred had washed the body and combed Sid's hair. Sid was dressed in a starched white shirt and woollen trousers. They buried him at the Coast Cemetery, beside the grave of Clea's father, the original leper of Lismore. Alice did not cry, and Will saw the effort this took, the way she arranged her face and held her mother's arm with white knuckles. He had to leave before they put the dirt on the grave; the trams were arriving from the city soon with the fresh influenza cases. Will turned and walked the narrow path back to the hospital. He did not have time to grieve.

# 14

*Jack*

**1919**

After disembarking the *Wandilla* in Sydney, Jack caught a train to Walgett with a stopover in Narrabri, and then another train to Brewarrina. He would not go home until this was done. He knew that Sally lived with her family. He felt the weight of Guy's death every waking moment.

It was strange, how the uniform and the wooden leg changed the way people treated him. Men slid over on trains now, patting the seat beside them. Strangers asked where he had fought, slapping him on the back. They shook his hand. Waiting for the train in Walgett, a man bought him a beer.

'You have no idea,' Jack wanted to say, 'what it was like.' Instead he smiled and nodded. Instead he was always polite.

He was still learning to walk with the wooden leg and it was different on his own, with no nurses to help. It was a matter of pride not to appear weak or tired. Still, he caught a ride to the Brewarrina mission with a man he met at the station. He drank a cup of over-sugared tea with the man's family and waited while enquiries were made as to Sally's whereabouts. And when a tall, sharp-boned woman stood in the doorway with the light behind her, shining through her yellow dress and illuminating the child on her hip, he forgot all the words he had practised. She had known for months, but it did not diminish her sorrow.

They walked along dusty streets to the other side of the mission, to the house she shared with her parents and sister. She walked fast and Jack struggled to keep up. Her ankles were narrow and sweat made damp dark patches under the arms of her cotton dress. At the house, the little girl, Lila, went inside with her cousins, and Jack and Sally sat on the steps at the front.

'You were there when he died?' she asked. Her voice was so soft, he strained to hear it.

'I was. It was at Beersheba. The whole campaign against the Turks hung on us capturing Beersheba, and we did.'

Jack hated his words as soon as they were out.

'Guy was the bravest. He took a bullet in the neck, and I carried him to the dressing tent. I was with him when he died, and he said to tell you he loved you. That was the last thing he said.'

She nodded slowly, scratching at a mosquito bite on her calf. He was too shy to look at her face.

'I have his papers, and his draughts set. His kit, too.' Jack rummaged in the bag at his feet. He passed the bundle to Sally, who held it on her lap.

'Will you keep something?' Sally asked. 'To remember him?'

Jack nodded. 'If you don't mind, I'll keep the draughts. Guy taught me. I think of him every time I play.'

Sally took the box and opened it, fingering the painted wooden pieces. She put her face against it, breathing in, then clasped it shut and handed it to Jack. He knew he ought to say she could keep it, but he wanted it too much.

'I promised I would look after you. I don't know what you need, but I can send money. I have to find work again, and I don't think I can ride, but I want to help. Guy was my friend through everything. I don't know how to go on without him.'

Then, to his shame, Jack's tears came again and it was Sally comforting him, passing him her hanky. Her hand on his shoulder. He loathed himself, then, for wanting everything Guy had. Even now that he was gone.

# 15

*Nellie*

**1903**

When a tree catches fire, it burns from the outside in. Flames lick the twiggy flappy parts that catch. Only when the wind has fanned the flames and the fire is crackling does it eat the heart. Only then does it burn the insides.

Leprosy is the same. It attacks the skin first and the nerve trunks later. By the time your skin is covered in tuberosities and sores, the destruction beneath the surface has begun.

When Ma had Dr Moffat come to look at Nellie, Nellie knew what Ma reckoned the doctor would find. At first she did not want him to touch her, but eventually she gave over. Like when Charlie touched her, Nellie's mind went elsewhere. He scraped at her skin with a razor. He pursed his lips tight, the edges whitening. He pricked her with pins to see what she could feel. Hilda watched him, big-eyed.

He examined Hilda and Hunter, and then he stood outside the house with Ma for a long time talking, his shiny shoes coated with a fine layer of dust.

Nellie did not think any more of it until he came back a month later with two constables in a police wagon. They were to take her to the Coast Hospital at Sydney's Little Bay, where her own father had died. They were to take her away from her children. From her husband. Nellie thought it was part of Ma's grand plan to have Hilda. Now she wanted Hunter too.

Ma said that Nellie was not to scare Hilda. She was to say goodbye as if she would only be gone for a week.

'You wanted this all along,' Nellie said. 'You set me up for this.'

'You're talking mad. It has gone to your head.'

'You wanted my children for your own.'

'I do not want to see you suffer as your pa did. They might fix you.'

'Like they fixed him?'

'He was too far along.'

'What will Hunter eat?'

'Cow's milk from a bottle. He will be fine. Come and say goodbye now. Don't get them worked up.'

The police stood by the wagon, watching, as Nellie kneeled in the yard and hugged Hilda to her breast. She buried her nose in the dandelion seed hair.

Hilda must've felt fear in Nellie's grip. 'Mama?'

'Listen to Gran,' Nellie said.

She lifted Hunter one last time from his basket. He smiled, blinking at the bright sun. His skin was perfect. His fingers sought her face, his hands small and star-shaped. She should not even touch him. She put him down quickly and he wailed at the emptiness around him. She hoped Charlie would not come close; he was watering the constables' horses.

They put Nellie in the back of the wagon, which smelled of sick, sour sweat. She sat on a small low bench, knees to her chest. The constables sat atop, in the front, in the fresh air. She was a thing to be feared now: a monster.

Charlie stood back, arms crossed over his chest. He would not say farewell.

Ma called to her. 'God bless.'

The wagon swayed and jolted, the horses trotted and the sky moved. Out of range of the house, she let go the wail that was trapped in her chest. Her breastbone creaked with the weight. A moan—a sound she did not even know she possessed. Milk darkened the front of her dress. A horse whinnied, recognising the animal depth of her pain.

•

The trip to Sydney was one Nellie wished to forget. A day of bumping in the back of the wagon, remembering the sound of Hunter's and Hilda's cries as she left; the lack of sorrow on Charlie's face. Then, when she thought she could take no more rattling, they were in Lismore. They kept her locked in a shed in the gaolyard for almost a week while building a hasty deckhouse for the coastal steamer which would take her to Sydney.

'Why am I locked away?' Nellie asked.

No one answered.

They opened the door of the shed to pass in a crust of bread, a tin bowl of watery stew. She relieved herself in a corner, squatting like a dog. The only light was that which came through cracks in the boards, showing rat-eaten planks, a few old shovels, a stained pallet and blanket they had left for her. She tried to break the door with one of the shovels, but only hurt her hand. She imagined she was in the deserted shack across the creek. The one she dreamed of living in alone. *Careful what you wish for,* her ma had always said.

The constables guarding the shed shouted at Nellie to stay back. She heard one of them saying the whole place would have to be torched when she left.

All she had to do to terrify someone, Nellie realised, was act as though she would touch them. This amused her for a time. When the constable finally came, she went as though to embrace him, and he stepped back and swore, brandishing his pistol to keep her at bay. When he turned to leave, Nellie spat at him. She flicked a scab pulled from her knee.

•

There was a small crowd gathered at the dock when they arrived to board the steamer. Nellie heard a man call out, 'There's the leper!' Some women shrieked. A man with a notebook tried to ask questions of her as the constables led her aboard the ship. She reached out to grasp his hand and he backed away. Women gawked at Nellie, touching their own faces. Was she really so ugly or disfigured? She pulled the blanket over her head like a shawl.

The deckhouse was a shoddily built construction: timber planks, a low ceiling and a tin roof. Hardly tall enough to stand in, there was barely space for a rough pallet. There was a door they chained shut when she was safely inside, with a slot so they would not have to open it. A bucket for waste, and a blanket, and a second bucket filled with water. Neither bucket was lidded.

Nellie lay down and closed her eyes.

She must have slept through the river voyage, but she woke sliding across the ground, everything wet. The cracks in the planks sluiced rain and the roof above leaked. The hut creaked as the ship rocked side to side. She was wet through. Nellie huddled in the corner, shivering in the dark, listening to the rain beating against tin, the waves breaking against the hull of the ship. At least she had not used the bucket yet, for it would have spilled, as the bucket of water had, in the rough seas. She would be sitting in more than just rain.

Morning brought sun and calm seas, and a voice called from the slot. 'Breakfast!' They shoved a tin dish of stew in.

'All my bedding is wet, the whole bloody thing leaks,' she shouted.

There was no reply.

Nellie ate without tasting, her hunger hardly sated. She licked the dish clean. The longer they treated her like an animal, the more she became one. She spent an hour picking at scabs on her legs, another pulling knots from her hair with her teeth.

Later, someone did push a dry blanket through the slot. It was stuck, and when Nellie came to pull it, she heard voices, 'Watch out!' 'Did the leper touch you?'

A pair of curious eyes peered in and were jerked away.

'Tommy! I told you to stay away from it. You want your fingers 'n' toes to drop off?'

There were nails sticking out of the rough walls and she hung last night's bedding on them, along with her dress which had been soaked through. She wrapped herself in the dry blanket, though it stank of unwashed bodies and grease. She placed her boots beside the slot in the hope they would dry in the ventilated air. She was staying alive through sheer fury, but fury is no small force.

They swabbed the deck around the deckhouse in carbolic. Nellie learned that she must eat everything on her tray or the rats would come. They came through cracks in the planks. They came at night, when she had no light to see by. She heard only their scraping claws. She woke once to a sharp pain; a rat had bitten her on the hand. She screamed and screamed. Afterwards she slept with her hands always covered. Twice she flung one off her by a scaly tail. They were heavy. The thud and squeak when they hit the wall was a sickening sound.

•

On the third day, movement ceased. Shouting on the deck, and close by ships' horns and flocks of gulls. Had they arrived? Nellie waited while what sounded like crowds of people walked past, sometimes peering through the slot. She was well aware of the stench inside the deckhouse, the bucket which she had kept upright but which was foul with her waste. The crusted stiffness of her clothes, sour milk from her leaking breasts, her matted hair. When they finally unlocked the padlocked door, the smell made them step back.

The light was too much. Nellie squinted, shading her eyes. She made out three men in uniform, and a boy with gold spectacles carrying a bag. 'She can be violent, watch out,' one of the men said.

Nellie stood from where she had been crouching in the corner and they all backed away. A policemen drew his pistol.

The boy pushed it down with his hand and stepped towards her. To Nellie's surprise, he touched her on the sleeve.

'You must be weary. I am Dr Stenger. There is only a short distance to travel, and we will be at the hospital.'

She let him lead her from the deckhouse into the bright sunlight, surrounded by the glinting water of the harbour. The deck was empty except for a few men sweeping, coiling ropes, polishing railings. It all hurt behind her eyes.

'You might have a bath there, and a sleep in your own bed. Have you injured your hand? Come, the treatment can only improve from here.'

Dr Stenger was not a boy, she realised, but a man. A small one, and different too. Nellie followed him down to the dock, along the quay, to the street. She had never been to such a city, a bustling place, but she was too ashamed to look around. All she noticed were the flies buzzing around her, the stench of her own clothes, the filth on her skin.

•

They travelled to the hospital in a horse-drawn ambulance with the policemen sitting as far from Nellie as they could. Dr Stenger sat facing her, speaking in that deep, calm voice. He had never met her father, but he had read all the notes of his case. He did not think Nellie's progression was as serious. He could not tell merely by looking at her, of course, but he had examined the specimens that Dr Moffat sent. He was looking forward to examining Nellie more closely, but first he would let her rest. As soon as he'd dealt with her hand, of course.

Nellie recalled very little of their arrival at the Coast, not the gates nor the path nor the door to the women's lazaret. But she did remember seeing the ocean—the sandstone-fringed bay that was her new home. More of that glittering sea. She wanted nothing to do with it. She wanted Hilda and Hunter, the only people in the world who needed her.

What use was she to them, though? Her paps were flat now; the milk was gone.

# 16

*Jack*

## 1923

It was five years after the war ended that the marks came. He had found work in Queensland, just over the border; work that suited a crippled digger. He sent money to Sally every week. The other diggers got soldier settler grants, but not him. The work was at a button factory, where he might sit all day among women and other damaged men sorting buttons into envelopes for shops. The buttons came in all different colours. The most common ones were black but there were also browns, blues, reds, greens, whites, yellows, purples and pinks. Jack's marks were the size and colour of the pale pink buttons, only not so perfectly round. The colour of a whitefella's skin, but just in patches. He could hear Guy in his head, ribbing him: *You're turning into one of them.* Jack had an easy camaraderie with the men in the factory, many of whom had been at war. They invited him to the pub after work, but he did not go. He would need his dog tags and his exemption certificate, and it would still be up to the proprietor whether or not he was allowed in.

When the spots became noticeable he went one afternoon to visit the doctor, whose office was in a residential house. The nurse asked him to pay upfront and told him to wait outside on the verandah. The doctor came outside to examine his teeth, the stump of his missing leg, the insides of his ears. There had been a sore in his mouth which had healed, Jack told the doctor. He was poked and prodded like a horse. Then the doctor told him to wait until the results were back to return to work. He said he would write him a letter for the factory boss.

•

The doctor rang the Board of Health before he rang Jack. They were waiting in a car outside the doctor's house when he gave Jack the results of the test. They put him on a train to Brisbane—a quarantine car, which was really just a boxcar they would burn when he arrived. From there they went to Cleveland, to the wharf.

When the government ferry *Karboora* came, they towed Jack in a double-ended clinker dinghy behind. There was one other leper in the dinghy, a man with a face so disfigured Jack could not decide whether he wanted to stare or could not bear to. When he held his hand out, though, Jack shook it.

'Name's Hugh,' the man said. 'This your first time?'

Jack nodded.

'Peel's not a bad place. D'ya like to fish?'

'Sure.' He thought of the Narran. Catfish long as a boy's arm.

'Plenty trevally. Snapper. Last week a kingfish.'

Jack was not used to the salt air. Hugh's voice was drowned out by the wind and the ferry engine. Jack could hardly tell where the water ended and the sky began, they were all such a bright glaring blue. The spray from the ferry drenched them and their clothes stuck heavy to their skin. On board were island staff, Hugh explained. They spent their time off getting pissed.

'That's us,' he said as an island covered in bush and fringed by white sand came into view. 'Horseshoe Bay. Not bad, eh?'

The lepers were on the mangrove side of the island. The ferry dropped them at the crumbling stone jetty alongside the rusting *Platypus* dredge. There was a man waiting to drive them to the village. Despite the segregation on the ferry, they all rode the cart together, with the mail and the milk cans, the clinking bottles of cordial, the meat delivery. It was a sandy trail through empty bush, only bird call and leaf rustle from lizards. On the way, Hugh pointed out the cemetery, among the cypress and eucalypts. 'When ya croak, they call it going to the gums,' he said. 'No marker. Just a number.'

Jack found he could not reply. He felt the air pressing down on him, the weight of dirt on his skin. This might be the last stop. He did not want to be buried nameless, so far from home.

•

They arrived at the cottages. At first glance, the place was like a seaside holiday village. There were carefully tended gardens and lawns, small tidy huts and larger buildings for the matron, hospital, caretaker and dining hall.

Jack laughed later, recalling the look on Hugh's face when the nurse came and called him the coloured patient. Hugh had not realised. Jack saw Hugh look at the hand which had shaken his. It was madness how a person who looked like *that* could be afraid of touching *him*.

The nurse took Jack to the clinic to check him over. She was thick-necked and spoke with a strange accent. She asked a lot of questions about Jack's life before and took a long time to write the answers in a book, in handwriting as neat as he had ever seen.

Finally, she asked, 'What would you like your new name to be?'

'Pardon?'

'People always choose a new name. To protect their families.'

He hardly took the time to think. He would not say 122.

'Guy,' he said. His lost friend.

The nurse closed her book and walked him to his quarters, and he saw the nice timber cottages with little verandahs and glass windows, electric lights.

'Those aren't for you,' she said.

She walked him behind the garden to where a series of corrugated-iron, low-ceilinged huts were scattered through the weeds. 'This is the coloured camp.' Some had concrete floors made from the island's middens. Others just dirt. Windows were only holes cut into the iron.

The nurse showed Jack-now-Guy to a hut he would share with two others. There were three beds made of chaff bags filled with leaves, sewn together. A flour sack hung across the door. It wasn't much more than his mother had at Angledool, but no one bothered to look after it. It felt nothing like home.

In their men's camp there were four Chinamen, an Arab, Kanakas and a Maori fella. Then there were blackfellas, six of them. The women were most of them black, plus the Maori fella's wife. That night he introduced himself as Guy to the others. The name would take a while to grow on Jack. At first, when people called it, he forgot to respond. Sometimes his heart skipped. Where was Guy? They sat around the fire as the sky darkened, seeing the electric lights through the trees in the white dining room, smelling the white patients' dinner.

'Who feeds us?' Guy asked the woman beside him, Mary, who reminded him of Aunty Rita. Except she had tumours on her face, and one of her eyes was a milky, rheumy hue.

She laughed. 'We do, yella fella. They give us raw rations, though. Tomorrow you can catch a fish.'

'Long time since I caught anything.'

''Cept leprosy,' she said. They both laughed.

They talked about where they were from. Most were from further north; Mary was Gubbi Gubbi. Someone passed meat. Bread that was hard to chew. Guy was so hungry he choked his down.

He learned that the coloured camp's residents looked after each other, because no one else would. They fetched their water from the well, collected melaleuca and boxwood to burn from the surrounding bush.

Some reckoned they were lucky not to have the cook making their food, because he was drunk half the time and filthy all of it. At the kitchen there was a list of rations. They gathered theirs every Monday.

|  | White | Others |
|---|---|---|
| Meat | 1½ lbs/day | 1½ lbs/day |
| Maizemeal | 2 oz/day | 2 oz/day |
| Bread | 1 lb/day | 1 lb/day |
| Vegetables | 1 lb/day | 1 lb/day |
| Milk | ½ pint/day | ½ pint/day |
| Butter | 1¼ oz/day | 1 oz/day |
| Bacon | 4 oz/week | – |
| Sugar | 1¼ lb /week | 1¼ lb /week |
| Tea | 4 oz/week | 4 oz/week |
| Rice/sago | ½ lb/week | ½ lb/week |
| Split peas | 2 oz/week | – |
| Flour | 1 lb/week | 1 lb/week |
| Fruit | 1 lb/week | 1 lb/week |
| Tobacco | 2 oz/week | 2 oz/week |
| Puddings | Three times/week | Once/week |

For the meat, there was a white patient who would kill and dress the sheep. The lazaret had a small flock. The lesser cuts were given to those in the coloured camp. The doctor came out once a month, if the weather was nice enough, if the boat could make the trip. He had a cursory look at the coloured patients after he checked all the whites in their camp.

'There any medicine for this, to make us better?' Guy asked the first time he saw the doctor.

The man looked at Guy as though he had not expected his patient to speak. Guy nearly didn't, after his experience with the doctor on the mainland. But what did he have to lose?

The doctor thought a moment, then told Guy that they were having some good results further south—in the Sydney leper hospital—with chaulmoogra, but one needed to have capsules or injections every day. 'Hurts like hell—I've heard people scream when you put it under the skin,' the doctor said.

One or two of the patients were taking it at Peel, he said, but they did not have the supplies to give it to everyone. Those patients bought it themselves, had it delivered in the post or when family visited. Guy guessed these were white patients. They were usually the ones who had their own food, medicine and clothing sent.

•

It was March then, the worst of the summer finished. He spent his days limping around—the island had many tracks.

There were discarded bottles everywhere: beer bottles, cordial bottles, soda bottles. They were piled up like middens, and broken glass glistened in every pile of dirt.

'You could make a fortune—why's nobody returning these for the deposit?' Guy had asked when he first arrived. That made the others laugh.

'Shop man's not going to take bottles from a leper colony, is he?'

'Those bottles are here to stay, just like us,' Mary said. 'Only way we leave is feet first, going to the gums.'

'Maybe the bottles,' Guy replied. 'Not me.'

He wandered through the cemetery, which never failed to make his skin prickle. There was a young fella Guy often came across in the mangroves, Cecil. He was always looking for birds, and he wanted to know all about Guy's wooden leg. He wanted to hear about the war, and Guy found he didn't mind telling him. It was different from trying to tell it to other men. Cecil did not come with so many preconceived ideas. Cecil showed Guy the sketches in his book: boobook owls, curlews, egrets, spoonbills and black ducks. Flipping through, Guy could see how Cecil's drawings were deteriorating. The boy was losing sensation in his fingers. He burned himself lighting a fire, not realising he was holding a smouldering stick. He was only ten and on his own, no parents or adults to look after him. Guy found himself waiting with Cecil in the hours of dusk, in spite of mosquitoes and biting midges. It was the best hour to see birds, Cecil insisted. Some evenings Guy brought the draughts and taught Cecil how to play. It was something to pass the time.

One of Guy's hut mates had built his own dinghy and they spent hours in it, more to get off the island than anything. Guy did not take a line but sat with the others. They talked about taking the boat all the way to the mainland, and there were stories of patients who did. But they always were caught. They always came back. Some even came back of their own accord. They'd got so used to being ostracised they ostracised themselves.

At night they listened to the wireless; when the whites got a new one, they gave them their old set. Sometimes Guy passed the whites' dining hall and heard the sound of piano music from within, saw the yellow light spilling onto squares of grass. Cecil's small head among them, at a table, bent over his sketchbook. Guy hated himself then for longing for something he wished he did not want.

There were two attendants and two nurses who worked in shifts—on for seven days and off for four, so there was always someone to watch them. Who exactly would take a job in a leper colony on an island, where there was no doctor, not enough medicine and the patients were angry and bored? A strange sort of person. Still, some were kind. The men were often drunks, the women sometimes too. The only thing Guy envied was their ability to come and go. Still, he wondered, did they tell people on the outside what it was they did? Guy figured they took the job because these were the people no one else would hire. They were accountable to no one, because no one was going to make sure the lepers were being treated right. You show up and the job's as good as done.

Guy found he could make money, here and there, unofficially doing work which others were too lazy or crippled to do. He cleared weeds in the gardens, and even with a wooden leg he could push the mower, chop wood. The pay was measly—he knew they paid him less than the whitefella who had done it before him—but it was something to send to Sally. Another man made money fixing clocks and watches. There was a woman who sewed clothes, another who washed and ironed. One fella was the barber; he was kept busy enough. *Just because our fingers and toes are falling off, doesn't mean our hair is,* he used to joke. They all had their jokes.

Attendants had schemes as well. One brought cigarettes and grog from Cleveland and sold it for a tidy profit. His wife would wash the leper-tainted money and hang it out on the line to dry. Guy would see her out there, in her housedress with a cup of tea, watching the bills flutter in the breeze.

Out birdwatching one evening, Cecil told him that in other leper colonies, in the Philippines, they had their own money printed. Then they did not have to worry about it going out among the general public. That way, patients were not going to escape and use their money on the outside, because it was useless there.

'How do you know these things,' Guy asked, 'little fella like you?'

Cecil tapped one ear with a pencil. 'The walls have ears,' he said.

Guy gave his other ear a gentle tweak.

Any mail was sent through the kitchen before going out. There, cook put it in the oven for ten minutes, to burn off the leper germs. Just him touching it probably gave it more germs than patients ever could. Guy never trusted his mail would reach its destination once he heard cook forgot a batch and torched it. Nothing but cinders at the bottom of the oven when he remembered.

Guy gave Cecil a detective job: discover the name of the leper hospital to the south. Cecil reported back that it was called the Coast. Guy traded his tobacco ration with one of the attendants for some paper and the cost of postage and began to write letters—multiple, in case they got burned. He was from Angledool, New South Wales, he wrote, and he was a Yuwaalaraay man. Just writing it gave him a bone-heavy feeling of homesickness. He wrote how he had been working across the border in Queensland because he had an exemption to live outside a mission. He'd fought in the Light Horse Brigade in the war and lost a leg at Khuweilfe. He was writing to ask if he might come to the Coast. He paid the same attendant extra to make sure his mail made it off Peel.

'You're not to lick the envelope,' the attendant said.

'I know. I used water.'

'What're all these letters to hospital for?' the man asked, suspicious.

'Old mate's laid up there. We fought together,' Guy said.

The attendant nodded. The war legitimised everything.

Guy wasn't allowed to affix the stamps himself either; the attendant did that for him.

•

Months passed. It was May when the attendant brought a letter for Guy.

'Looks like your mate's finally written you back, eh?'

The return address was the Coast Hospital, Sydney. He tore it open.

Dear Mr Flint,

I have heard unhappy stories about the hospital to the north, and now you have confirmed my suspicion that it is less a hospital than a place where men and women are left to die. I was very surprised to receive your letter because, as you might imagine, a leprosy hospital is not a place to which people often write requesting admission.

You are correct that we do not segregate the patients by race here, merely by sex, as the women and men have separate lazarets. And because we are first and foremost a hospital—and the lazaret is only a small proportion of our patients—we do focus on what we might do to treat the disease, regardless of the difficulty. However, in the case of leprosy, the patients are rarely cured.

Patients are assigned cottages within the lazaret and, whilst they are allowed to use a section of the beach and a fishing boat we have, they are not allowed to leave the hospital or mix with the general population of patients. I am sure you understand the reasons behind this. I have my own opinions about the segregation of those suffering from leprosy, but I will not go into those here, as that is not why you wrote. The space allotted to leprosy patients is smaller than that at Peel, but the level of medical care is far superior.

I will write a letter to the Chief Leprologist of Queensland and the Protector of Aborigines requesting your transfer to our institution. As you are originally from this state, I will insist it is our responsibility to look after you. The Chief Leprologist considers it his primary duty to segregate those who suffer from leprosy. However, I do not believe that he desires to hold on to any leprosy patients unnecessarily, so I would not be surprised if he relents and allows you to travel south. We also look after quite a few returned servicemen at this hospital, which I shall use to give additional weight to my request—though for obvious reasons we could not allow you to stay in the diggers' ward.

Meanwhile, I urge you, do not speak of this to the other patients. If you keep it to yourself, our chances of success will improve. I shall write immediately and hope that we have the opportunity to welcome you soon to the Coast Hospital at Little Bay.

Sincerely yours, etc.
Dr William Stenger

Hope is a fragile feeling; Guy tried not to be overwhelmed with it. Why would the Chief Leprologist allow him to travel south? And then there was the guilt he felt at his silence. The others in the camp had done nothing but help him, and he was just trying to save himself. Only Cecil knew of Guy's plan, but Guy trusted him. Cecil said he would not wish to leave Peel, because his family was coming to get him one day, and if he left they would not know where he had gone. Guy hoped Cecil was right. The boy had stepped on a mangrove root and injured his foot, so Guy visited him now in his cottage. Cecil's foot was infected, and he could no longer walk.

Still, Guy had moments of feeling as light as a seed pod floating in the wind. He bided his time. He let Cecil win at draughts sometimes. He chopped melaleuca, taking small pleasure in the way logs split from the axe. He limped along the paths, careful of his one good foot. He rowed out with the other men, who sat in the early dawn to fish, watching for ripples and bubbles in the calm surface. He sat in the mangroves without Cecil, whittling, slapping mosquitoes, listening for the rustle of birds. But most of all he waited. He knew how to do this; he had spent most of his life waiting.

•

Strange how the past comes back unbidden. Guy woke on the train to Sydney, certain he was on a ship to Egypt, the smell of horses in the hold, the rock and sway of the waves and the thump, thump of the engines beneath. Then they had been jittery with the thought of battle, their oiled rifles used only in practice, the creased uniforms carefully packed. The ship zigged and zagged en route to Cairo to avoid mines and the German U-boats. They had heard stories of other ships blown apart. Guy had been disappointed to be going to Egypt. The war he knew of, the enemy he knew of, was in Europe. It seemed cruel to send them from one sun-baked land to another.

When he woke, though, he was not on board the ship, but in the cargo car of a train. The floor was straw and horse manure, which explained the memory of smell, and the car did sway from side to side. In the open doorway was the man Guy recognised to be his police guard. Tim had traded places with Ian at the border. Ian had only sneered at Guy over a curled moustache, but Tim avoided his eyes. Tim looked to be less than twenty. The hair on his chin grew sparse like grass that had been eaten away. He was probably terrified to have been given this job of looking after the black leper. Guy reassured him early on that he was going to keep his distance. He wondered what frightened them more—his blackness or his leprosy. He was not game to ask.

Tim asked what kind of sandwich Guy wanted when the train stopped in Newcastle. Guy said nothing, but Tim brought ham, on white bread, with a limp slice of tomato. Guy was unused to kindness from unexpected places, and when it came it overwhelmed him. He found himself blinking back tears as he chewed the dry bread and salty ham, face towards the floor. Tim stayed silent and Guy was grateful, for silence was always easier than questions.

Guy had spent his childhood learning the Bible from the brothers at the Home, but it was not until recently that he began to think on it. The idea that we are all born sinners and must rise out of those ashes towards goodness, righteousness. What if we were born innocent and are taught by the world to sin? The white man taught him to lie about who he was, to kill others in war. Guy figured that people were born to feel love, sorrow and pity. It was all he knew before they took him away from his mother and Aunty Rita at Angledool. Funny that the ones teaching him the Bible were the ones who taught him coldness and cruelty. Before he was taken away, he had not known what sin was.

•

Tim wished him luck when he left Guy at the Coast. They had gone in a motor ambulance from the train station. He was a fine fellow, and Guy told him as much. In another life he would have shaken Tim's hand.

Dr Stenger was there to meet the ambulance, a more fragile man than Guy had pictured, with thinning red hair and eyes that flicked here and there behind gold spectacles. He was jumpy as well, like a horse that was mistreated once, easy to spook forever after. But his hands were steady and calm—he touched Guy without a moment of hesitation to examine his skin. Guy watched Dr Stenger's fingers rest on the inside of his wrist to take his pulse. They were long and pale, the nails clean.

'You will be in a cottage with a fellow from the East Indies,' Dr Stenger said. 'Goes by the name of Java Jim. Fairly advanced case, but we like the more well-off ones to go with those who are worse off. Only one attendant for the men's lazaret, so you can help Jim out a bit here and there. Sound alright?'

'Yep.'

'You're from up north then. Angledool?'

'Know of it?'

Dr Stenger nodded. 'From Walgett myself.'

'Not far from me then. How'd you end up here?'

Dr Stenger shrugged. 'I made a better doctor than sheep farmer. Come along then. You manage well with that leg. Where're your things?'

All Guy had was the draughts set, but he gave it to Cecil when he left Peel.

'Haven't got any.'

# 17

*Alice*

## 1924

Visiting days were Sundays and Fridays, between two and five in the afternoon, but in fourteen years I had only been visited by relatives from Jiggi twice. I did not hold it against them; it was a long way to travel. The first was Gran, only three years after she left me. She brought a slab of ham, half-a-dozen peaches and a bunch of daffodils. She was here less than an hour before she turned around and left. The flowers were wilted, and the ham must have been too long in the same heat. Mama and I retched until the following morning. The most recent visitor was Hunter. He was grown, my dear brother, a head taller than me. He sat in the small sitting room in our cottage, across from Mama and me, staring at his hat, which he turned around and around in his lap.

Mama asked him questions about Jiggi Creek and he answered them dutifully. Gran had died two years back but Charlie was still around. They raised pigs now. He talked of the price of pork and the agricultural show he was in Sydney to attend.

Hunter had heard of Sid's death from a letter I wrote, but it was different, hearing it in person from kin. I kept Sid's marbles in a box beside my bed. The grief I felt when he was gone was like nothing I imagined. The loneliness insurmountable. The possibility of love vanished from the world. Mama tried to reach me, but I pushed her away. She was no comfort to me.

Gran keeled over lighting the stove, Hunter said. He had found her there, face in the cold kindling, when he came in from feeding the pigs one morning. Mama said, 'It was her time, I suppose.' There was no love lost between her and Gran, yet her voice hinted at a more complicated grief. Annie and Irene had left (and who could blame them?), but Charlie did not take long to move a young woman in. It was not fathomable for him to make his own tea. I touched my face as Hunter spoke, unaware I was even doing it until I caught myself. Sid would have laughed. Hunter and I had lips that were the same, different eyes, a similar plane of cheek. It was like looking in a mirror at a not-gruesome version of myself. I could not stop staring. He barely glanced up from the floor at me.

'What about you?' Ma asked. 'Have you got yourself a wife?'

Hunter went red to where the barber had cut around his ears—just that morning, it appeared.

'There's someone,' he mumbled. 'I'm courtin'.'

'Someone I might know?'

'Jane Fletcher. From Goolmangar?'

'Oh, yes. Those Fletchers. Be surprised if *her* parents would agree,' she said.

'Mama!' I said.

'I'm not saying he's not good enough. And I'd bet money he's better-looking than anyone in a hundred miles. But I'm sure there are plenty of rumours still about our family in the district. It's why Avery moved away and never came back. We haven't made it easy for you.'

Hunter was working his jaw furiously. When he was a little boy, it was how he coped when the others teased him. How he had worked out not to cry. It hurt to see it now, a grown man on the verge of tears.

After a moment he spoke, his voice cracking. 'Her parents aren't so agreeable. But she is, so we're trying to convince them.'

'They'll come around,' I said.

The new nurse, Sue Hull, came to the door.

'Time to change your dressings, Alice.'

'Now?'

'Go on, Alice,' Mama said. 'Hunter will still be here when Sue is finished.'

I heard their murmuring voices in the next room as Sue unwound the bandages, applied the ointment, wrapped fresh ones.

'Be quick,' I whispered.

'Doing my very best,' Sue replied. Olive had gone to help her daughter who had just had a baby in Brisbane, and Sue was a probationer nurse who Matron had roped in to helping in the lazaret. She quickly became indispensable. We had not realised how old and frail Olive had become.

When I returned to the sitting room Hunter was standing. Mama was offering more tea, to stay for dinner, anything she could think of.

'I promised a mate I would meet him at the pub, and the tram will take at least an hour,' he said, looking towards the clock on the wall.

'Let me walk you to the gate,' I said.

Mama frowned—I knew she wanted to come, but she'd had him to herself already. She came with us to the door of the cottage, put her hand on his arm, the woollen fabric and cotton shirt protecting him from her taint. 'Travel safe,' she said.

'Goodbye, Mama,' Hunter's voice wavered again, and the muscle behind his cheek twitched. His whole life he hadn't known her, and now only this.

I followed him down the stairs of the verandah. I could not get enough of watching him. Here was the little boy who had curled beside me for years, who wept when I left. Now he towered over me, smooth-skinned, healthy.

'I regret that I've never visited,' he said, as we walked along the path to the lazaret gate. 'I wanted to come when Charlie brought George, but he wouldn't let me.'

'You're here now. When do you—'

'What's she like?' he interrupted.

'Mama?'

'Yes.'

'Stubborn. Sneaks off at night, drinks too much. But she looks after me, too. She misses you something awful. She makes a life here but she would rather be with you, at Jiggi.'

'And you?'

'I had to stop thinking of it. It is too hard.'

'Forgive me.'

'It's not your fault.' I shrugged. 'Life is so small here. Sometimes I think death would be easier.'

We were at the lazaret gate.

'Mama looks well, mostly.'

'She has what the doctor calls tuberculoid. Borderline. Heals spontaneously. Mine they don't think will ever heal. It's like Si— like George's was, only he had gone without any treatment too long before they brought him in.'

Hunter shook his head. 'They didn't want to admit it was happening again. I tried to talk sense into them. It was awful . . .'

We continued in silence for a moment. 'I was with him when he died.' Now I was fighting tears, recalling Sid's struggle to breathe in his final hours.

'I'm sorry. But I'm glad, too, that he wasn't alone. How far can you come?'

'We can go to the hospital entrance.'

'If you go further?'

'They send police. It's a law, you know, that we must stay confined.'

I rarely left the lazaret now, knowing how others watched me when I did. I would never touch something or sit on a bench outside the lazaret. Having Hunter beside me seemed

176

different, though. We walked along the path that ran beside the tennis courts, a plumbago hedge and the shade of the tall pines. The air was warm and smelled of jasmine.

'Charlie was awful to you,' Hunter said. 'I wish I could have protected you.'

'You were little.'

'I never understood why it came to you and George and not me. I always feared it. I check my skin all the time; any little rash makes me sick with dread.'

'But you've had nothing?'

'No.'

'And what is Charlie like now?'

We passed a group of off-duty nurses headed for the tram in their day clothes. They were chatting loudly but grew silent as we passed. They all must have known of me, but I had never seen any of their faces before.

'Easier. I'm not scared of him now. A few times I stood up to him, and he didn't know how to take it. I wish I could do my own thing, but I haven't the money. The farm is all there is. I wish I could have gone to war, but I was too young. They wouldn't take me.'

'I'm glad you didn't.'

'It hasn't been easy. A lot of people talk about us still, in the district.'

'Where do you say we went?'

'We said it was TB, that you went to a sanitorium in Sydney. But there were always rumours, because of Grandad and Mama.'

'You mustn't pay them any mind,' I told him.

'That's what Gran always said. And when I start to feel sorry for myself, I think of you. At least I am free.'

'So be free,' I said, grabbing his sleeve. 'Take advantage of your freedom.' I tried to tone down my urgency, but he had the chances I would never have.

'You're right.' He did not shrink from my touch. 'I will. I'll visit again Hil— I mean Alice. It won't be so long.' Hunter put on his hat. We were at the hospital gates, the sandstone pillars, the road to the outside world. The tram shed was just there, out the front.

'Good luck with Jane,' I said. 'Write and let us know.'

I wasn't going to touch him again, but then he leaned in and embraced me. His lips brushed my cheek. I pulled away, and he was already walking off, turning back to wave, 'Bye, Hil. Write me a letter.'

He didn't come back. He did not even write. But I would do the same, given half the chance. I'd run as far as I could. I don't blame him at all. I only hope he found his freedom. I hope that he and Jane went far from Jiggi, from a past which no one there can forget.

•

When Matron Wilson retired we knew things would change, but none of us realised to what degree. She saw the lazaret as an integral mission of the hospital and made an effort to visit us whenever she could. Matron Wilson had been at the Coast for nearly twenty years, but she was getting old and she wished to return home, to Scotland. When her dog, Judy, was gone there was nothing to keep her in Sydney; she always said that Judy wouldn't survive a sea voyage.

The new matron, Matron Broom, had been a nursing student at the Coast years before. Matron Broom was everything Matron Wilson was not: tall, cold, more interested in the science of nursing than the feeling of patients. She had a little car she drove from place to place around the Coast rather than walk, but she did not often park it outside the gates of the lazarets.

We were hopeless cases—no cure had been found—and a young matron was interested in things she might change, patients who could be healed. Matron Broom wrote a letter to the Board of Health, and Dr Stenger showed me what she wrote about the lazaret:

These patients are particularly trying—they are constantly quarrelling with the attendants and between themselves, their complaints and wants are endless and all fall to my care, and each time I visit them there is a fresh difficulty to settle.

I can honestly assure you that my duties in connection with the Lazaret are more onerous to me than those of the whole hospital.

I engage and supervise the attendants employed there, keep books in connection with the wards and stock for which I am responsible. I buy all clothing for the patients, which may require advancing my own money for the purpose.

It is a peculiarity of their malady that they are most difficult to please.

I am expected to do their shopping for them and spend hours in search of the particular article they want.

I buy as economically as possible and try to some extent to limit their demands, which at times are excessive. Their clothing must be bought by some responsible person; if their friends were allowed to buy and present the accounts to the Board of Health there would be no limit to their expenditure, for they demand the best of everything and their friends would get it for them at the expense of the Government.

A piano has been supplied for these patients.
I frequently play for them, playing accompaniments for those who are able to sing, thus endeavouring to ameliorate their condition.

These patients are suffering from a disease considered sufficiently dangerous to the public to justify them being isolated. This being the case, I would reasonably submit that I can hardly be expected to undertake this work without some remuneration.

Is it reasonable to expect that with the duties of the Matron of the Coast Hospital (with over two hundred beds) and the supervision of a large nursing staff, I should be called upon at great personal discomfort to attend the Lazaret?

'I've never heard her play piano,' I said to Dr Stenger. 'She just whooshes in and out, complaining that we ask for too many things—and we have paid her back for all the purchases she has made.'

Dr Stenger sighed and folded the letter, placing it back inside his case. 'You know she's here to stay, though,' he said. 'I will put a suggestion in with the board, though, that she truly visit the lazaret if she wishes to complain about it at such length.'

'Perhaps she plays piano for the men,' I said.

'Doubtful.'

•

Sometimes I went to the men's lazaret myself now. Matron Wilson used to read aloud to Red, who had been blind nearly fifteen years. Now that she was gone, he could sometimes persuade the attendant, another patient or a nurse to do it, but he was particular about his readers. He was obstreperous— a word he taught me. He had studied at Oxford, which he never failed to bring up, and his favourite thing was poetry. He had caught leprosy while serving in the Indian Army, or so he claimed.

He would send for me, and I would drop everything to go to the Arts Cottage in the men's lazaret where he would be waiting, expectant, a pile of books beside him.

'What took you so long?' he demanded, on a recent visit.

'Am I paid for this?'

'It's not nice to keep an old blind leper waiting.'

He was grumpy, but I liked his books. That afternoon, Keats was on top of the pile, so I read him the Odes, and 'The Eve of St Agnes', 'The day is gone, and all its sweets are gone!'

When the dusk holiday—or holinight
Of fragrant-curtain'd love begins to weave
The woof of darkness thick, for hid delight

'What does that even mean?' A voice came from near the
shelves towards the back of the cottage—I jumped in my seat.
'Woof of darkness? Woof's the sound a dog makes.'

I turned. I had been so preoccupied I hadn't seen the man
there, and I didn't recognise him. He had his leg crossed over his
knee and a book in one hand, held open. His skin was tanned,
and in the light streaming through the high window his eyes were
the colour of toffee. He had a wide mouth and a strong chin.

'If you would kindly hold your words,' Red said. 'Alice is
reading to me, not you.'

'I think it means weave as well as the bark of a dog. Sorry—I
don't know your name.'

'Guy. The name's Guy. At least, here it is.'

'Listen, Guy,' Red said, 'I'd like to hear some more today,
so if you don't mind keeping your mouth shut or going elsewhere, I'd appreciate it vastly.'

Guy leaned back in his chair and I rolled my eyes at him,
mouthing the word, 'Sorry.'

'I'll be off then,' he said, and left the room, letting the
flyscreen bang shut behind him.

'You could be nicer,' I said to Red, trying to find where in
the poem I'd left off. But I was flustered and could not focus.

'What's the point?' Red replied.

I knew what he meant. What was the point of manners? Of
being polite when you were old and blind, dying of leprosy in

a hospital-prison? When you had to rely on half-literate girls in order to hear the poetry you loved?

I was glad to read again when I found my place, to roll the words over my tongue, even if there were some I did not understand. The way they sounded made me feel the way music sometimes did. It brought me a strange and rare peace.

When I'd finished, I rang the bell for Ted to take Red back to his cottage. Then I tucked the small stack of books he had lent me under my arm, turned off the light and left.

Guy was on the verandah, leaning against a post, smoking a cigarette. He ashed it against the railing and gave me a little wave.

'Sorry,' I said. 'Red's like that. Rude to everyone.'

'It's alright,' he said. 'Nice hearing you read Keats. I didn't catch your name.' It was impossible not to return his smile. He leaned towards me when he spoke, like he was afraid he might not catch my reply.

'Alice.'

'Good to meet you, Alice. How long have you been here?'

'Forever,' I said. It did not feel like a lie. I leaned against another post, the weight of books under my arm satisfying. The afternoon sun warmed my face. It had been chilly in the cottage. 'When did you get here?'

'Last week.'

'You look fine,' I said. 'Have you been for a swim yet?' I could hear my own voice but not control it. Was I flirting with him? He would steer clear of me from then on, I was certain.

'Nup.'

'There's a leper beach. And a boat, if you like to fish. The swimming is good.' I did not go in the salt water anymore as my own legs were riddled with tuberosities, little ulcers, but they were covered by my long skirt. The cicadas were screeching and I felt as though the noise was in my head.

'Thanks, Alice—lovely to meet ya.'

He took off then, and I noticed what I hadn't before: that he had a false leg. He must have been in the war. And I had told him he looked fine. I felt like a fool.

I walked off with the books, wishing the earth would swallow me. He was probably horrified by my face. He was probably hiding in his hut, quaking in alternate fits of fear and laughter, having just met the ugliest woman alive.

# 18

*Guy*

Compared to Peel, the Coast was a day at the races. There was even a golf course—a huge swathe of grass cut short and watered daily just for a handful of doctors to play on. That was the thing: there were doctors, and the fact that the hospital was not only for lepers gave Guy hope. It was not, like Peel, a place to wait for the grave. There would be treatment, and tests, perhaps even people cured. There were fewer lepers and each received the same treatment, regardless of colour.

The day after Guy arrived, he wandered through the male lazaret. Past the worn, weatherboard cottages, carefully tended vegie garden and the espaliered fruit trees along the brick wall. He exchanged greetings with a few other men—they were all curious. News travels fast when there's little to do other than gossip, but Guy was determined to keep to himself. In the Arts

Cottage, he discovered a small library. He was flipping through books when a woman came in to read to the old blind man. She was not a nurse but another patient, wearing a skirt and blouse rather than the uniform apron and cap. She was the first woman he had seen inside the men's lazaret. She helped the old man get comfortable in his chair and began reading to him. Guy knew this man was called Red but had not met him. According to Jim he was the orneriest man in the lazaret.

'Doesn't like our kind,' Jim had said, 'so keep your distance.'

Guy knew the type, and he was not about to pick an argument, not after this narrow escape. His attention was drawn to the woman, though. Or was she a girl? She was reading Keats and she spoke every line like she lived each one of the words. He was back in that tent in the Sinai desert, with Guy and Johnno and Rich. He could not turn away. Her disfigurement was striking because there were glimpses—in her plaited honey-coloured hair, her narrow waist—of the beauty she might have been. Guy could not stop himself from interrupting, just to get her attention. It was a senseless question, but he wasn't thinking. When Red became furious, Guy stepped outside. He would wait for her; he had all the time in the world.

When she emerged, she walked with caution, like a soldier stepping among mines. He learned her name was Alice. She turned towards the winter sun like a flower, full-faced, leaning the stem of herself against the wooden post. Yet she flinched when he brushed against her. Was she afraid of him? Or was she, like so many horses he'd known, easy to startle? Guy hoped, as he watched her leave the men's lazaret, that he might find out.

•

Guy took his wooden leg off every night to sleep, leaning it against the bed beside him, so if he needed to rise in the night he might attach it—but also to remind him, because sometimes he forgot that his real leg was gone. He woke his third morning at the Coast when dawn was grainy and pale, not certain for a moment whether he was at Peel still, in a dormitory of other boys or under the bough shed in Angledool. The sound of the surf and Jim's gentle snore placed him. He put his hand to where his leg had once been, as he did every morning. Sometimes that foot had pins and needles, and sometimes his missing knee ached. The scar of his stump was ridged with pink, shiny tissue. The skin where his prosthetic leg buckled on was worn and smooth. He rose and moved stiffly, emptying the chamber-pots, boiling the kettle for tea. Jim stayed in bed late, and Guy brought him the breakfast tray which was delivered to their cottage from the hospital kitchen. There were boiled eggs that quivered in their brown shells, toast and porridge. There were pats of pale butter and pots of jewel-coloured jam. None of it was hot, but Guy ate regardless, taking his time, watching a pair of rainbow lorikeets feed from a grevillea tree, squawking and chattering.

The attendant, Ted, visited mid-morning to dress Jim's sores and give them their chaulmoogra tablets. 'I can use your help, that's for sure,' he said. 'If you watch me clean and dress these, you can do it yourself in the evenings.'

Guy forced himself to watch, and he tried not to wince at the misshapen lumps, the ridged and raw skin, the sores leaking pus. It would keep him busy, like splitting wood at Peel. Jim saw his gritted teeth and shrugged his shoulders in apology.

'Been out in the boat yet?' Jim asked.

'Heard about it.'

'I'll take you sometime.'

'Sounds good.'

'You can push me over the edge. Put me out of my misery.'

'Quit feeling sorry for yerself,' Ted said. 'And hold still, will ya? I'm almost done here.'

'Old leper like you, even the sharks'll turn up their noses,' Guy said.

'Yeah they'll come after you then. You won't have a leg to stand on.' Jim grinned.

Ted handed Guy the roll of gauze. 'You two are like a married couple already. Here, do the sore on his foot now. Too busy bickering to see how it was done.'

Guy applied the ointment, the dressing, and wound the clean gauze around Jim's swollen ankle. He was slow but gentle. The smell of carbolic, the heat: the dressing shed at Beersheba was just there at the edge of his conscience. He took the sharp scissors and sliced the gauze, tucking it in.

'Not bad,' Ted said, standing and gathering his kit. 'You'll make a good wife for Jim.'

# 19

*Will*

Will had read a theory that leprosy was latent until the body
was under duress. And if the duress continued, the leprosy
rapidly worsened. It would make sense in many of the patients
he dealt with, including the new patient, Guy, who had returned
from war, one of many damaged men. At the Coast they built
four wards for returned soldiers and spent a great deal of time
learning how best to treat their wounds and unfamiliar diseases.
The influenza epidemic was by far the worst of it. There was
little that could be done for these men besides sit with them,
bathe them, and watch them die.

Guy had lost most of a leg in the war, but it wasn't until
he came home that he learned he'd contracted leprosy. He
still looked unblemished, apart from the missing leg and the
occasional rash. Some of the other doctors thought that Will

went too far for Guy, having him brought from Peel after he wrote letters from the coloured camp. Will replied that, in all consciousness, he could not ignore the man's plea for help. These people were not being treated, only left to die.

Dr Cillen scolded Will when he learned of it. 'You cannot bring all of them, all the half-castes and coloured lepers mistreated up north.'

'I do not plan to. Only the ones who write to me as Guy did.'

But he didn't say he also softened when he learned that Guy was from the same part of the country as he was. When the families in Walgett complained about Aboriginal children in the schools there, the Aboriginal families had been sent to Angledool. Will would not have been surprised if his father was one of those who complained. But Guy had not gone to school in Angledool, Will discovered; he had been put in a boys' home. He did not say much more on that subject, though, and Will was not one to pry.

Guy had an easy smile, a way of listening. Will felt understood. Perhaps because he was different too, they sought one another out.

This was the second Sunday morning Will would meet him in the Arts Cottage for a game of draughts. The day was grey and blustery. Waves crashed into the cliffs either side of the beach and the wind rattled the gate of the men's lazaret as Will fumbled with the latch. He hurried in, wishing he had brought his umbrella. Guy had set up the draughts board at a small table. His wooden leg stuck out at a strange angle. He looked up and grinned.

'Look what the cat dragged in.'

Will smoothed his hair; the wind had made it stand on end and every which way. He wished his face did not colour so easily.

'How are you, Doc?'

'Exhausted.'

'Try having nothing to do but feel sorry for yourself.'

They began at once. Guy seemed distracted, and his eyes kept going to the windows, which were rattling in the gale.

'Penny for your thoughts,' Will offered.

'I'm not telling you how I'll win, if that's what you're after.'

'You are thinking of other things.'

Guy ran his hands over his face and looked up at the doctor. The whites of his eyes were bloodshot, the irises brown flecked with yellow.

'D'you look after the women lepers too?'

Will nodded, eyeing the board. He had a habit of putting his tongue between his teeth while thinking, and he kept catching himself, pulling it in.

'You know Alice, then?'

'She has been here since she was nine; she is like a daughter to me.'

Guy turned to the window again, which was streaked with thin rivers of rain.

'What happened to her?' he asked.

'Her mother—Clea—was taken away first. Well, first it was Clea's father, Joe. Then Clea, then Alice and finally her half-brother Sid. Small community, Northern Rivers.'

'Where is Joe then, and Sid?'

'The graveyard,' Will said, tilting his chin towards the south-east. 'She has known a great deal of suffering in her short life, but she knows nothing of how the world works.'

'And I know too much,' Guy said.

Will was losing. Guy's smile was half ashamed, as if he felt bad about all the pieces he collected.

'What do you think it does, locking us up like this?' Guy asked.

'What do you mean?'

'What's the point of it?'

Will set the draughts board and pieces on the shelf, brushing the dust with the sleeve of his coat. He wanted a drink, though it was not yet noon. At the chapel, the Sunday service would just be ending, and the other doctors, nurses and patients who could walk would be leaving, pulling their coats around them rather than standing and chatting in the battering wind.

'The point is . . .' Will sighed. 'The point is that it makes everyone else feel safe—it's not for *your* good. We know leprosy is not as infectious or dangerous as, say, tuberculosis. But we treat lepers like criminals, while tuberculosis sufferers are treated in the hospital, normally. Leprosy is the only disease with that stigma. Because we separate lepers from their families and homes, people are terrified of contracting it, and rather than admit to it they'll hide the symptoms as long as possible. But who's to say we can't treat people at home? Just keeping them away from young children would be the only real requirement. It would never be allowed, though. Not in the world we live in today.'

'You ought to be in charge,' Guy said. He stood, wincing as he moved his wooden leg. He would not complain, but Will could see the straps might be too tight, or irritating the skin. Perhaps there were active sores on the stump. He would check it the next time he examined Guy. If he asked to see it now, he would cross that fine line that allowed them to converse and play draughts as equals. He would once again be his doctor rather than his friend.

The wind slammed the door behind Guy as he left and Will looked at his watch again. Sometimes, he had to remind himself that he had chosen this life. Without work, Sundays were interminably long. The Coast doctors all had three Sundays off out of four, and they took turns looking after all the patients on the fourth. Three Sundays out of four were meant to be days of leisure; he was meant to play cricket, or picnic, or simply smoke in the sun. Those were the days his loneliness felt well-deep, as though it extended to the centre of the earth. Will would have worked every Sunday happily to avoid that sensation. Work allowed him to forget what was missing from his life: a family of his own. At least he had patients, like Alice, who felt like family.

•

There are so many secrets a doctor must keep. The human body holds multitudes. An examination is a prising open and it is important not to expose all the flaws to the light. Will learned early on how to hold a neutral expression, for it was dangerous to frown or smile—even worse to cry out or laugh. He could never gag, even when faced with the most putrescent limb, rotting with gangrene, or pus-filled boil. He swallowed his own bile rather than show how sick something made him.

And the worst thing was to show fear. That he must always hide. For if he showed fear, the patient knew they had no hope. Will had become an expert at hiding the truth: he had a lifetime of experience. But he had never been asked before to pretend a well patient was sick.

Clea had always been an interesting case because her leprosy was latent for so long, and when it came, it was tuberculoid. Tuberculoid patients suffered patches of dead skin, the loss of sensation and some nerve damage but not extensive disfigurement. There were times she seemed to recover completely, and then something would trigger the bacilli and her immune system would react and there would be a flare-up. Will knew that the tuberculoid patients were most likely to heal spontaneously; they were the ones who might one day leave the lazaret. The lepromatous ones, like Alice and Sid, lacked any natural immunity to the disease. He had never heard of one leaving.

Patients were not released until they had given eleven consecutive negative smears at an interval of not less than one month for a period of fifteen months. In August, Will returned to Clea the results of her eleventh negative smear. She had been a patient at the Coast for twenty-one years.

'You're free to leave,' he said, steam rising from the cup of tea before him in Clea and Alice's cottage. Alice was off somewhere, probably reading to Red. 'We will always look after Alice.'

Clea shook her head. 'I'm staying here.'

'But there are—'

She interrupted. 'You must not say the tests are clear. You have to say I'm still sick.'

'But I—'

'She cannot know. She'd insist I leave. She wouldn't shut up until I agreed to go.'

Will put up his hand. 'Let me finish. What if you stay and your next smear is positive? You will have to wait sixteen more months, at least. This might be your only chance. You have to consider it carefully.'

He drank the last of his tea, setting the cup in the saucer. 'You don't need to decide now,' he said, standing and brushing his trousers, retrieving his case. 'Take your time.'

Clea did not reply, but stared out of the window, which looked directly out to the high fence surrounding the women's lazaret.

Will was meant to go to the laboratory, but instead he walked down the sandy path through bracken and brush to the beach. The sight of the ocean always calmed him, even when, as on that day, the sea was wilder than usual, waves crashing into the cliffs either side of their normally placid little bay. A few patients from the men's lazaret had taken the clinker out, and Will saw a speck which might be them on the horizon. Further off was a distant ship. He knew he had given Clea an impossible choice: her daughter, or freedom. He wished Alice could know the truth. But he knew that things were never so simple. What bound them together was too complex to unknit, too tangled to think the truth would smooth it.

# 20

*Clea*

It had been that long since she'd drunk so much rum: Clea was surprised by the lightness she felt. She was a filly again, leaping over stones on the path to the Coast Cemetery. But she had to keep an eye out for snakes. Someone had seen a brown, she'd heard, and it would be just her luck to be killed by a snake the day she learned she was free of leprosy.

At the cemetery Clea pulled her hat off to feel the sun's heat on her dyed-black hair. Alice assumed when Clea left their cottage that she always went to the men's lazaret. Clea did not mind her thinking that—sometimes she did. But sometimes she just walked the headlands, or she went to her father's grave. He had died years before Clea arrived at Little Bay. Years before her own ma told her he had. Only Dr Cillen remembered him, and never kindly, but Clea could still recall the smell of his ointments and the feel of his hair in her fingers, how tall she was when she rode on his shoulders. He was buried among the gravestones of dysentery deaths and victims of tuberculosis, typhoid and Spanish flu. Among the gravestones of other lepers. Clea was not the type to sit beside his grave and speak to him, but she walked through the cemetery, running her hands over the gravestones, thinking of him and Elma, the sister she killed.

There was Fred's headstone—it tore at her. There was the boy's grave, too, and she still felt ashamed for wishing he had never come. For feeling secretly glad when he died, because he gave her daughter back to her. Clea knew she was greedy. This was her problem, it was why she was drunk now and why she never knew to say enough, no more. She found a patch of grass and lay down.

She had dreamed of this day so long. And now it was here and she lay in the grass in a boneyard, filled with sorrow.

These are the things she planned to do:

Go dancing.

Watch a picture show.

Ride a horse.

Return to Jiggi.

She'd like to give Charlie a shock, point a rifle at him—not to do him any harm; just to frighten him. She would find Hunter and see if he had any children, if he ended up with Jane Fletcher. She would like to hold a grandbaby in her arms, eyes blinking up at her, fingers small as a doll's.

To even just take the tram south along Broad Road to the Lapa loop and see the carnival Sue told her of: dogs pushing baby strollers and the snake show, where the snake man let red-bellies and browns wrap around his arms and neck, and fished tiger snakes from potato sacks with his curved metal hoop. *You think that's brave*, she wanted to say, *try living twenty-one years as a leper, never leaving. Try learning you're better but your own daughter's still got it, and to be free you'd have to leave her. Try every man you ever had leaving, whether on a horse, with your ma or with strychnine. Try this for a life.*

She belched and smelled the sharpness of her own breath, and rolled so her cheek was against the scurfy yellow brittle grass. A bindi-eye poked through the shoulder of her blouse. She shut her eyes.

She felt the rock and sway of the ship again, and the smell of her own piss. The sound of Charlie's belt as it came off, the clink of the metal as it hit the floor. A lifetime of others telling her where to go and what to do. Where she was not allowed. What a woman like her might never become. She brushed away the flies at the corners of her mouth and eyes.

Clea could smell the hay and sunshine of Alice's hair sometimes, when Alice let her close enough. It was a rare occasion.

The world spun, the edges of her vision blurring. Her chance might never come again. Could she really leave her? Clea rolled on her hands and knees, spewing yellow foam, watching the ants scurry from the acid flood.

What kind of mother had she been anyway? Alice would be better off without her. Clea knew she was not clever, but even a fool could see that this much was true.

# 21

*Guy*

Guy had long ago abandoned the careful schedules of the boys' home and the military. Besides meals and medication, assisting with Jim, he took each day as it came. Each day he felt lucky not to be shot or bayoneted, his bones buried in a shallow, unmarked grave. Guy attempted to explain this to Dr Stenger as they walked along the sand. It was Sunday, and Guy knew that Dr Stenger needed to fill his time. He did not allow himself pleasure. Guy sensed in Dr Stenger a great reticence; he was always punishing himself. The sand was slow going for Guy, but Dr Stenger matched his pace. 'Is not pleasure the purest joy we can seek?' Guy asked. He thought of Mariam's gentle hands.

Dr Stenger stopped in his tracks. It was a bright, humid day already, and he squinted, shaking his head.

'Pure joy is in work,' he said, 'hard work. Helping others. Staying busy rather than idle.'

'You sound like the brothers I grew up among.'

Stenger threw up his hands. 'I sound like my own father. I'm sorry, Guy. Far be it from me to tell you how to live.'

Guy knew that Stenger came from landowners. Sheep farmers bred hard and merciless.

'In the desert,' Guy said, 'the Sinai, the thing which scared us most was thirst. Here we were with rifles, knives, guns, all the equipment of war, but it was not death in battle we feared; it was water—the absence of it. On marches we were only given one pannikin of water for the day. We were not allowed to drink until noon. I would spend the morning thinking only of that first sip. The way it would moisten my tongue, cool my throat, how I had to keep from guzzling it all in a single gulp. We take water for granted until we do not have it—then it is all we think of. Now look at me. I am surrounded by water. I could drink and drink and still there would be more.'

'Sea water will not quench your thirst.'

'No, but all I need to do is open a tap. There are creeks, lakes, bottles of beer, flagons of rum, pots of tea. Endless sources. I will never be thirsty again.'

'Does that mean you should drown yourself in it? Or drink so much you make yourself ill?'

'No, but I will not take it for granted again. I will take the pleasure I can find, where I can find it. Does it make you better, to deny yourself that which you desire?'

Dr Stenger turned away, towards the ocean, and Guy could see his cheeks were flushed. When he spoke his voice was tight in his throat.

'I cannot say.' He picked up a shell and tossed it into the surf. It sunk, disappearing, and he did it again.

Guy felt Stenger's unease. 'Never mind. I am keeping you. You must have other things to occupy you.'

Dr Stenger turned towards him and Guy saw that his eyes were wet behind his spectacles.

'You have learned to adapt. I wish I had too. I have only learned to avoid those things which bring me discomfort. It is why I am here, safe, among people who will always need my help, who will always be worse off than me.'

Guy shifted. His phantom leg ached, as it did when he stood too long. They began to walk again, towards the path which led away from the beach, towards the lazarets and the rest of the hospital.

'It is like you were saying about the water,' Dr Stenger said. 'I have denied myself of it, so it occupies my thoughts. The more I try to push it away, the more incessantly it pushes in. It is evil.'

The path leading from the beach was steep and rocky, and Dr Stenger was behind Guy, watching in case he lost his footing.

'I don't think it is evil,' Guy said. He did not turn to look at Dr Stenger. He did not need to look to know his face would be pink with shame.

'I am certain it is.'

Guy paused at the top of the trail and caught his breath. The herd of cows was on the hill to the north, and their black-and-white coats gleamed against the green. The seaside daisies were spots of yellow and orange against the carpeting grass.

'Taking children from their mother is evil. Shooting men in the back as they run from battle is evil. Locking people away because they suffer from a disease is evil. Love is not evil, Dr Stenger. You could spend all Sunday arguing and still not convince me that is true.'

# 22

*Alice*

The day dawned cloudless and hot, and when I told Mama I was going down to the leper beach she said she would come too. My face must have fallen.

'You don't want company?'

'I'm going there to be alone.'

I was and I was not. I knew that it was the sort of day the men from the lazaret were likely to take the boat out, and that Guy might be on that boat. The last thing I wanted was for him to see me with my mother. I had been thinking of his smile, the ease of it. I felt silly for thinking of him, because I was certain he was not thinking of me.

I picked my way down the rocky path to the leper beach. My eyes had started clouding, but I lied about it, because I could still read. I could get around.

Once down the steep rocky slope and past the trickle of creek I saw our beach was empty. There were a few nurses in their swimming costumes to the south, and I tried not to stare at their smooth skin, their long perfect legs. I would not compare them to my own. I had put my hair up in a new fashion, but I always wore the same long skirt. There was a boat out on the horizon—I wondered if it was the men. Better if it was, because if he were here Guy would probably just stare at the gorgeous nurses with their lithe bodies.

The sun was behind a violet cloud. I sat on a rock that jutted from the sand and watched for the big ships on the horizon. I longed to walk up a ship's gangway—not just a North Coast steamer but one going abroad—and watch the streamers stretch and snap as it drew away. I longed to forget my history.

Mama told me once how her pa was taken away by the police. He had to ride in a specially built timber box on the deck of a ship under police guard. There was a slot in the side of the box where they passed his food and water, and a bucket inside where he passed waste. On rough seas, that bucket spilled. There was little air. Mama came the same way.

Mama said, 'They treated us like animals. I nearly died.' It was why she had Gran bring me herself, before Dr Moffat could tell the authorities. She did not want me to endure the same shameful journey that she and my grandad had made.

When Dr Cillen first met me, he said, 'You're the granddaughter of Joe, the original leper of Lismore.' He frowned. 'He was of a particularly drunk and dissipated habit.'

Before Grandad was taken away they lived in a slab hut with a dirt floor which the health department came and burned down after. Mama spoke of the fire sometimes, how it blackened the sky, the way the people in town came to see it. The shame of being so dirty they burn your house to the ground.

'The government gave us money to build a new house,' she said. 'I didn't know it, but Ma was a widow then. And that's who your father was: one of the men who came to build it. Named Ned. I was fourteen.'

'Does he know of me?'

'He disappeared. But then Charlie came along, and we had Hunter.'

'And then he had Gran.'

'Hush.'

There were still things which Mama did not wish to speak of.

The pale white flannel flowers and fiery red bottlebrush coloured the bush around and birds hunted food for their nestlings. There were plovers screeching and dive-bombing when I came too close and honey eaters who had made a nest in the eaves of our roof. I wanted what they had, those birds: a mate—a match. I thought that I had accepted this would never happen. I leaned against the cool sandstone, watching skink tails disappear between crevices of rock, and smelled the sun on seaweed. The skinks were probably going home to their skink families. All I'd ever have was Mama.

The boat was getting closer. It was the clinker and I hoped that Guy was on board. Tailor were running and I could ask if they had caught any. Curiosity would be as good an excuse to speak to him as any. But as the boat slid into the shore, as the tattered, wind-whipped trio of men stepped out with their pants rolled and their buckets and rods, I was stuck to the rock. They waved, and I waved back. Guy *was* among them. They dragged the clinker to the slip rails and hauled it up the beach. I saw the easy strength in Guy's arms despite his limp, his stiff leg. His broad shoulders straining the back of his white shirt. He must have felt my eyes burning a hole in the cotton.

He said something to the other men—Ah Foo and Jim— and began walking towards me. I looked down at my lap, the stone, my hands, anything. He was coming to tell me it was rude to stare. He was making slow and awkward progress over the stones and the soft sand.

'You're a sight for sore eyes,' he said, and I smiled in spite of myself.

'You're a terrible liar. Now you'll say you caught a fish as long as that oar.'

'I did—it's just in that bucket Jim's got. Want me to call him over to show ya?'

We both grinned.

'It was that hot out there. Got any water?'

I had a pannikin and passed it to him. He drank in that way men drink, where they tip back their heads and just let the water run down their throats, Adam's apple bobbing, excess just spilling out and dribbling down the chin. I never felt so thrilled to watch someone drink.

He passed the pannikin back and I took it, our fingers brushing.

I would put myself out of this misery.

'I am not looking for a sweetheart, in case you were wondering.'

'Oh. Do you have someone then?' Guy sat on the sandstone beside me, so I could feel the warmth emanating from his skin.

'No! Who would want . . .' My face burned. 'I only mean . . . you needn't worry that I'm going to go all moony on you.'

'What if I like the moon?'

Guy slid down the sandstone to rest on the sand, his legs straight out in front of him, with bits of driftwood and broken shell around us. He scooped up a handful and let it run through his fingers. I shifted down to sit beside him, spreading my skirt around me. I felt so conscious of every move I made. I glanced over. The nurses were still at the south end of the beach, splashing one another in the calm water.

'You don't,' I said.

'I'll be the judge of that.'

'Let's talk of something else. Tell me how you came to be here.'

Guy started to tell me about the war, about being shot and losing his leg in a hospital. He fought asepsis and thought he would die there, but the nurses saved his life. He told me how he came home and moved in with his mother and his aunty, who lived near the Queensland border, at Angledool. But he was getting in their way and went up to Brisbane to find work. That was where he started noticing some marks on his skin.

'Besides the marks I was awfully tired and losing weight. I went to the doctor to see if it was something to do with my leg, some sort of infection. But then the doctor, when he heard where I had been, decided to run the test for leprosy. He told the police before he told me. And that is why I'm here.'

'That's rotten,' I said, frowning into the sunlight, which had come from behind the cloud and was now glittering on the small waves rolling into shore. He had not even glanced at the nurses swimming.

'We had so many diggers after the war,' I said, 'but they have their own ward and I hardly saw them. But I would hear them sometimes at night. Screaming. And then there was the flu. Every day the trams brought more and more patients from the city. It was the worst if they'd been to war. Surviving that, only to die here.'

'Awful.' Guy stared out at the horizon and I was furious with myself. Now I'd made him feel guilty for being alive.

He cleared his throat. 'I'm going to jump in the water and cool off. D'ya fancy a swim?'

I shook my head. 'No, thanks.' He was probably desperate to get away from me, the ugly leper girl with the sad stories.

Guy unbuttoned his shirt. He struggled to his feet and shook off his trousers. He was unselfconscious. I averted my eyes. He was wearing a swimming costume beneath his clothes of navy wool with narrow straps over the shoulders. His chest was hairless, smooth as a tree stripped of bark. He leaned over and unbuckled his wooden leg. It looked raw and sore around the stump.

'I might need some help getting there,' he said.

'Of course!' Had he seen me staring at his stump? He must have thought me horrid.

I took off my own shoes and unrolled my stockings. I tucked up my skirt; he would see the ulcers on my legs, but somehow it seemed less important now. I put my arm around him, touching his torso. At first gingerly and then, as he leaned his weight on me, with all the strength I had. He was the first man I had ever touched of my own volition. Together with our three legs we walked to the sea. The water was cold on our feet and I gasped.

'Reminds you you're alive,' he said, and when I looked at him his face was lit by a smile. I wanted to take off my stupid skirt and swim with him. Instead, I went in to the tops of my thighs, watching for submerged stones, ignoring the sting of salt water on the open sores, until it was deep enough for him to swim and he went under. Surfacing, he took great strokes with his arms, out past the rocks. The muscles on his back rippled. He could swim with only one leg better than I might with two. He stopped to tread water and wave to me. I waved back. My skirt was soaked and floating on the water as it foamed. The stinging had subsided and my legs just tingled now. I turned to walk back to shore, careful of rocks, strands of seaweed clinging to my ankles. My skirt sucked and dragged around me. The sand was pocked with holes where the pipis hid beneath the surface; beyond that were little balls where sand crabs dug.

Guy's wooden leg looked so strange sitting alone there on the beach. A seagull had landed on it, curious, to check if it were somehow food. It pecked and flew away. I stood on the hard sand where the high tide had been, wringing sea water from my skirt and watching his distant figure. I felt as though he was the world come to me. I had lived in isolation so long. He had been amid the chaos of battle and the streets of far-off countries, the stories of other men. I only had to ask—I only had to overcome my fear.

I forgot my embarrassment. I smiled so much my cheeks hurt. I even forgot my midday dose of chaulmoogra.

•

Mama scolded me when I returned that evening.

'Why's your skirt soaked through?'

I told her about Guy. How I'd helped him into the water to swim.

Mama clapped her hands together and her face was split by a grin. 'Finally!' she said. 'Alice is keen on a fella.'

'I am not keen. He's new and I felt sorry for him because he's a digger and he's lost a leg.'

'Let's hope it's only his leg that don't work.'

'Mama!'

'What? Besides, I happen to know of him, and from what I hear he is too handsome to say you only feel sorry for him. Alice has a beau!'

'I am never speaking to you again.'

'Yes, you will—there's no one else,' she said.

Nurse Hull brought me warm water to soak the sand from the sores on my legs. The pain as I scrubbed them hardly mattered when I recalled Guy in the surf, his strong arms slicing through the water. How buoyant he must feel swimming, not dragging his prosthetic leg. I let my feet float to the top of the basin, feeling that same intoxicating lightness.

# 23

*Clea*

Alice would kill her if she knew. Clea walked right up to Guy's cottage. He was helping Jim prune the rosebush which Jim nurtured. Jim no longer had enough left of his fingers to work the shears.

Jim saw her approaching and grinned, toothless old fella that he was. They'd had some good times before he went downhill.

'Queen Cleopatra, to what do we owe this honour?' Jim croaked.

Clea curtsied. 'I've come to introduce myself to Guy. Hear he's new.'

'Too young for you, I reckon,' Jim said, laughing, and Guy straightened up, wiping perspiration from his forehead with the back of his shirtsleeve. He was handsome, Clea thought, with no small pleasure.

'Pleased to meet you, Mrs . . .' Guy brushed his hands on his trousers.

'Just call me Clea, love. Everyone else does. Either that or "sweetheart".' She looked hard at him. He did not look away.

'Come inside for a cuppa,' Jim said, and led the way, limping across the threshold.

Guy took over in the kitchen, boiling the kettle, and Clea found an extra chair on the verandah. They did keep the place clean, she noticed. Some of the men's cottages smelled like ulcerating flesh. She could not bear a foul smell.

'You've met my daughter Alice?' Clea asked as Guy threw some leaves in the pot.

'In the Arts Cottage. Reading to that cranky old fella, Red. She's got a lovely voice.'

'She's clever,' Clea said. 'But she's lived in here since she was a child. Hasn't been much of a life.'

Guy brought over the teapot and three tin mugs, then sat. His wooden leg stuck straight out.

'She needs a bit of a lark,' Clea said. 'I'm glad you're here.'

She saw Guy blink. He was not expecting that, she reckoned. She smiled a little, and Jim winked at her across the small table. Perhaps, if Alice had Guy, Clea could leave, knowing her daughter was looked after. Knowing she was not alone.

'Have you got any of them ginger biscuits, Guy?' Jim asked, licking his dry old lips.

'I'll get them.' Guy got up to go look in the cupboard.

Jim put his hand out across the worn table and Clea took the mangled stubs of fingers in her own. 'You looking for a boyfriend as well?' Jim asked.

Clea shook her head but smiled anyway.

'You still got it, Jim? I thought it might've fallen off when your fingers did.'

They had a good cackle.

'Still 'ere, still works.'

'Well, I'm too old for all that now,' Clea said.

'Never too old for love,' Jim replied, as Guy clomped back to the table.

'True,' said Clea, but she was thinking of Alice.

# 24

## Alice

I did what I said I would not. I mooned over Guy. I spent hours unpicking our conversation like a too-short hem. What did he think of me? He smiled, yet he might smile like that at anyone. For days I stayed in the women's lazaret: scrubbing the floors of our cottage, pulling weeds from the garden. Hoping the physical work would tire me so I did not think of him—but there I was, picturing his strong back, feeling how his skin was smooth and warm against mine. I yanked another weed, the sound of roots ripping in sandy soil. I had to rip myself from the thoughts. They'd bring me nothing but sorrow.

•

Agatha had been bedridden for a year. The cupboard beside the stove in her cottage was filled with the various 'cures' she had tried: Eno's Fruit Salt, Ayer's Sarsaparilla, Zam-Buk ointment, Bile Beans, Beecham's Pills, Bonnington's Irish Moss and Cockle's Antibilious Pills. I loved to read the labels and boxes, what they offered. Shiny hair, clear skin, perfect vision, return of courses, regularity of bowels and a slim figure. She sent away for all of them, took them enthusiastically for weeks, and then gradually abandoned them when she realised they would not deliver on their promises.

Then, she followed recipes for potions mailed to her by fortune tellers. *Mix an ounce of potash, a drachm of powdered brimstone and half an ounce of saltpetre. Anoint the parts which are suffering.* Or: *Mix a pint of house-leek, half a pint of verjuice and a pint and a half of posset. Drink.* Or: *Drink a decoction of burdock leaves for a month, morning and night.* She sent Nurse Hull to fetch the strange ingredients. She drank the potion one-handed, keeping her rosary beads in the other hand, hedging her bets.

When I came to visit, she sat up in bed dealing the cards for our gin rummy and I turned the teapot three times in each direction, as she taught me. Agatha was difficult company, but Mama said to visit and play cards with her once a week would not kill me. It was a small act of kindness, Mama said. 'Unlike calling her "the Mick",' I replied.

Every week I played gin rummy against Agatha and every week I lost. I thought it might kill her if I won, so I always gave up towards the end of the game. Agatha glared at me over the tops of her spectacles, looking for a change in my condition. She would point out gleefully any new swellings or sores, as if I did not know they existed.

Agatha kept busy with tatting—she continued making the fine-detailed doilies that decorated her little cottage even as her hands began to deteriorate. There were doilies on every surface—some places they overlapped—and every doctor and nurse who came near the lazaret had been gifted more lacework than they knew what to do with. For a person with a penchant for delicate work, she had a very coarse way of speaking.

I poured her tea and dumped in the three spoons of sugar which had, over the years, turned her teeth as brown as the liquid she drank.

She fanned her cards in front of her, then held them to her chest. 'What's this I hear of you being sweet on a fella named Guy?'

I stared at my cards. I would kill Mama. 'He's new. I was just being kind, helping him into the water.'

She snorted. 'Not what I've heard.'

'What have you heard, exactly?'

I took a sip of my tea too soon. It scalded my tongue. I arranged what I had in sets and runs.

'He's an Abo's one thing.'

I had not known, but I wasn't going to let Agatha in on that. 'Have you heard he was in the Light Horse Brigade during the war?' I replied. 'That he lost a leg?'

'Hmm. He tell you he was in the coloured camps at Peel first, before he came here?'

He had not.

Agatha arranged her sets, laying them out. My cards were better than hers.

'Are you two having relations?'

I feigned ignorance. 'Relations?'

'Surely with *your* mother you know what I mean.'

I gritted my teeth, laid out my own sets.

'At least you don't have to worry about getting pregnant,' Agatha said. 'Your insides are all rotten.' She grinned at me. Her teeth were surely the rottenest things in the room.

I picked an ace of diamonds from the pile and laid out my final set. 'Gin. Rummy.'

'Think you're good now, do you?' Agatha slammed one hand on the flimsy table.

'I've got to go. Someone's waiting on me.'

'Just watch yourself, Alice. Don't let him think he's better than he is.'

I left the tea things untidied on the card table beside her. The flyscreen slammed behind me. I wanted to stick my fingers inside the tatting of her doilies and pull until I felt them rip.

But I could not stop recollecting her diagnosis. Rotten insides. A pile of overripe fruit, mouldering in the sun. Fly-blown mush. There was nothing pure about me. Nothing as it was meant to be.

•

In bed that night I tossed and turned. My hands found a new lump behind my knee. Thoughts churned and festered.

'What's wrong, Alice?' Mama asked, her voice heavy with sleep.

'Nothing.'

'Go on.'

'Is Guy Aboriginal?'

'He's not white, is he?'

'I just thought he was like Jim, maybe. Javanese. I didn't know. I guess I've never known someone who is.'

'There's a lot you've never known.'

'No fault of *mine*.' I swallowed. 'Agatha says such awful things.'

Mama got up and shuffled over. The springs creaked as she sat on the edge of my bed. Her hand stroked my forehead.

'There's always going to be people like Agatha, love. People that say things about everyone else to try'n make themselves seem better. Best thing is just to ignore them. Agatha'd only be happy if everyone around her was a misery guts too.'

'Why'd you tell her I was sweet on Guy then?'

Mama took her hand away. 'I didn't.'

'Who did then?'

'Don't know. Just try not to worry about what everyone else thinks. They'll talk about us no matter what we do. So live your life, whatever you can of it.'

She planted a kiss on my temple; she smelled of Pond's Cold Cream. I wiped away the slippery residue.

'Thank you, Mama.'

'Night.'

I heard the creak and shift of her climbing back into her own narrow bed.

•

I went to the men's lazaret the next day. Red had sent a note asking me to come and read to him. Which was not why I spent an hour fixing my hair in front of the glass. I read until my eyes ached and then told Red I was going home for tea, but I did not walk towards the gates. I walked instead towards the furthest cottage, the one I knew that Guy shared with Jim.

He was sitting and smoking on the verandah as I approached, and I felt everyone's eyes following my footsteps.

'Alice.' He grinned and stood, putting the cigarette out on the railing and slipping it in his pocket. 'Come sit. Would you like a cuppa?'

'I would. Milk and two sugars. Shall I fix it?'

'Not as my guest. Sit down—I'll be right back.'

I heard Jim inside asking Guy in a muffled voice who it was, and then a low, long cackle and Guy telling him to shut his gob. My face was hot. The warm breeze rattled the corrugated-iron roof and the floorboards of the verandah were soft, rotted away in places. The whole place needed a lick of paint. But it was swept spotless and the garden was bursting with flowering bushes—azaleas and gardenias, even the half-bare branches of a rosebush. A fat lazy bee hovered.

Guy came limping back with two full mugs in his fists. He set them down and pulled his chair up close beside mine, studying me with his toffee eyes.

'Who's the gardener?' I asked.

'That's Jim. He's not feeling so great today, but he's good at keepin' anything alive—even himself. He says to give you his hellos. You been reading to Red?'

I nodded. 'Dante's *Inferno* today.'

'How come Red gets so much of your time then?'

I swallowed my fear and looked him straight in the eye. 'He asks me.'

'Well, that's my own fault then. Want to go out in the boat with me tomorrow? I'll bring a picnic.'

I nodded, not trusting my voice to speak.

We sipped our tea. I left when Ted came around to check the dressings, and the men's eyes followed me again on my way out. It hardly mattered. Guy and I were going to sea.

•

We met on the beach early, after breakfast but before the heat of the day turned oppressive.

'Will you fish?' I asked, as we dragged the boat down on the slip rails. The beach was littered with washed-up bluebottles, their tentacles trailing in the sand, their translucent blue-tinged bodies sagging in the heat.

'Not today,' he said, grunting and pushing.

I asked him a dozen questions: about the war, the desert, and how he came to ride horses. It took ages, with his bad leg and my lack of strength, with my constant chatter and his monosyllabic replies, to get the boat in the water and climb in without toppling. I was learning that without something we take for granted, a person becomes more interesting. They must learn to do without, and that makes them stretch the world that remains. Once we were in the boat, Guy handled the oars. A wave nearly toppled us and I screamed—more out of excitement than fear—and then we were past the breakers and dripping wet, out beneath the sky. In the distance, Guy pointed out the black triangle of a shark fin. It did not worry me.

'Look at your smile,' Guy said. 'You're a thrill seeker.'

'I suppose,' I said, wiping the droplets from my face with the back of my hand. 'I haven't had many thrills to seek.'

'Perhaps that's due to change,' Guy said, squinting out to sea, trying to hide his grin.

I fixed the button at the neck of my blouse. He was watching me, and I did not know whether it was his gaze or the chop of the sea which made me feel strange. Detached, somehow. As if this woman in this boat with this man was not me.

'Let's hope it does,' I said, dizzy with my own courage.

Guy unpacked the picnic from the wicker basket at his feet. There were liver-paste sandwiches, apples and shortbread biscuits. We ate our sandwiches with the sound of water slapping the timber hull, and the gentle rocking from the sea. Guy ate fast, in bites which seemed too big to swallow.

'What's the hurry?'

'This.' He stood and the boat rocked more perilously.

'Careful!'

He inched towards the bench where I sat, behind the oars. He lowered himself to sit.

'What're you doing?' I was still laughing at the sight of him trying to move, and nearly choked on my last bite.

'May I sit beside you?'

I scooted to the side. His good leg, pressed against mine, was warm from the sun on his black trousers. He put the backs of his fingers against the skin of my cheek.

'You're getting sun. Where's your hat, young lady?'

'Same place you left your manners.'

He knew I was only teasing, for his fingers went to my neck and stroked the unblemished skin there, his thumb to the pulse behind my ear. He must have felt my heart pounding.

A fish jumped nearby and we both turned towards the splash. A cloud covered the sun and the water turned steely grey, then bright blue again. I pulled away.

'What's wrong?' he asked.

'Why would you want to touch me?' I replied. 'With my horrid face. Don't you see?'

'I see your eyes. The lovely grey of 'em. The sweetness of your smile, the light on your hair. I see that you're strong because you've suffered. That's in this . . .' He touched the scurfy skin on my cheek, the swollen bridge of my nose. The rough patches on my ears. 'Like it's here.' He grazed his bad leg with the back of his hand.

I knew the blood had gone to my face.

'I hear it in your voice, too, Alice. Like when you go under a wave on a hot day, the way that cold water makes your skin tingle. You know it isn't just about what we see. That's not even a sliver of it.'

Guy's face against mine was sudden. I did not know how our lips would fit until they did. It was skin feeling and something else too, inside, down into my belly and below, a shiver between my legs. I closed my eyes and put my hand on the place beneath his ear where his neck met the sharp corner of his jaw. I touched the bone and felt the movement of his mouth against mine. Behind my eyelids the sky turned red and pink. I pulled away to breathe.

'You alright there?'

I nodded, blinking the water from the corners of my eyes.

The words from 'Ode to Psyche' were all I could think to say:

*'And in the midst of this wide quietness*
*A rosy sanctuary I will dress.'*

'Come back here.' He put his hand on the back of my skull and pulled me gently towards him. There were no more words.

I had grown so used to pain, I did not know what to make of pleasure.

# 25

*Guy*

When he brought the clinker hull in with Ah Foo and Jim, Guy was surprised by his own relief at finding Alice waiting on the beach. He had been in a fog for so long, but here was something else. He should know better, he told himself, but she was not just a distraction from the tedium of the lazaret. She was curious about the world, about him. She wanted to know all he carried inside his head.

'Do you still feel your leg, though it is no longer there?' she asked.

'Do you believe in God?'

'Do you think that fear has a smell? Did you smell it during the war?'

He answered as best as he could. He told her his leg felt as though it were still there. It sometimes ached—the doc had told him these were called phantom pains. He told her he believed in his family, his ancestors. He told her how fear smelled sharp—somewhere between sweat and urine. Emanating from hundreds of men, it was a smell he hoped never to encounter again.

In the outside world Guy would never have spoken with a white woman. He knew that was not acceptable. But since escaping Peel he was letting down his guard. Here at the Coast their shared disease was foremost. Alice was not like him—she was both impetuous and fearful, and she was always causing herself injury through thoughtlessness; forgetting to look after what she could not feel. If you stick your hand into a candle flame and do not feel the pain, are you still burned? If your flesh sizzles and curls, and the nerves beneath it die, is absence of feeling preferable? Alice made up for the lack of feeling in her limbs with an excess in her heart. She was skinless to the world.

Alice thought Dr Stenger could do no wrong. Guy tried not to be jealous of her love for the doctor. He had, after all, guided her since girlhood. He had not healed her, but he was the only one who comprehended her disease. Guy understood what she wanted: a chance to feel. Scared, alive, in love, all of it. She had been walled up in her broken body for too long.

Clea was different, though. She pushed Alice into Guy's arms. There was something distinctly unmaternal about her; a battle raged beneath the surface. In spite of her disfigurement she was carefully put together, her blouses starched and ironed, hair coiffed, smelling of the perfume she ordered by mail. There ought to have been strands of grey in her black hair but there were not. Her eyes were small and watchful. Guy felt them on him at the strangest moments. Hers were the kinds of expressions which were practised in the glass before they were shown in public. She was not someone he ever wanted to be alone with. There was no telling what she might convince him, unwittingly, to do. He did not tell Alice that Clea had visited him, to tell him they ought to have 'fun'. He knew how upset Alice would be.

•

There was a wireless installed in the Arts Cottage, and the matron had eased some of the restrictions on women coming to the men's lazaret because the women did not have one. The popular radio shows aired on Saturday evenings. Clea, he knew, would be in the Arts Cottage with the others. He had found a note beneath his door that Saturday morning:

*And there shall be for thee all soft delight*
*That shadowy thought can win,*
*A bright torch, and a casement ope at night,*
*To let the warm love in!*

When the others had gathered around the radio, he went to Alice's cottage. Even the matron would not look for them on a Saturday evening. The entire hospital sat beside wireless sets, listening to the latest radio concerts and plays.

The window casement was open, but Guy knew that with his leg Alice would not mind him using the door. He knocked, and she was there as though she had been waiting beside it.

'You came.'

'How could I resist?'

Alice and Clea's cottage was nothing like the one Jim and Guy shared. There was a deep clutter of pictures and trinkets, so many small things. It was evident how long they had lived there by the sheer quantity of what they had collected.

'Did you like my note?' Alice asked.

'"Ode to Psyche"?'

'Yes.'

She looked so happy. She offered tea, biscuits neatly arranged on a tray. They sat stiff on the sofa, alert to any noise, knowing they might be discovered at any moment. They did not let down their guard until he led her to the narrow bed.

'Put out the lamp,' she said.

He turned down the wick until the lamp was out: the glass clouding with smoke, the smell of burnt wick. He focused his attention on the parts of her body which he knew were not numb, the islets of normal skin, and she muffled her cries in the quilt. They forgot to listen for the creak of unoiled hinges, footfalls on the verandah. She made him feel as though he were whole again. And it was not false, as it was for the rest of them, crowded around a radio play. Her guilelessness was the most beautiful thing about her. That and just inside her hip, where the bone curved beneath the skin in an unblemished hollow.

•

He walked back to the men's lazaret in darkness, listening to the bell frogs croak. In the cottage, Jim was sitting up in bed with the lamp on, waiting for him.

'Where ya been?'

'Walkin'.'

'In the dark? With a bum leg?'

'What of it?'

'People notice when it's just the two of you missing. You be careful, eh, fella? It's dangerous what you're getting yerself into.'

# 26

*Alice*

The new matron watched us with hawk eyes. She began to visit the women's lazaret.

She would appear on our verandah, looking prim and stiff. 'Just here to check everything is shipshape,' she'd say, and wander through our cottage. She was looking for Guy. As though I might hide him in a closet, or beneath the kitchen table. I began to call her the Queen of Hearts. I imagined her finding him one day, in my narrow bed. 'Off with his head!' she would cry. Her knaves would come running.

We knew the best times to avoid eyes. Distracted times, or the middle of the night. I was slower than I had been at fourteen, but I still knew of places. The pockets in the cliffs at the beach, where there was space for two bodies, pressed together. The scrubby hillside above the men's lazaret, behind the banksia rubble. One night we went to the cemetery and spread a rug among the gravestones. No one would dare look for us there. I held up the lantern and showed him Grandad's headstone. 'The original leper of Lismore,' I said, mimicking Dr Cillen. I showed him Sid. 'There is space here beside him for me one day.'

He held me close to his ribs. 'I prefer you here.'

Guy told me how his namesake had died in battle at Beersheba, and how he helped dig the graves for him and others. 'I'm not ready for death,' he said. 'It can come all at once, too soon.'

He told me about the Guy he'd met on the ride to the boys' home, when he was taken from his mother. I asked why they took him and his whole body shook when he spoke of it. His aunty hiding him, how he sneezed. He was a boy again, doubled on a horse, the sound of his mother's wail behind him.

I extinguished the lantern before he undressed me, ashamed of how my body looked, but he said I was beautiful. He knew where I had feeling still, the patches of skin that were sensitive—behind my ears, my breasts, below my navel. He touched me in the dark like I had been certain no one would ever touch me. It was heat lightning, small flashes of pleasure and pain. I kissed the stump of his bad leg. He shivered and moaned.

All I wanted was to be alone with him, away from prying eyes. It was what I spent every waking moment thinking of. I loved Guy for his quick smile, his easy laugh. I loved him for showing me that fear was not the only reaction to my body. That I was not all ugly, inside and out. I loved his broad shoulders, his narrow hips, the long shank of his thighbone to the round curve of bum, his beautiful brown skin. I had never touched a man's sex until I touched his, and I loved the mystery of it, how something small and shrivelled could change. Marvelling at it, I understood for the first time some of my own mother's thrall.

•

The boat was one place we could be alone. One still, windless day we lay listening to the gentle sound of water against the hull. The lapping water, his body above mine, the sun casting a halo around his shape. The sky was yellow with light. There was a sharp pain when he entered me, a sense it was not possible until it was.

'Will I stop?' he asked.

'No.' I took a deep breath in. The pain was fading already, pleasure pooling in its place.

Afterwards, we lay side by side. I studied the mole on his shoulder, the small scar beside his eye.

'Let's keep going. All the way north, to Queensland,' I said.

'Not Queensland. Out to sea. We could row to an island somewhere. Just the two of us.'

'You did not tell me you'd been to Peel.'

'Prefer to forget,' he said.

'Was it worse than here?'

He shrugged, sitting up, putting on his shirt. His fingers were quick with the buttons.

'Back to our island then. What would we eat?'

'Coconuts. Fish. And we would walk around with no clothes.'

'Now you're going too far!'

'I'm just getting started,' Guy said, covering me with a blanket we'd brought, lying back down beside me.

I wondered what it was about Peel he wanted to forget. I did not bring it up again; instead I spoke of where we would go. We both dreamed of being elsewhere.

'*Let us away, my love, with happy speed,*' I said.

'You just let me know when.'

'I'm serious.'

'Me too.'

He pulled tiny splinters from my back and I did not feel them. That afternoon we rowed to shore, laughing.

•

Matron Broom found me later. 'We cannot have fraternisation between the male and female lepers,' she said. 'You're to stop seeing Guy.'

I wondered if she smelled it on me. Or if it was the light in my eyes. The pink of my cheeks from too much sun.

'Besides, he is Aboriginal.'

'*Really?*'

'You cannot. It is not done. If you were to become *with child*, that child—mixed race, the child of lepers—would be taken away.'

'You need not concern yourself,' I said.

'I realise your mother has not been the best example of chastity and temperance. I know your road has been a difficult one. However, I cannot excuse this behaviour. This cannot occur in my hospital.'

'Off with his head,' I cried.

'What are you on about? I think you have had too much sun.'

I knew then that Matron Broom was concerned only with appearance, so it was no surprise she cared little for the lepers, because we were the ones who looked the worst. The ones the outside world feared the most. Imagine two lepers having a leper baby, she was thinking. A part-Aboriginal leper baby. *The horror.*

The thought pained me, though. I knew Agatha must be right. A baby was not possible. I thought of how Sid used to curl into me to sleep.

I would never have a child of my own.

•

Being told I cannot do something has always made me more determined to try. The next time I saw Guy I said as much.

'You want to run away?'

'I have six pounds saved up. We can rent a room together, sleep in the same bed. No more hiding from Matron. No more sitting around imagining other lives.'

'What do we do when the money runs out?'

'Go to work?'

Guy raised an eyebrow. The bumps on my face were not so visible then as they had been. They were not inflamed; there were just patches of swollen skin. The weeping sores on my knees and wrists were easily covered. My sight was failing, but I had found ways to hide that.

'How will we travel?'

'By tram.'

'They'll catch us straightaway.'

'You look normal. Do you have your uniform still?'

'I can get one.'

'Good. Do. You will be a returned serviceman, cured of TB.'

'And you?'

'A mother who has been visiting her little fella with diphtheria. I'll wear a broad-brimmed hat. A hanky pressed to my face because I'm on the verge of tears. We cannot catch the same tram, though, in case one of us is caught.'

'I'll find a uniform,' he said. 'But we need to plan this carefully, Alice. They could throw us in gaol, or worse. We cannot muck this up.'

# 27

*Will*

A bob-a-day man delivered the telegram to Will as he was leaving the men's lazaret.

In Sydney next Saturday for medical conference. Dinner at the club Saturday night? Has been far too long.

His knees went soft, and he had to steady himself against the lazaret's fence. A bee landed on the jutting edge of his ulna and sat there for a moment before it flew off. He wished it had stung him, for immediate pain to usurp imminent.

He went to visit other patients, and the new women's attendant, Nurse Hull—out of breath—joined him as he walked to the women's lazaret.

'Sorry, Doctor. The matron was giving a lecture.'

'I managed perfectly well on my own,' he said, sounding sharper than he meant to. He moderated his tone. 'What was the topic?'

'Personal hygiene.' Nurse Hull rolled her eyes. 'Some of the probationer nurses have longer than desired fingernails and patients are getting scratched.'

Will realised as she took his bag and the box of specimen slides how reliant on the new nurse he had become. Most of the work he did in the lazaret she was perfectly capable of doing herself. She noticed things. Will had decided the best doctors and nurses were ones who watched the world closely: who paid attention.

'Is everything alright, Dr Stenger?' she asked, proving his theory. 'You seem a little pale.'

'I'm fine—truly, I am. She ought to look at your fingernails before she lectures you.'

'So only keep behind the ones with long fingernails?'

'Yes. You oughtn't all be punished for the sins of a few.'

'I'll pass on your suggestion.'

'Just don't tell her who suggested it, please.'

'You're scared of her too, aren't you?'

'Hush.'

'You *are*.'

He smiled in spite of his nerves.

They knocked at Clea and Alice's cottage first, as if by unspoken agreement, and Nurse Hull practically skipped ahead when Clea opened the door, swinging the kit. 'Dr Stenger just admitted he's scared to death of Matron Broom,' she announced.

'Not to death,' he said, but the two women were off, arm in arm, to share the news with Alice.

Alice came out of the bedroom laughing as he hung his coat beside the door. He protested over their laughter, 'I simply meant that she is a little intimidating. It doesn't mean she has made me cry. Well, not today, at least.'

That brought a fresh gale of laughter and he let their merriment engulf him, hoping it might drown his thoughts.

Alice was light-hearted; he had not heard her laugh so much since before Sid died. Was it because of Guy? Will had seen them ducking off towards the headland together, and had heard rumours that they took the clinker hull out alone. He was secretly glad; they each deserved the pleasure. The matron was in a lather, but he told her that neither of them were children, and that he did not consider their private lives his public concern. She had stormed off, saying, 'Well, I suppose I shall have to reprimand them completely on my own.'

He had to tell Isaac that he could not meet him. It would be worse to hope than to accept it could never be.

Busy Saturday. Sorry I will miss you. Will

•

On Saturday he swam in the bay as dawn broke, skin tingling from the cold. With every stroke he changed his mind. He would see Isaac. He would not. It was worse to know than not. It was worse to feel than to suppress. His arms felt like lead weights. He wondered what Isaac would look like now. He thought of his own body: not much changed, though the skin was looser, a small pouch of belly where it used to be flat. He rarely considered his body except as a vehicle—a tool to work with, to get him from place to place. But he wondered about Isaac. Was he stouter? Had his hair thinned? The nurses at the Coast made it a sport to speculate over Will's bachelorhood. He was surrounded by lovely, industrious women; why had he not found a wife? Perhaps it would have been easier—to pretend to be a thing which he was not in order to fit into the world; to ease the constant speculation.

But it was for the woman's sake that he couldn't. He might choose to live a lie, but she would have no choice. She would be with a man who must force himself to touch her, who closed his eyes and imagined she was someone else entirely.

Will thought of Nurse Hull—who'd insisted he call her Sue when they danced at the last Nurses' Social. They waltzed around the room to the music from the gramophone. Her hair smelled of gardenias and she smiled up at him with a hopeful expression as he led her clumsily. They smoked cigarettes outside afterwards, and she touched his arm often, and ran her fingers through her short, dark hair. She wanted him to kiss her, that much he knew, and he was glad she was not brave enough to make the first move. He wanted to tell her the truth, but that truth could finish him. He stood to lose everything. So he made an excuse about an early shift and left, and things were strange between them for weeks afterwards. Later she told him about a new boyfriend, a man she'd met at the tram shed—he'd been visiting his brother in the diggers' ward. He envied her the ability to find someone else. For him it would only ever be Isaac.

Drying off on the beach it came to him that he had no choice. He had to go, or he would die wondering.

•

The day was a blur of small tasks on the wards, patients checked with only half his attention and instruments fumbled. A distracted doctor could mean a dead patient, they were taught in medical school, and those words came back to him. But they also brought the memory of Isaac's arm on the desk beside his, the black hairs sprouting from his cuffs, the way he held his pen. Luckily he killed no one, though whether his distraction skewed his diagnoses would take weeks to determine.

After work, he bathed and changed, shaving and running a comb through what was left of his hair. Too long at the neck, he decided, but there was no time for the barber. He hoped the lights at the club would be dim and Isaac would not notice.

As he waited at the tram shed, he realised he had not told Isaac he had changed his mind, that he was coming. Perhaps Isaac would not be at the club. But Isaac was not satisfied with his own company; in this way they were different. He would always go out rather than stay in.

There were a few nurses and pros in their city clothes, and relatives returning home from visiting sick ones, looking red-eyed, careworn. Another doctor exchanged a few words with Will about their destinations. 'Meeting an old friend,' Will told him. Luckily this doctor was not going to the club as well, but to his mother's, in Coogee, for dinner. Will found a seat alone. The tram screeched and rattled along Broad Road towards the city. He looked out at the dark, at his own pale face reflected in the glass. It was a face he'd spent most of his life loathing. A face, a manner, a disposition. And yet, to know Isaac loved it gave him some relief. To recall how Isaac smiled at him in their first week of medical school and suggested they study together. The jolt that ran through Will the first time their legs touched beneath the table in the library. A stronger jolt the second time, because he had stopped wondering if it was accidental.

There was the time they walked home, drunk, after the first-year party and fumbled into Will's bed together, Isaac even clumsier than Will, even more halting and uncertain.

Afterwards Isaac cried, facing the wall, his back shaking with deep sobs.

'What is it?' Will asked.

'I'm a degenerate.'

'No, we both chose to—'

'But you must think—'

'I think you are—I can't even find the word, Isaac. I think you are what I thought I would never find.'

'You don't loathe me?'

'No. Please. Never.'

Isaac turned and his eyelashes were clumped into tiny triangles from tears. Will put his lips to Isaac's and tasted salt, rum. Their teeth clashed.

'Sorry,' he said. 'I'm such a lout.'

'Shhhh.'

This time they kissed more gently. And they took it slow, as slow as each could bear to go.

•

The club was spilling out smoke, deep voices, the laughter of self-important men. It smelled of whisky and woollen carpet that was damp and never thoroughly dried. Men clustered near the platters of food, the fireplace, the bar. It was a small world, the world of medical men in Sydney, and Will was soon caught up in unbearable small talk with a friend of Dr Cillen's, Dr Cecil Johnson, who wanted to speak of Moloka'i and Peel and what island off Sydney they might send their lepers to. He felt Isaac's presence before he saw him. A tingle in the tips of his fingers; a sense he was being watched.

'Stenger, Johnson, wonderful to see you both.' Isaac clapped Will on the back in a quick, manly greeting.

Johnson smiled his shark smile at Isaac and began asking ingratiating questions of his practice in Melbourne. Isaac was a star in his field, and Johnson one of those men who thought being in the proximity of stars would cause him to glow too. Will stood for a few interminable minutes, minutes forever lost with Isaac, and then interrupted.

'Can I get you fellows a drink?'

Isaac turned his gaze to Will. 'I'll come with you. I've got an important question for you about a patient with some interesting skin lesions. You'll excuse us, won't you, Johnson? I don't want to bore you with rashes on a Saturday night.'

Isaac had always possessed the social skills Will lacked. He extricated them painlessly, and soon they were in a dimly lit corner, sitting in armchairs with drinks beside them. He leaned towards Will, arms on his knees. 'I thought you weren't coming.'

Will stared into the deep gold of his drink. Again he felt Isaac's gaze on him. He had studied Isaac earlier, while he was speaking to Johnson. He was one of those men whom age distinguishes: some threads of silver in the hair, smile lines around the eyes and mouth. Deep crevasses where his dimples once were.

'I could not stay away.'

'I'm glad.' Isaac's voice cracked, and there were tears beneath it. 'I'm sorry, Will. I wish life did not turn out this way.'

'It isn't your fault.'

'It is. I am weak. I let my parents bully me into marrying.'

'How is she? And the children?'

'Fine, they're all fine. I wish you could meet the children. My boy, Leo, is gentle but quick-witted. Lily, is fierce-tempered and strong-willed. Rose despairs of her, but I think she'll go far in the world.'

'I would like to meet them very much.' Will poured the whisky down his throat, emptying his glass. He felt light-headed, spun by an unseen hand, his limbs too large for the rest of him. He did not know where to place his hands, and shoved one down the side of the leather chair, the cushion hard against it. He hated the feel of leather, the slipperiness and squeak. He wanted to feel Isaac's skin—alive and warm—not this dead, cold cow.

'You had a question,' Will asked, 'about a patient?'

Isaac laughed.

'An excuse to get away from that awful bore. Come now. Let's enjoy each other's company—we only have a night. Will

242

you come for a walk with me? I feel as though we are among too many people here. Too many eyes.'

Isaac downed the rest of his drink and they departed, practically running down the flights of stairs to leave the building. Outside the streetlights hissed and glittered with warmth.

Isaac took Will's arm, his touch gentle now, and they walked down to the harbour where ferries still came and went across the velvety black water, their lights rippling reflections. Will wished for another drink, something to numb him.

He put his hands in his pockets.

'I have a room,' Isaac said, 'in the Harbour View Hotel. There is no reception, besides the bar, and there is a stairwell that goes to the street.'

They passed a cluster of young men pushing and jostling one another, edging to fight.

'It must be loud,' Will said. 'A room in a pub, on a Saturday night.'

'I imagine it is.'

One of Isaac's eyes, his left, squinted when he smiled. Will had forgotten until it was right there in front of him.

'Lead the way.'

•

There are things one can be taught, and things which one must do to learn. Will read in a textbook a dozen times how to cannulate a vein, but until he actually performed the procedure he was useless. He could spend years thinking of Isaac's body, but it was nothing like being beside him, sprawled in bed.

'Have there been others?' Will asked afterwards, when Isaac got up to use the toilet. He left the door open.

'Other men?'

'Yes.' Will steeled himself for the answer.

'No. You must have been with others, though. I always think of that, though I try not to.'

Will sat, pulling on his underclothes, his trousers, adjusting his braces.

'I haven't, Isaac.'

'Women, then?' Isaac ducked his head out of the bathroom door. His hair was tousled, his smile relaxed now.

'Not interested,' Will said. 'How do you manage? Is it hard, sometimes?'

Isaac sighed, springing back onto the bed beside him. 'Not anymore. She's done, now that we have the children. So we have separate bedrooms. It has been'—he paused, counting back in his head—'seven years.'

'How did you, though?'

'How do I do so many things, Will? Wishing I did not have to. Remember, I never wanted to be a doctor; I only studied medicine to please my family. I still am frightened by what I do. Every day I must enter rooms I wish I never had to.'

'I have not forgotten. How are you so successful then?'

'Probably because I am still trying to please my parents. While most doctors are brimming with ambition, I have none.'

'That's true.'

'Not you, though; you've always loved it. I wish I had your passion. Please don't get dressed because you're leaving. Stay longer.'

Will glanced at his wristwatch. 'The last tram is in twenty minutes.'

'Then stay the night.'

He let himself drop backwards, back onto Isaac's bed. That was the thing with Isaac, Will could never refuse him.

# 28

*Alice*

We had to wait weeks for Guy to find a uniform, but this gave us time to plan. We studied the tram schedule. 'I will go first,' he said. 'I'll wait for you.'

'Where?'

'The Lord Nelson in the Rocks. We can get a room there. I stayed there once, before the war. There are places I want to show you, Alice. How are your feet?'

'They're fine,' I lied.

'They'll be even better once you're free.'

He was catching the 1.32 and I would take the 3.11. They would be unlikely to look for us between lunch and dinner, and I would be travelling at the time frequented by schoolchildren.

'A crowd is the easiest place to hide,' Guy said.

•

Once the midday meal was finished and I had taken my chaul-moogra capsules, I began to fidget. Mama asked was I alright. She had been watching me lately; perhaps she suspected. I told her I was going for a walk to the beach, that I was meeting Guy. 'Don't wait for me for supper,' I said, on my way out the door.

'Don't spoil your nice clothes with sand,' she replied.

They were my good clothes. A long silk velvet dark blue skirt—hemlines were growing shorter, but I knew better than to show my legs—and a white blouse with lacework at the neck and sleeves. I did not tell Agatha, but I had stolen her wide straw hat. What did she need it for anyway, bedridden as she was? I got a small thrill out of how she would disapprove of the purpose. The ribbons were frayed, but the brim was floppy enough to hide my face. It was not fashionable, but it would have to do.

The difficulty was luggage. That morning, before dawn, I had placed my little case behind a bush just outside the women's lazaret. Mama would never let me go if she saw me carrying it. There was only a change of clothes, my nightgown, a toothbrush, hairbrush and as many chaulmoogra capsules as I had been able to hoard in the past week—two dozen, which was barely any. It would have to do.

I slipped out the door of the lazaret. To be off on my own, to be free.

I had to look busy, determined, as though there were some-where I had to be. The worst outcome would be to encounter a doctor or sister, so I took the path behind the wards up past the stables and chook sheds, staying clear of the reception cottage. I kept my head down and did my best not to trip. It was easier for leprosy patients to twist an ankle, Dr Stenger said, because the reaction of those with full feeling to an ankle twist was to take the weight on the other leg, for the knee of the twisted leg to go soft and the leg to bend. It looked awkward, but it enabled them to avoid a sprain. Those of us with numb ankles and feet did not have that reaction, so our ankles sprained frequently without our knowledge.

Dr Stenger had been telling me that I needed to train myself to look after those parts I did not feel. That it was not pain that was the enemy, but painlessness. Pain was a signal our bodies sent to avoid injury. I thought of this as I set one foot in front of the other. I imagined them as Guy's. They were precious; I had to look after them.

Yet I also had to move, because I saw the clock tower beside the gate and the tram left in two minutes. I was cutting it close intentionally. The tram might have nurses, even doctors, and I had to situate myself as far as possible from them.

I heard the bell as I hurried out through the iron gates. There was a sign with its destination on the front of the tram: George Street. I was the last on. There were seats in rows rather than facing one another. Guy said I'd be lucky to get one of these; it was called a toast rack. I took a seat towards the back, tucking my case at my feet, and pretended to be fascinated by the scenery. There were several nurses in their day clothes but none familiar. I heard them chattering of the strawberries and cream they were going to buy at David Jones, the gloves they wished for, how sore their feet were. Guy had instructed me in how to interact with the ticket collector. He would come through asking for tickets, selling to those who had none. My palms were sweating by the time the uniformed man reached me.

'Central, please,' I said, and handed him my coins.

'One way?'

'Yes, thank you.'

'That's quite a hat.'

'I thought the sun would be stronger today.'

He tore off a ticket from his roll, punched it, and handed it to me. As he moved on to the next person, I let out the breath I was holding and settled against the timber seat. I thought of Greta's advice from long ago, 'You'll only draw attention if you act guilty.'

We passed weatherboard houses, dunes and sand-whipped streets then stopped again outside the gaol. A tired-looking woman with stockings that sagged around her ankles sat in the empty place beside me. I pulled the brim of my hat closer to my face, lest it brush against her cheek.

The woman rummaged in the handbag on her lap and took a handkerchief out, dabbing at her eyes. I wanted so badly to ask her what was the matter, whether there was anything I might do. I imagined her son was a prisoner, that she was coming from visiting hours. She sniffled and dabbed beside me, and I kept my mouth shut.

'Whatever you do, keep quiet,' Guy had said. 'No chatting on the tram. No making up stories about where you're going or where you've been unless you have to, unless someone asks you. The more stories you tell, the more lies you've got to keep straight.'

'What are you, some master criminal?' I had asked.

'I worry it will be too much for you out there.'

'I know how to lie.'

'Should I be worried?'

'Perhaps.'

As soon as we were out of the sand dunes I no longer had to pretend to watch the scenery. Everything was different from what it had once been. The houses were closer together, larger, and there were cars, motor cars like I had never seen. I had to keep from grinning like a fool. Why had I not done this earlier? I was crossing the creek at Jiggi on my first day of school, skipping up the opposite bank.

As the tram neared the city we passed advertisements painted on signs for products I had never even heard of, shops I never knew existed. I was in a changed world, one I could not have imagined from reading newspapers, listening to the radio or asking a thousand questions of Guy. People crowded onto the tram and chattered in loud voices. There was a cluster of women with red lipstick and short bobbed haircuts. They all wore dresses that finished at the knee and their legs were slim and shapely in stockings, perfect unblemished legs, and I had to remind myself not to stare.

Guy said when the buildings grew taller I had to pay close attention because it meant Central was coming up soon. I would see the Grace Brothers building, the Empire and finally, on my right, the Clock Tower, which meant we had arrived. I stood and excused myself, bumping against the weepy mother's knees. She waved her handkerchief, apologising. I gripped my overnight bag, steadied myself on the rail and waited my turn to get off.

On the street, even the smells were different. There was coal burning, cigarettes and petrol fumes from the cars. Bitumen in the heat. Something fishy from the barrow down the road where a man called, 'Fresh prawns 'ere!'

I moved to the side of the footpath. Where was this hotel? I had to take another tram, Guy had said, to the Rocks. But now that I was in the city I wanted to walk. I was free. It was the strangest feeling, one I had never known, to walk alone down an unfamiliar street. I was giddy: the world was spilling from every shopfront and street corner. I kept stopping to take it in. How loud and frantic it all was. How thrilling.

It was dark by the time I reached the hotel. Acetylene lamps spluttered and hissed, a street sweeper passed with his horses. I had walked, then, realising I was doing my feet more harm, looked for a tram, but at that stage I was lost. Finally I asked an old man who gave directions. The hotel was tall, unnerving. The bar was crowded with men and loud voices, a dense cloud of smoke and the floor sticky with spilt beer. I felt out of place in my long skirt and floppy hat. I saw Guy's back immediately; he was still in uniform, the khaki, his broad shoulders, his black hair cut close. 'Hello,' I said, tapping his arm. The men around gave us a wide berth. He grabbed my hand. 'Where've you been?'

'I began to walk, but realised how far it was and found a cab,' I said.

He had been drinking; his words ran together. He was so worried, he said, he nearly called the Coast. He nearly gave up the whole thing.

'Come, dear wife,' he said, for the sake of the barman who was watching us now through narrowed eyes. 'I'll show you to our room. We can get you a drink in the ladies' lounge.'

I followed him up a narrow stairwell, his sideways slow climb, dragging his leg. It smelled of piss and more spilt beer.

'I'm sorry I—'

He turned and put a finger over his lips. 'Let's talk when we're in our room.'

Guy put my bag on the worn floorboards and took a key from his pocket. All these things were so unfamiliar: keys in locks, the sounds and smells of a hotel. The door was open, then, and it was a simple room—one bed—with a dingy coverlet and a rust-stained sink. Beside the open window were two chairs and a small table, an ashtray, a teacup which was half full. It was paradise.

As soon as the door was shut Guy put his arms around my waist, his chin on the top of my head. 'You took so bloody long. Did you have enough to pay the cab?'

'Sorry, darling, yes. I wasn't thinking. There's so much new.'

'You must be weary.'

I sat in a chair and bent to unlace my boots, then thought better of it. 'Where is the tea from?'

'The bar downstairs. Would you like some?'

'That would be wonderful. And have you eaten? I'm starving.'

'Yes, I meant to wait but I was famished. They have steak pie, lamb cutlets or beef stew.'

'What, no tripe? Tongue? Mystery soup? Chicken neck fricassee?'

'Ah, you are used to finer dishes from the tea lady, madam. We are no longer dining at Chez Little Bay.'

'So be it. The pie, good sir.'

Guy went off to order at the bar.

Really, I wanted him to be out of the room as I took off my boots. Inside, my feet were as I had imagined. Bloody and purple-skinned, with blisters that were broken and rubbed away. Red, raw places which would take weeks, months to heal. I had brought some ointment, and I stumbled to my bag to get it. Clean dressings, ointment, and I was finished by the time Guy was back with tea.

'Just how you like it,' he said, 'milk and two.' He stopped short inside the door, staring at the floor. There, on the worn floorboards, were bloody footprints. I nearly swore. He set the tea tray by the door and came to examine my feet, his wooden leg scraping the floor. 'Leave them,' I said. 'It won't do any good to unwrap the dressings now.'

Guy stood. 'I'm taking you back,' he said. 'I will go out and fetch a cab now. We can't do this. I was foolish to think—'

'No! I'll rest. You can nurse me. If they don't heal, I promise I'll go back. Not now, though. Let me have a little while with you, alone.'

Guy sat there, the glow of the lamp behind him casting a circle of gold, considering. He blinked, and I could have sworn I was done for. He was silent, though, as he stood and poured the tea, set it beside me.

'Right, then. I'll take you out tomorrow, my girl.'

When the barmaid brought the food, later, we had made up through kisses.

That night, together in the one bed, I kept waking with nerve pain, then wondering where I was. What strange place was this, what shape beside me in the dark? His leg leaned against the bedframe where he'd unstrapped it. Earlier, he had lain beside me and moved carefully until I said he must not. Be careful, that was.

I spent too long living carefully.

# 29

*Guy*

To escape was dangerous, but he wanted Alice to see the outside. He wanted to show her that a world still existed outside the lazaret. He imagined them walking on a beach that was not the leper beach, swimming at Coogee, or Bondi. But he knew that he could not walk on the street beside her without drawing the wrong kind of attention. There were those who would never approve, and he wondered whether this would come as a surprise to Alice.

As soon as he disembarked from the tram, Guy went to the telegraph office to send his mother a message at Angledool and tell her he was in Sydney now, to ask how they were. To do this from the Coast he would have had to ask Ted or the matron, or Dr Stenger, and he had grown so weary of asking favours. He could picture his mother hurrying to the post office from the reserve at Angledool. Did she need money? Medicine? Were the rations sufficient, did she have enough to eat?

After that, he sat in the Domain for a while, watching birds—ibises and magpies—that watched picnickers, waiting for a crumb to fall. The magpies were quicker but the ibises had a slow kind of patience. They watched for so long you forgot they were still there. They ate more that way, he decided. Pure aggression was not always the thing.

A mother scolded her son for lying in the dirt, getting his trousers filthy. The boy was only four or so. A group of schoolgirls came along in their calf-length skirts, chattering and shrieking, less conscious of watching where they were going than of being watched. Alice would have never known that world—the false humility, the intense pressure to be like the others. She did not apologise for who she was.

At the hotel he ordered a beer, waiting for her arrival. Some men were eyeing him from a table, and he overheard the words *Abo pub*. He had already paid for the room; would they kick him out? He would not have been allowed in if not for his uniform. He knew the kind of men watching him, and what they hoped for: a fight. If the real Guy were here, he would have fought them, and come away bloody-mouthed, knuckle-grazed but bold. The only fights Jack had ever been in were at Guy's behest. It was always about whether they belonged where they were. The thought of it tired him now. He would avoid their gaze. The danger seemed too great.

When Alice finally arrived, he saw how badly off she was. Her wide hat did little to hide the puffiness of her face, her swollen nose and her unsteady walk. He hurried her upstairs.

(The barmaid had been kind to him, earlier. She had found him a room on the middle floor rather than the top, waited for him on the steep stairs.) Guy realised, seeing Alice, how she used the familiarity of the Coast to hide her condition—her failing eyesight, her crippled feet. When he saw her bloody footprints, he was furious at himself for letting it come to that. He was furious at her, for how much she was willing to suffer.

Still, they had moments of forgetting together, of shutting out the world and creating this secret shelter between them. Their bed was a respite, a place where words melted to touch, and tenderness was the only currency. But her numbness was spreading. There were more and more of his touches that she never felt.

•

The next day, the walls of that cheap hotel room were closing in on him. He had to get out, but Alice wanted to stay in bed. 'I won't be long,' he said. He went straight back to the telegraph office, where there was a reply from his mother.

Aunty Rita died last month. Miss you. No need to send money.

Guy walked out of the office gasping for breath. He had to gather his thoughts. He limped through the parks and streets until his stump was raw. First Granny, now Aunty Rita. He could still feel the warmth of her lap, encircled by her arms. He'd not even known she was sick. Aunty Rita had no children of her own and had always blamed herself for Guy being taken.

She ought to have hidden him better, she said. What was she thinking, a flour bag? It was never her fault, but had he actually told her? Did she know he never blamed her? He felt empty inside, scraped clean. His mother would be beside herself with grief. He ought to have been making money, looking after his family, looking after Sally as he promised, not stuck in another bloody institution, smoking and staring at the sea. He wanted to be there for his mother. He wanted to be there for Alice. He wanted to cry, but he had to be a man. He could not cry in public. He had to tell Alice. He had to send another telegram.

So sorry, will come home as soon as I can. Love, Jack.

After sending it he got on a tram to go back to the Lord Nelson, and there was a folded-up newspaper left on the empty seat beside him. He was only scanning what he could see, biting back tears, trying to distract his mind when he saw the words. Aunty Rita's death was overshadowed by a more urgent piece of information.

# 30

*Clea*

At first she had been glad for her. The cheek of the girl, running off like that, it was something Clea wished she'd done herself at that age. Truth be told, she had been suspicious at the clothes Alice was wearing—*to go to the beach.* My giddy aunt you're going to the beach like that, but Clea kept her mouth shut. As if she didn't notice the bag go missing, or the clothes. She pretended not to see because she wanted Alice to be happy. But then worry set in like one of the storm clouds, heavy over the headland, threatening to break. What if people found out the truth of them? What if Alice had one of her pain days? What if she hurt herself, and Guy did not know what to do?

She did not mind Guy, but who was to say he would not abandon Alice at the first sign of a better thing, leave her to find her own way back to the lazaret? Clea knew better than to ever trust a man. She sat on the verandah and worried, tapping her foot against the worn boards. The same verandah she had seen Alice walk up, only she was Hilda then, and only as tall as Clea's ribs. Clea couldn't believe her eyes. She was no good at telling her as much, but that was the best day of her life, when Alice came. She had a purpose then. A reason to claw back some kind of dignity, some form of a life.

When Alice read to Clea, her first Christmas at the Coast, Clea's pride swelled. She sat up in her own bed, watching Alice's blonde head bent over the book, her small hands turning the pages. Alice's clear voice made sense of letters so easily, breaking the code which had baffled her mother. Here was this child who was hers yet was capable of more than Clea ever was. She felt as though her chest would burst. When Alice finished reading, Clea pretended to be asleep. She did not want Alice to see how soft she was, how easily moved.

She saw Alice feel the same thing, near to, when Sid came along. And then something altogether new with Guy. She remembered it with Ned, but the pleasure was so short-lived the memories were always tinged by the longing of after. That skinny black dog going alongside the wagon, while she was left behind.

Clea was still stewing when Dr Stenger walked up the path, his face as worried as she felt. He was carrying a piece of paper.

She stood and brushed her skirts. That morning she had not even combed her hair.

'Any news, Doctor?'

'Not yet, I'm afraid. We've put a note out to the police and other hospitals, and we're publishing this in the evening edition of the paper.'

Dr Stenger thrust the paper towards her. She blinked, holding the page, and he stared for a second, waiting, before he realised.

'Sorry, Clea—it has been that sort of day. Let me read it to you.'

Alice had given up years ago trying to convince her to learn.

'I'm too old and too stupid,' Clea always said.

'Mama, you're only fourteen years older than me.'

'I prefer listening to you read.'

'What if my eyes go?'

'We'll find a nice handsome young'un to read to us both. Like Red does with you.' She'd winked, and that had shut Alice right up.

Dr Stenger read her the descriptions of Alice and Guy.

'What makes you think people won't try to harm them?' Clea asked.

'You know as well as I do people will be too fearful to get near.'

Clea convinced Dr Stenger to stay for a cup of tea and they sat together for a while, the wind such that they could hear the ocean and smell the salt on the breeze. Dr Stenger was better than a father to Alice, because the fathers she'd had—Ned and Charlie—proved rubbish.

'She loves you, you know,' Clea said, watching his eyes behind his little gold spectacles. 'Probably more than she loves me.'

'Nonsense,' Dr Stenger said. 'Though you know I love her too. She has never let this place confine her spirit, has she?'

Clea shook her head. Bloody tears. She swiped them with the back of her hand.

'I swing between wanting them to get far, far away and wishing they would return. I know one is selfish but I cannot help it. She is all I have.'

'You see perhaps why she would want the same for you then,' Dr Stenger said.

Clea shook her head. 'You always have to be so bloody sensible. Drives me mad.'

Dr Stenger smiled, a sight as rare as rocking horse manure.

She pressed her lips together and they sat in silence while the tea grew cold.

# 31

*Alice*

Not long after the sun was up Guy grew restless. I could not keep him in the room. He needed to check for a reply to a telegram, he said; he had sent one to his mother. Could he take me to the beach? The picture show? A walk on the quay, to see the ferries?

My bloody feet. I told him to go, I'd be fine. I was going to spend the day in bed to let my feet heal, but I'd be up and ready to walk again tomorrow. We might go to all of those places. He brought me tea, a plate of biscuits, a red apple. He bent over to kiss me before he left, his cheek smooth, his hair smelling of pomade.

As soon as he was gone, I got up and washed myself at the sink. Perhaps he regretted coming with me. Perhaps he was visiting a lady friend. 'Hush,' I said out loud. 'Fix yourself.'

My hair was tangled. I brushed and plaited it. My face was puffy and swollen, but to a person with little knowledge of the disease I would have looked only tired. Beneath my arm was a gland which was starting to ache, to swell, and my tooth hurt as well, one of the back ones. I swallowed my chaulmoogra capsules and fought the desire to gag. I chewed a dry biscuit to cover the foul taste.

I had brought a book with me, but when I lay in bed again my eyes just swam and blurred. It was to be one of the days Mama called my pain days. I missed her. She would be beside herself with worry.

The curtains were open and lifted in the breeze, I could ignore the stains on them when they fluttered so prettily. The breeze did not smell of the sea, rather of cooking grease and rubbish which has sat too long in the sun. There were marks—smudges and sometimes tears—in the wallpaper, and I imagined how they would have come about. Lovers fighting, men too drunk to stand, children left to occupy themselves while their parents drank downstairs. I must have lain for hours studying the room, noticing the cracks and crevices. I had never been on my own so long. Since I arrived at the Coast as a girl, Mama was always there. She drove me mad at times, but she was there, asking what I needed, and there were the doctors, nurses and attendants, too, and the others in the lazaret. They would be frantic by now, realising we were gone. The police surely had been notified. Dr Stenger would be trying to keep it out of the papers, trying to quell the panic. Here, on the outside, we were pariahs.

A knock on the door made me jump. If it were police, I reassured myself, I would have heard more footsteps. It was a light knock. My voice quavered as I called, 'Come in.'

A scrawny girl opened the door, her apron covered in food stains. 'Would missus like some tea? Your husband said you was laid up and to check on you at noon.'

'Why, come in.' I sat up straight and patted the bed beside me. She looked at me as if I were mad. Perhaps I was. I was not used to strangers.

'I sprained an ankle coming here last night and it's terribly swollen today, so I'm afraid I can't get up to come downstairs. Might I have some food brought up to me?'

She hovered, as though if she got too close to the bed I might reach out an arm and grab her. Where her sleeves were rolled there was a bruise, marks like fingers, on her forearm.

'Would you like me to fetch a doctor to look at it? We have one who sometimes calls. There's a few ladies who stay here that he looks after.'

'Oh no. If I just stay off it for a day I'm sure it will be fine. Now, what is there to eat?'

'They can make you a sandwich, 'am or roast beef. Or there's a plate of cold meats—and a pickled egg.'

'A roast beef sandwich sounds perfect, if it's not too much trouble.'

'Not a'tall. I'll be back in a bit.'

'Thank you—sorry I did not catch your name?'

'Sarah.'

'I'm Alice.'

Sarah ducked her head and hurried out of the room. It made me wonder how bad I must look. If word were to get out that Guy and I were lepers, we would be out on the street in a moment: our dishes smashed, our bedding burned, the room scrubbed cleaner than it had ever been.

•

Guy returned in the early evening. I was dreaming that Agatha discovered her hat missing and came after me, only she turned into a giant peacock, shaking her feathers in aggravation.

*Why, you might make an even better hat with peacock feathers*, I was telling her, when Guy shook me awake.

'Sorry I'm late,' he said. 'Did you eat?'

I nodded, sitting up, my bedclothes crumpled around me. I had meant to look lovely and serene when he returned, not like this. I noticed then his clothes were wet, stuck to his skin, and there were droplets of rain in his lashes.

'Is it raining?' The window had been shut and the curtains drawn while I slept.

'Pouring. I'm surprised it did not wake you. Lightning and everything. Huge cracks. I had to shelter in a tram stop till it was safe to run here.'

'Did you shut the window?'

'No. It was closed when I came in.'

'Sarah must have come and done it. Are you alright?' He looked wan.

Guy pulled a newspaper out of the inside pocket of his jacket. 'Bad news.'

There, on the third page inside, was an article towards the bottom. LEPER LOVERS ABSCOND FROM LAZARET.

'Oh no. Read it to me.' I lay back, gripping the sheets between my fists, trying to calm the rising fear.

'*Two lepers—a light-brown-haired girl of twenty-three, five feet two inches, and a half-caste, twenty-five, five feet nine inches in possession of a wooden leg absconded from the Coast Hospital Lazaret yesterday. Authorities are searching for them in order to bring them back in. It is the law that lepers must be segregated from the rest of the population because of the highly contagious nature of the disease.*'

'What will we do?'

'Not even a man,' Guy said.

'Not hard to spot in a crowd, are we?'

'Let's sleep—you look tired. We can get up at dawn and make a fresh plan.'

I knew neither of us would sleep. We lay together in bed, staring at the ceiling.

'My Aunty Rita died,' he said.

I took him in my arms and felt him soften against me. He'd told me how she had blamed herself when he was taken. 'You must go home.'

'I know,' he said. I waited for him to ask me to go with him, though I knew how impossible it would be. But the words never came.

'My real name's Jack,' he told me, his finger tracing the ruined line of my jaw. 'What about you?'

'Hilda,' I said.

I felt her stir. Maybe she was still there, inside me.

A drop of water from his nose fell on my face. I pulled him closer to kiss.

'Which do you prefer?' he asked.

'Alice. What about you?'

'Jack.'

'I'll call you that then.' I stroked his hair off his forehead.

'I don't want to get you wet. I'll change.'

'Have there been many others?'

'Women?'

'Yes.'

'Just one, in Egypt, a nurse during the war. What about you?'

'You are a darling. Don't change into dry clothes. What do you need clothes for?'

'I guess you missed me then.'

'I did.' I pulled him near.

Things are sweeter when you know they will disappear.

•

Later that night Jack woke me and said I had been crying out in my sleep. The gland was swollen even more, so that it was the size of a cricket ball. I was frightened it would burst, though I had never heard of such a thing. The pain was excruciating.

'Let me take you back,' Jack said.

I shook my head.

I was falling in and out of consciousness then, skating towards delirium, and the thought I might die without Mama struck like a wave and pulled me under.

'Call Dr Stenger,' I managed to say. 'But you go—be with your mother. Don't you dare come back with me.'

Jack was gone the next time I opened my eyes and the room was lit only by a small lamp. I was alone again.

I shut my eyes. I opened them.

There was Dr Stenger.

•

We rode back to the Coast in an ambulance car with a police escort. I lay in the back, on a stretcher, with the doctor beside me. Jack had refused to stay behind. He was on the other side. Dr Stenger lectured us on how reckless we had been.

'It's the public I'm most worried about. You saw the article?'

Jack nodded. 'It's my fault,' he said. 'It was my idea.'

'He's lying. I dragged him along. I am solely responsible for any damage that has occurred.'

Dr Stenger sighed. 'Will you both stop trying to take all the blame? You are each responsible for your own actions, and you both snuck out of the lazaret. I worry more, Alice, that you've done yourself irreparable harm. And you, Guy, have had so many negative smears, but now I worry that Matron Broom may try to make you start over. But I will stop the lecturing. I am sure she will give you a tongue-lashing of her own. And your mother, Alice—Clea's been beside herself.'

'You cannot punish him. I told you, it was my idea. And you must understand why.'

'Why you had to leave?'

'Why we had to try.'

Dr Stenger took my hand in his own. Outside the sky was pink and orange with streaks of dawn, and the soft light made his face look as young as it did when I first came to the Coast as a girl. When I still thought he could save me.

'I do,' he said.

# 32

*Will*

1925

He squeezed Guy's skin between finger and thumb, then made a small cut with a scalpel, no more than a millimetre deep. Tissue fluid oozed as the sides of the incision separated, and Guy flinched, which was a good sign in itself. Patients with more advanced leprosy did not even feel it. Will turned the blade of the scalpel to scrape this fluid on the surface of the blade, and then transferred the fluid to a microscopic slide.

The smears were conducted monthly. In all his time at the Coast, only five patients had been cleared to leave, most recently Clea.

When he was done, he scrubbed his hands at Guy and Jim's kitchen basin. Jim refused to have any more smears, he said: what was the point? They would never be clean.

'I've had ten clean smears, counting the ones from Peel,' Guy said to Will.

'I'm surprised you are in here in the first place. You only ever had one which showed the bacilli.'

'That's more clean than dirty.'

'You were good to come back with her, to look after her.' Will had been fielding calls from the newspapers and Dr Cillen ever since. The papers all wanted to do a piece on the leper lovers. Dr Cillen wanted to shut the lazaret down. Will finally stopped going to the telephone when a call came in for him and studied each envelope he received in case it came from Isaac. But there had been no word from Isaac since he returned to Melbourne. Will did not expect it.

Guy leaned against the small kitchen table.

'I love her, you know. But I have to go home. I know where I belong, and it's not here.'

Will nodded. 'I'm sure Alice understands. She will understand. She wants as much for you.'

Guy's head was lowered. 'How long do you think she has?' he asked.

Will shrugged. 'A year, perhaps two?'

He gathered his instruments to leave.

He was on his way to the next cottage when Ted called his name.

'Clea was looking for you,' he said.

•

Clea stood in her small kitchen. She had an answer, she said, about the smears. She blinked and tears gathered at her bottom lashes.

'I won't leave her. Not again.'

'Very well,' Will said. He had guessed, since the beginning, that she would not.

'You will come in with me and tell her?'

'Lie for you?'

'I will say it, I only need you not to disagree.'

The bedroom was dark. Alice was awake, though, and she held a hand out to Will.

'Why have you come today?' she asked. Her voice was hoarse, hard to hear.

'He was checking on me, Alice,' Clea said. 'You know this was my eleventh smear? It was positive. It has come back.'

'Mama! Is that true? Dr Stenger?'

He sat on the edge of her bed and patted her arm. 'Your mother has had a setback, but it is a small one. You can't let it worry you, Alice. You must think about your own health. Focus on that.'

'What about Guy?' she whispered.

'I have done his smear today.'

'You must let him go, Doctor.'

'I will if I can.' Will stood, needing to be out in the air, away from the perfume Clea had doused herself with. He was weary to the soles of his feet, involved in all of these lives more deeply than his own. His night with Isaac weighed heavily on his mind. What life had he chosen? What purpose did he serve? Slicing and cutting, speaking of what must be done.

Clea walked him out. She paused at the door, her hand on his arm. 'Thank you, Doctor.'

'I thought you said I would not have to lie.'

'I'm sorry.'

He did not like to lie, but he was an expert. He had a lifetime of experience. The problem with lies was that you forgot the truth. Why it was so dangerous in the first place, or if it even was. There was no simple answer. In this case, Clea might nurse Alice, and they could only hope that afterwards she would still be free to go.

'You are a good mother, Clea, in spite of what you think.'

He walked away quickly, the dry leaves crunching beneath his feet. He would not turn back, but he could hear that his words had made her weep.

# 33

*Alice*

There was a story once of a white woman and a black man who fell in love and wished to marry.

She took his blood, the blood that ran red in his veins, and with a syringe she put some of his blood in herself.

They went before a magistrate, then, asking to marry.

'Do you have any black blood in your veins?' the magistrate asked the woman, and she smiled wide in her knowing.

'I most certainly do.'

•

Mama came to fetch me. Jack was on our verandah in a white shirt with the sleeves rolled up, his arms gleaming in the sun. I had been bedridden for two months since we had returned. It did not stop Matron Broom from coming and shouting at me for an hour about bringing bad press to the hospital and being a shameless hussy. Mama had finally ushered her out, insisting I had to rest.

'You'll be in trouble if the Queen catches you here,' I said to Jack, hobbling to a cane chair. We had been banned from seeing one another. I spent my days in bed longing to be back in the hotel with him, in that room with the fluttering curtains, his leg unstrapped and leaning against the bed. Or in the clinker hull, staring up at the sky, his shadow moving above me. But here he was now, on the verandah, and I smiled in spite of the pain I was in.

My nerve pain was sharp—it felt as though every move was through mud, pushing aside some invisible weight. The swollen gland had receded, but my eyes were worse. Dr Stenger said it was iritis, that the nerves in my face had become damaged so I could no longer close my eyes completely. Mama brought out a pot of tea and two cups and saucers, as if I were a normal young woman entertaining a suitor. I had a newspaper cutting about the leper lovebirds being caught that I had clipped to show Jack. There was a quote from Dr Stenger saying that leprosy was not contagious and most of the population had a natural immunity to the disease.

I have worked in close contact with the lazarets at Little Bay for more than twenty years and in that time none of our doctors, nurses or attendants has contracted leprosy.

There was also a quote from the owner of the Lord Nelson, saying he had fumigated the room and burned the bedclothes—he had taken every precaution and spared no cost to rid the place of our taint.

But before I could show him, Jack stood up and pulled a folded letter from his trouser pocket. I could see it had been opened and refolded many times, the creases soft. He was looking down at the wide planks of the verandah. His eyes were light brown, amber in the sun. I could not look too long, or I'd get stuck inside them. He shifted his weight to his real leg.

'Last smear was clean, Alice. Stenger argued my case and Broom is happy to be rid of me. I'm free to go.'

He gave me the page so I could read it for myself, but I could not see the words.

'This is perfect,' I said, setting my face in a fierce smile. 'This is wonderful news.'

'I don't want to leave you, Alice.'

'You will. I will not let you stay.'

I stood and stepped towards Jack, leaning into him, wrapping my arms around his waist. He rested his chin on my scalp and I felt his heart beating close to my mouth. I wanted to feel it beat inside me. I wanted his baby then, even if it would be taken away from me; I wanted him to leave me something. But he had already given me so much. He had seen beyond my ruined skin and deformities; he saw *me*.

And he loved me.

He sat with me for an hour and we filled the silence somehow. He was clear, but he was not afraid to touch me, touch the places where I once had feeling. I pretended I still did. He was leaving but I never would. I knew it, we both did, but he spoke of when I would get my clean smears, how we would be together again. I nodded because the lie was easier than the truth. I kept the article in my pocket. When he left I walked inside, kicking the door as hard as I could. I threw the cutting in the stove. My toes were black for weeks afterwards, but they did not hurt.

Painlessness can break your heart far worse than pain.

•

Jack kissed me for the last time at the hospital gate, with Mama, the matron, Dr Stenger and all who passed by watching. I kept my eyes open while our lips touched; I could not bear to look away. He had a new set of clothes and a train ticket. He had my travelling case: I knew I would never need it again. I kept the silver teaspoon I stole from the hotel wrapped in my shawl, a memento of our escape.

I watched him walk out to the tram shed and wait, his back so straight, his shoulders squared. Mama and I stood until the tram came, and then he waved at me one last time and climbed aboard.

'Goodbye, love,' I called, no longer caring who heard me.

We walked back to the women's lazaret, passing banksia trees, their warty, knobbly bark mocking the growths on my skin. Once inside the gate, I screamed, biting my own nerveless fist. Mama tried to shush me, to hold me, and I fought her, and Nurse Hull even Dr Stenger. I was on the ground. Finally they all left me. Long after the sun had lost its sting I lay there, watching ants make slow trails across my wretched skin.

Hilda betrayed me with her tears.

•

Jack did not leave me with child; he left me with syphilis.

The sores I developed went unnoticed at first, for they were assumed to be from the leprosy. I did draw them to the attention of Dr Stenger, but he did not find them different or strange. But a flat, red rash on the palms of my hands caught his eye one day, months later.

'How long have you had this?'

'It's just come up.'

'Any other new symptoms?'

I shrugged. His eyebrows were low. He drew blood—some days I felt like little more than a pincushion—and later that week told me he had run a Wassermann test and it came back positive. I had syphilis. I was glad we were alone. Sue had gone to take the specimens to the laboratory. Mama was playing cards with Agatha, because I had given up.

'I must have missed the symptoms in Guy. Sometimes people have no external symptoms. I now believe his leprosy diagnosis was mistaken. That would make sense, given how short his stay here was.' Dr Stenger looked up, realising he had been muttering more to himself than me.

'I'm sorry, Alice. You must be terribly upset. I feel somewhat to blame.'

'It was my doing, Doctor.'

I poured him more tea. I could not look him in the eye. I knew that behind his gold-rimmed spectacles his expression would be full of sympathy.

'We do not need to tell the others; we can just adjust your treatment. But I need you to stay celibate.'

'Of course. I'm not—Guy was the only one. Will you tell him?'

'I will write him. He needs to start treatment. Tell me, though, if there are any new symptoms, anything at all. We must keep a close eye on it. And we must hope it does not trigger other reactions.'

I promised. He left, and I studied my palms. The rash was flat, harmless-looking.

Mama walked in the door, and I looked up at her, frowning.

'What's wrong, love?'

'I've got syphilis.'

'That's rotten.' Mama threw herself onto the sofa beside me and poured tea into what had been Dr Stenger's cup. 'It shouldn't kill you, though. What bad luck.' She put her arms around me and held me tight. One good thing about a mother with loose morals is she's not so likely to judge you.

I thought of the nurse in Egypt Jack had mentioned, wondered whether she was the source. I could not hate her, for he would never have been in the lazaret if not for the lesions. Without them, I would have never met him. With or without syphilis, I knew that I was dying.

●

'Syphilis,' Dr Stenger said, 'is problematic because it can exacerbate the symptoms of leprosy.'

'Can you say that in English?' Mama sounded cross. They were both standing in front of the window, blocking the light.

They were blurring, but I had the memory of how they looked only months before. Dr Stenger's soft eyes and his thinning reddish hair. Mama's black knot of hair and her square jaw.

'He means it makes the leprosy worse,' I said.

Dr Stenger was coming more often, spending longer than ever before in our cottage. I knew he was worried. I knew that he blamed himself for my decline. The therapy for syphilis can be poisonous for those with leprosy, so there was not much treatment he could prescribe.

I asked him if there was a danger Jack might have caught leprosy from me, as I caught syphilis from him. I could not bear the thought.

'You mean Guy?'

'Yes.'

'Well, it's certainly a possibility. Though there has to be a susceptibility. And that has been found in Aboriginal patients. I have written him several times but I've not heard back. I will send another letter and tell him to be mindful for symptoms. I imagine he will not be rushing back to the doctor any time soon, though.'

My vision grew worse each day. It was as though my eyes had given up. My feet were bad too, but that was my own doing; I had broken several toes kicking the door and they were healing badly: purple and brown. Dr Stenger worried they would become necrotic. I had lain in bed for several weeks, the pains in my legs and thighs had grown worse. At first, I was there from sorrow, but then my body grew trapped there. The world around me shrank and shrank, until it was the size of a bed. Dr Stenger brought me a cane and encouraged me to try walking with it. At first I merely refused to get up and walk around, but soon I found it impossible. My limbs were wasting. My senses shrivelled like a worm in the sun. All this mattered more to Mama and Dr Stenger than it did to me.

There were others in the lazaret—both during my time and before—who had killed themselves. The stories were there if you sought them. It was whispered of, seen as shameful, but I thought they were the clever ones. Fred, whose sense of humour hid his suffering, had poisoned himself with strychnine; those in the men's lazaret that day had not forgotten his screams. Mama never showed her grief. There was the Chinaman, Ting Lun, who was admitted one day and found hanging from a beam in his cottage the next. I wanted something quick and blanking, like a gunshot, but I did not want a mess for Mama to have to clean. I did not want to gasp and struggle—to fight. I knew pain like the inside of my eyelids, but I had known enough. There was a bottle of Lysol in the cupboard I might drink. There was the ocean, rocks in my pockets, the struggle to stay under.

Mama tried to keep me tethered to the world. She spent her days beside me. Her boyfriends would grow tired of waiting for her, I said, but she told me to shut my trap.

'If you are going to sit there all day at least entertain me,' I said.

She told me stories. Bushranger stories and ghost stories. Nurses who died young at the Coast and still haunted the wards. I had heard them all before, but I was comforted by the dead.

# 34

It was four days' travel to get there. A train as far as Walgett and then the back of a bottle truck. The bottles were encased in straw, but he bounced until his arse was sore. He asked to be let off at the bank of the Narran. The river water tasted earthy and sweet. The Narran was flooding and the coolabah trees were flowering. The river rose beside him, at walking pace. Beneath the cracked ground he could hear the water flowing, coming to the surface. He remembered catching fish at the weir, and the bigger boys catching catfish, carrying them home in sugar bags, mindful of the spikes.

Following the road to the village, he waved away shoals of flies, skirted the Old Bark Pub, Hatfield's General Store. He saw people he recognised, but they did not recognise him. He walked past the Chinese garden, smelling the tomatoes on the vine, that sappy green scent. At the reserve there was the smell of a campfire, of roasted meat, and he was doubled on a horse again, fear rising like dust, a back with sprigs of purple against brown.

At their hut his mother was not alone. He called out from the path and she came to the doorway, crying out so they all came to see, 'Jack's home!'

There was family: his sister Daisy, a woman now. His mother small and withered, the bones on her face sharp. He did not stand back and wait for her embrace. Other hands rubbed his uniform, touched his skin, voices exclaiming over the stump where his leg had once been.

'They said I'm cured,' he said, and his mother shook her head, laughing.

'Don't worry,' she said, 'we got good bush medicine here that will fix you if you're not.'

•

They went inside and the others melted away. His mother brought him a plate of food, a drink. She sat across from him, watching him eat, hands spread on the scrubbed tabletop. Her hands were chapped from years of work.

'How are you?' he asked, between bites. It was a foolish question.

She shook her head. Shrugged. She had lived beside her sister all her life. Jack saw the healing cuts on her arms. Later he would go to Aunty Rita's grave, the painted upright posts decorated with stones, broken glass.

'The river's flooding.'

She nodded. 'They'll be glad at the station.'

'Are you working there still?'

She shook her head. 'Just being a lazy old woman.' But she smiled, and he knew she was busy enough.

'Let me do that,' Jack said when she stood to clear his plate.

'Pshhhh.' She waved her hand. He went outside for a smoke, sitting on a metal chair, still warm from the day's sun. There was rustling in the bushes nearby—perhaps a goanna or a snake—and the warning chirps of birds woken in their nests.

Alice would be in her narrow bed. If the wind blew inland and the window was ajar she might hear the ocean from her bed, water washing the coarse sand. He could see her clearly in his mind.

He turned to watch his mother through the yellow square of window, wiping his plate and cup, finding the place on the shelf where they belonged. The cup was the cup from the Home, which sat now among his mother's dishes, chipped and beaten.

The land was different here; the river had its own way of surprising them. It sat dry for months and then flooded all at once, filling the cracks in the earth. Just when you think the dry will go on forever the rains come, the floods come, the land is green again.

The night grew louder, the frogs pitching their cries, multiplying in the floodplain. He closed his eyes. The noise filled his head, pulsing against temples, the fragile stretched tight drum of his ears. It came in waves like the ocean. Like memories, Jack thought, and their undertow. He would get on with his life. For the sake of them. For the sheer luck of surviving.

The ghosts gathered around in the dark; they were beside him now, rather than in the distant sky. Guy beside him smoking, Alice resting her feet. Aunty Rita with her dice clicking, the gap in her wide smile. Granny sitting cross-legged in the shade, singing. His leg—not the shrapnel-ridden gangrenous one they had amputated, but the healthy strong one, the one which had carried him, told horses where to go. They would be there always, his ghosts, just at the edge of the darkness.

His mother called, her voice that same clear note. He stood up, stretching stiff limbs. It was harder to be home than away, because here was everything he missed; all he'd lost. But he was older, and steadfast now.

'I'm here,' he called back. 'I'm home.'

# 35

*Will*

**1926**

Will opened the pages of his *Medical Journal of Australia* and read a diatribe from a famous leprologist, Cecil Cook. Dr Cook had been to study the patients at the Coast and wrote extolling the benefits of segregation for patients with leprosy.

> What is the explanation of the disturbing fact that in Australia, with every hygienic advantage, a sparse population and purity of race, leprosy after thirty years of compulsory notification and isolation, is increasingly prevalent among Europeans?

Worse, he continued:

During 1909, four lepers were discovered amongst aboriginals at Roebourne, Western Australia, other cases were subsequently found and natives in the district were subjected to periodic medical examination. All lepers were promptly isolated on an island. The result has been the stamping out of the disease in that locality, no case having been reported for some years; I was unable during my survey of the district to detect a leper amongst the natives examined. This would appear to be a striking indication of the efficacy of notification and isolation in the combating of leprosy. Why then has this same procedure failed completely to purge Norway and Australia generally when applied to the more intelligent and less insanitary white population?

What did Cook know of intelligence? Will fumed. Who was Cook to make rules about who could be around whom, which people were superior?

He had been segregated too, Will realised, just like his patients. It had been self-segregation but also a matter of survival.

Will was surprised at how coherently the argument flowed. Finally he would speak out against unjust segregation of his patients. He did not sleep that night, for writing. In the morning there were twenty pages. The next night he cut it down to three. During the day he had moments of terror. Would he lose his position? Perhaps. But he could no longer stand the ignorance.

In his letter to the editor, Will began with the segregation of leprosy patients. To his knowledge, he wrote, it has caused nothing but isolation, secrecy and pain.

Compulsory segregation is now recognised as productive of harm rather than good, since it has been proved to determine concealment of the disease in order to avoid separation from home and family.

Our lazarets should be immediately converted into refuges for patients in the terminal stages of the disease, places where they may find some release from their pain and distress, but they must no longer be prisons into which the patients are cast against their free will. The doors of our lazarets must remain open to receive those who wish to enter and to permit those who wish it to depart. Segregation as a measure for the combating of a chronic disease has been tried and has been found wanting.

Will listed the cases he knew of where patients lived for years outside of lazarets without passing along their illness to anyone at all. The fact that at the Coast none of the attendants, doctors or nurses who frequented the lazarets had ever contracted the disease. He wrote of Father Damien's ill hygiene, how he shared bedding and utensils with leprous patients and was in constant, long-term contact with their open sores. To use him as an example of leprosy's contagion is ridiculous, Will wrote.

The following morning he rushed to get the letter off to the postbox before he could change his mind. Dawn was breaking, it was a grey and drizzly day, and once the envelope was inside the postbox he could do no more. He felt worse than he ought to. Perhaps it was not the answer.

Will had an hour before he was due in the wards; he relinquished his swim for bed. He slept restlessly, dreaming of Isaac swimming in the bay. Watching from the shore, he saw a wave, a freakishly large wave, looming on the horizon. He tried to call to Isaac, to warn him, but his voice was like Alice's, strangled to the point of silence. Almost gone. He woke in sheets damp with sweat, his nerves frayed. Isaac had not written since their night together. Surely he regretted it, as Will regretted his letter. What had he done?

•

Will's letter ran in the *Medical Journal of Australia*. Dr Cillen summoned him to his Macquarie Street office for a meeting and allowed Will to argue his case, but insisted he seek permission next time he took a stand in such a publication.

'Is now a good time,' Will asked, 'to tell you about the editorial they have asked me to write?'

'A doctor's place is not the pulpit,' Dr Cillen said.

'I agree. But we ought to share what we have learned from clinical experience, and *MJA* is hardly a pulpit.'

'Write the editorial, but send it my way first,' Dr Cillen told him.

Will stepped from Dr Cillen's office into the rainy streets of central Sydney, the cobblestones glistening with water, the gutters full and rushing. He did not feel a drop of it. There was something he might do—small though it was—to change the world he had worked in for so long. To give the patients some of what they had lost.

•

At the Coast lazaret, families of patients are allowed to take the bodies of their loved ones when they die, but most chose not to. They are frightened that other cemeteries will refuse them. They are often relieved by the death. The last thing they want is that flesh—the contamination—still on their hands. So the Coast Cemetery has a high proportion of leprosy victims. There is a small, low fence around the graveyard, and inside it is kept mowed. There are dead flowers and chipped glass vases. Graves with Chinese characters, graves with only a few letters and a date. Alice's grandfather's grave says only: *Joe.* Sid is beside him. Will knew that Alice would be buried in that windswept place. Her time was coming soon: cachexia had commenced; her body was wasting away.

Some days he hoped it would come sooner; what did she have to live for? The loss of sight and touch, the deformity and pain were extreme. But he also knew that behind those unseeing eyes, that leonine face and those clawed, stub-like hands she had the same spark of soul he saw when she was a child of nine. The smile that lit her face like a lamp, the innocence she brought to his weary work, the endless-seeming days.

There were no walls that could hold Alice, and no diagnosis that could define her. He wished he had some blood claim; a justification for the grief. He was only her doctor, and a useless one at that. He could not save her.

# 36

*Alice*

Mama helps me to the sitting room in our cottage. Nurse Hull tunes the wireless. Each day we are allowed two ounces of brandy or rum. Sue pours it to the precise line. Mama will give anything for yours if you haven't the need, but I have gained a taste for it, the brief giddy flush, the slippage. The day's pain is muted for a moment, but still it gathers and sharpens, gaining focus where it had been dispersed. And the dark thoughts come with it. As Sue helps me back into bed and changes my dressings, she gives me gynocardate of magnesia, the capsules of chaulmoogra, one-tenth of a grain of strychnine, and a spoonful of jam to allay their foul taste, but still I gag.

Sue never grimaces or gasps. She does not look away. She touches me with both hands, winds the bandages for dressings, asks me what I feel.

'Why do you work here?' I ask tonight, feeling the darkness within me. 'I cannot think of anything worse.'

'They weren't hiring clowns at the circus,' she says.

'I am serious.'

'I like it here. You lot are tough. But I also know what to expect. And I am not so good with blood, or trauma, but I understand leprosy now—and how unfairly the world treats you, the prejudice.'

'People surely treat you that way when they know where you work?'

'I stopped caring. But my parents think I work in a different ward. Diphtheria. They never wanted me to be a nurse.'

'Why?'

'They wanted me to marry. My father said, "The war is over, you'll never be Florence Nightingale."'

'How kind.'

'I know. He was right, in some ways. What is my compulsion to work with those who suffer?'

'Tell me of suffering. I want to hear of someone else's pain.'

She sits back. I know she has small, stubby thick-fingered hands: working hands, with nails that are bitten to the quick.

'There was a nurse here who died last week, did you hear?'

'No. Who was it?'

'May Timms was her name.'

I lay back on the pillow. 'I don't know her. Tell me, though.'

Sue does not mind gossip, and she knows I am desperate. She takes a deep breath and launches into the story. I close my eyes, picturing everything.

May was waiting for a tram into town when the ambulance drivers pulled up. If they were taking an ambulance into town to pick up patients but had an empty ambulance on the way in, nurses might hitch a ride. This ambulance was full with four nurses and the two ambulance workers. May sat in the front on the knee of the second ambulance officer.

I imagined how it would feel, as a grown woman, to sit on a man's knee. The bones of his legs beneath me, his arms encircling my waist. The man became Jack in my head.

But the ambulance skidded, hit a telegraph pole and rolled over. May was thrown out. She died of her injuries.

'What kind of horses were they?' I ask.

'Silly girl, they are motor ambulances now.'

'Of course. Like the one that Jack called for me.'

'Imagine how he feels,' I say, my voice muffled, still picturing Jack, just before he left.

'Lucky to be alive.'

•

I have this old habit of scanning over my body before I sleep. What is numb now, what is aching, what is sloughing away? When I came here aged nine I wanted to scream at the sight of some of the lepers, particularly those in the men's lazaret. Billy with his face a hideous mess of sores, his hands mittens, fingers shrunken to stumps. *I would rather die*, I said, *than look that way*. It is a slow eking of feeling, though. Not as drastic as I thought. I am like a glacier. Bit by bit I melt away.

They are trying a new method, Dr Stenger says; he is corresponding with the American doctors at Carville, a leprosy hospital in Louisiana in the United States. They have had some good results. I listen and nod, for he might try anything now and I would not protest. To feel something I touch it with my lips—the fabric that Mama bought in the mail, the soft feather she found in the garden.

If you were to ask which I missed more, the sense of touch or sight, I would say touch. If I could feel something I might feel the breeze, Mama's hand on my forehead, the warmth of Nurse Hull's body on the edge of the bed. I could remind myself how it was when Jack touched me. If I was able to feel, I could read Braille, so I would not miss my sight so much. I would stroke a dog. Run my hand across silk. Feel the size of a child's hand in my own.

To lose your sense of touch does not mean that the pain goes, for it is still there, living beneath the skin. Deep in the nerves it aches, in the bones and muscle. A pure pain like white ash on the hottest coal.

My voice is nearly gone; it is a hoarse whisper.

There are still things I am glad for. I can hear. There's the gramophone in the Arts Cottage and now—thanks to Dr Stenger—we have our own wireless. Just the other day I listened to Helen Keller on the radio, and she spoke of how if she could choose to see or hear, she would choose to hear, because then people could describe what the world looks like to her. She could then imagine it. I still have that as well. My imagination. Memory.

Sue is with Dr Stenger today. She tells me that he is mixing the heated chaulmoogra oil with a camphor-resorcin solution in order to inject it. My nose is blocked today but still I can taste the chaulmoogra, the heavy rancid cloying smell of the yellow oil.

'It's called Antileprol,' she says, and the name makes me giggle, though it sounds more like I am choking.

'I know,' she says. 'What a stupid name.'

I don't feel them preparing my arm, but the doctor tells me they are. I do not feel the needle but the nerves beneath it ache. Sue speaks in a calm and soothing voice.

'Not long to go,' Dr Stenger says, and it is burning me, like fire.

I hold as still as I can as I feel it spread, flames beneath my skin. Like a snake slithering beneath a sheet. I grit my teeth.

'Does it hurt?' Sue asks.

I shake my head and wait to gather my voice. I think of Helen Keller, living in silence and darkness.

'No,' I say. 'It's fine.'

# 37

*Clea*

Clea did not sleep. She sat beside Alice's bed, angry at Nurse Hull, at Dr Stenger—they all did the wrong thing. Alice needed cold cloths, not hot ones. Small sips of sweetened tea. Nothing was right, nothing that anyone else did was right, so Clea had to stay awake to give Alice what she needed. Clea was the only one who knew. Alice was struggling to breathe and it was awful to watch. Clea wanted to blow the air from her own lungs wholly into Alice's.

When she did finally drift off in a chair beside her daughter's bed she dreamed she took her back into her belly, where her babies once grew. She was safe there, coiled inside Clea like a carpet snake. It was the only place. Clea woke wishing it were true. She would carry Alice—there is not much left of her—and Clea has grown fat in her middle age. She would carry Alice inside and protect her. Clea's stomach could stretch to breaking, her legs could crumble beneath her, as long as Alice was safe.

Her daughter's breathing was so loud, the struggle of getting the air in and out, of being strangled from the inside. So many times Clea has wished she might take Alice's pain as her own. She lay down beside Alice. As a baby, Alice surprised strangers with her beauty. She could stop them with her smile. All that is gone; strangers would shudder to see her.

To Clea, she is more beautiful than anything, than anyone has ever been.

•

She remembered how Olive read the first letter from Jiggi to her in the small cottage at the lazaret. It was the only letter from her ma, and it carried the worst news. Alice had the disease. Clea gave Olive the words to write in reply: *Alice must not come the way I did. You must not let Moffat report her. You must bring her yourself.*

Clea knew she was not the mother Alice hoped for or the daughter Ma wished she would be. But at this place she was free of her ma for the first time, and it was a wonderful thing. To be her own person, with no one criticising her for the way she boiled the water or poured the tea. She had never been able to make Ma happy. It was strange because she did have what she wished for as a girl. She was diseased, but there were small joys. The other women in the lazaret did not tell her she was stupid, and the men were funny and kind. It pleased her to be around men, particularly if they flirted. It was easy to make them happy. It was harder to make Alice happy, but nothing had prepared her for how it was to have Alice with her: the joy only coloured by the pain of seeing her suffer.

She never told Alice what it has meant to have her company, she did not know how. But she would lie curled beside her, hoping until the end to show her.

Clea nestled against her daughter, her hand resting on Alice's ribcage, feeling the shudder, the frail rise and fall.

Each new breath she hoped was not the last.

Or hoped it was.

# 38

*Alice*

I have shrunk now, so small I might fit through the eye of a needle. So small I might finally disappear.

I hear Mama's voice, Dr Stenger's and Nurse Hull's.

I feel beneath me Jiggi Creek, the muddy bottom of it, the suck and silt. To go under, you must shut your mouth. Your eyes. But some things, your ears, your nose, will get water in them anyway. No matter how you try.

I have stolen Gran's hat and I am running running from her, my legs are small but so fast. When I look at the sky it is endless blue the ground blurs beneath. Charlie is red-faced and angry, but I am slippery, so small he cannot hold me.

Jack is there, his leg grown back so he is whole and small like me, and we are running together across the grass, holding hands.

•

I am cold, always cold—maybe it is to do with having shrunk so only a microscope can see me—but Mama piles quilt after quilt on top of me and I hear in her voice how worried she is, how weary this has made her.

When I am gone she will be free.

I want to cut my hair short and wear a dress that falls just to my knees.

To kiss the man I choose and drink whisky by the light of fires.

I want to breathe.

Air.

Free, Mama

I

will be

# Epilogue

*Clea*

**Hornsby, New South Wales**
**July 1967**

It is the last thing she expects, the letter from Dr Stenger.

Dear Clea,

I hope this finds you well, and I apologise for the belated-
ness of my birthday wishes. Did you think you would live
to see eighty? And how the world has changed.

Changes are underway here as well. Prince Henry
(formerly our Coast) has become a teaching hospital for
the University of New South Wales, and there is much
in the way of construction and demolition. Because of the
sulphone drugs, those with what we now call Hansen's

303

disease have been moved into the Tropical Medicine
Pavilion, and the lazarets are to be burned. I think that the
hospital would like to forget that dark corner of history.
Our medical men hope never to acknowledge that for a
barely infectious disease, they thought it worthwhile to
imprison innocent people and lock them away for life.

I think still of Alice, of the bravery and spirit she
showed in the all-too-brief life she lived. I am retired, but I
still volunteer in the Tropical Medicine ward. I have a soft
spot for those patients who are ravaged by Hansen's. It is
no longer a death sentence, but it is still approached with
equal amounts of ignorance and prejudice.

I wonder—forgive me if this is out of place, no need
to reply if it is—if you would be interested in coming to
watch them burn the lazarets? A few of us associated
with the place are going to be there. Not out of joy, or
celebration, but because we all spent such a long time
there, and because of the memories attached. We will
gather in recognition. To say goodbye.

If you can come, it will be Wednesday the thirteenth of
July at nine in the morning, and I would be happy to pick
you up (I know you live across the bridge these days, but
I still drive, despite my age). Though I understand if the
prospect is too much. I am not quite sure how I will find
it myself.

With love,
Dr Will Stenger

•

Clea is awake most of the night, old stories coming back to haunt her. By the time the doctor rings the bell her eyes feel sore already from the light of day. If it were a normal day she would go back to sleep in her recliner beside the oil heater and the radio, her simple comforts. Hunter bought her the tiny flat in a level block of six, all occupied by elderly people with not many needs or much rubbish to fill their bins. He lives only a few minutes away, having sold the land at Jiggi years ago and moved to the city with Jane when their children left home. When the sulphones came, Promin and Dapsone, Clea took them to be sure. The leprosy was gone then, but she wanted to keep it at bay. Clea left the lazaret not long after Alice died, but Dr Stenger still made sure she had the drugs.

He said she needed to find something to stay alive for, to keep her busy. What he did not say was something to stay sober for, but that was true as well.

Clea ignored him for a long time. She woke in strange beds more times than she could count, after nights in pubs where the lights were dim enough that no one could see the scars. But the numbness of thought from desire was gone. Her mind stayed, hovering above, recalling Alice, demanding too much of her. One morning Hunter showed up hours before she would normally be out of bed and took her to the library, to a free adult education class in literacy. A woman as old as she was, learning to read: what a ridiculous thing! But no one laughed. It took a long time; she was too old, she kept saying. But Hunter would say that was rubbish. 'For Alice's sake,' he said. 'She loved her books.'

Clea worked harder than she had ever worked. Ma's voice stayed in her head, saying she was too stupid to learn. The first thing she read aloud was a children's reader they gave out in class. *The cat sat on the mat*—that sort of thing. She was not going to waste a lifetime of not being able to read on those. The next book she read aloud was Alice's copy of *Alice's Adventures in Wonderland*. It did not bring her daughter back, but her brittle shell, as stiff and fragile as the spine in that old book, cracked a little. Her head ached behind her eyes. The breeze felt softer than it had in years.

Clea now has a subscription to *The Star* out of Carville Hospital in Louisiana, a magazine a patient named Stanley Stein started in the 1940s, which is working to change the perception of leprosy. They have convinced the world to call it Hansen's disease. Carville is where, in the 1940s, Dr Faget first began using the Promin injections. Only six patients volunteered and the results were hard to believe. Clea has seen it in person, the way the lesions recede, the ulcers disappear. The bones which were resorbed do not grow back, but there are prostheses, even plastic surgery, offering noses and hands and feet for those who have lost theirs. Clea had surgery on one of her hands which was clawed, but the scars on her face just combined with the ravages of age. It took years for the drugs to come to Australia. Dr Stenger had fought to bring them over, insisting his patients should have access to them and that leprosy should no longer be considered a terminal disease that saw patients isolated for life.

Carville is a hospital for the whole of the United States: they have as many as four hundred patients. They have their own school, a nine-hole golf course, tennis courts and baseball diamond. They have a lake to fish or boat in and cottages for the patients who marry. And at Carville, patients are free to leave.

The first letter Clea ever wrote was to *The Star*. In it, she detailed the treatment of patients in Australia and described the laws of segregation which had been so slow to change. She had not realised that seeing her name in print would bring such joy. She had not thought that kind of happiness still possible.

•

Clea opens the door to Dr Stenger and thinks, *He looks as old as I do*. His red hair is gone, his loose skin pleats at his neck. They kiss dry cheeks with wrinkled lips and she holds his elbow as they walk to the car, the kind a retired doctor ought to drive, a shiny black Mercedes. Another man steps out of the passenger seat as Dr Stenger ushers Clea over. He holds out his hand.

'This is my friend, Isaac,' Dr Stenger says. 'He's coming along today as moral support.'

'Pleased to meet you.' And she shakes the man's hand—he is as old as them—and looks into his warm brown eyes.

'Likewise.'

Clea tries to protest that he should stay in the front seat, but he is quicker to climb into the back. Dr Stenger shuts the passenger door with a solid click, and Isaac puts his hand on Clea's shoulder from the back seat. She does not trust her neck to turn back and look him in the eye, so she glances at the rear-vision mirror.

'It is so good to meet you,' Isaac says. 'Will has talked about you often. What an honour to accompany you both today.'

She nods, keeping silent. There is no honour, she wants to say—only silence and shame.

Dr Stenger slides into the driver's seat, clapping his hands together to warm them.

'Let's get the heat on full,' he said, adjusting the dials. 'Are you warm enough, Clea? Let me know if there's anything you need.'

'So comfortable, Dr Stenger.'

'Please call me Will.'

The two of them try their best to keep the conversation light on their way south, driving across the Sydney Harbour Bridge with the morning rush-hour traffic and the glints of light hitting steel. Clea is lost in a rabbit hole with Alice, the life she might have lived. They drive and drive, and Dr Stenger puts a hand on her arm and Clea realises she has not heard his question.

'Pardon?' She blinks, surprised at the wetness of her eyes.

'I was saying I've not heard from Guy—have you?'

'No.'

'I've tried to find him but haven't had any luck. I worry, sometimes, that he ended up catching it from Alice, in the end, and took it back to Angledool. They were moved to Brewarrina in 1936, all of Angledool, on the back of government trucks in the middle of the night. There were some cases of sandy blight, supposedly, and so the Aboriginal Protection Board razed all their houses, the entire mission.'

'That's awful,' Clea says, and the car is silent.

'I wrote to the manager at Brewarrina, but he had no record of Guy.'

'Remember when they ran off? I nearly died of worry.'

'And they called us to rescue them from that hotel.'

'Oh, I was furious!'

They are past the prison then, on Anzac Parade, out at Little Bay, and it is all so different. The hospital is shiny modern buildings and pathways linking the glass and steel. Only a few cottages remain—they look so small and derelict beside the new buildings.

Clea swallows. They drive down the narrow road towards the sea, passing the tall, elegant pines, what were once the doctors' cottages, the gardens, the bob-a-day men's bunkhouses.

Dr Stenger pulls onto the verge, tyres biting gravel. 'We'll have to walk. It's no longer a road from here.'

The two men flank Clea, in their smart woollen coats and scarves, their closely cropped hair. It comes to Clea, why it is that the doctor never married. She takes Will's hand, and Isaac's. How funny after all these years to realise. She wants to kiss them both. More than anything she wishes she might tell Alice.

She notices the fire trucks then, three of them, parked alongside the boundary with hoses unspooled. A small cluster of people, some in medical uniforms, stand at a safe distance from the enclosure. There are bulldozers parked in the distance which will come through afterwards and clear the charred remains.

'The women's lazaret will be first, then the men's,' Will says, leading Clea towards the cluster.

Two of the firefighters spread fuel through the lazaret, and there are sandbags at the edges, as well as more firefighters in their uniforms with hoses at the ready. Clea closes her eyes for a moment, smelling the sea as it has always smelled from here, the eucalypts and pine, a catch of carbolic still beneath it all.

Eyes shut she sees Fred in the firelight, his kind eyes, his knuckles on the oars of the boat. Alice as a girl in her travelling dress, unknowing. How she ran—oof—into Clea's stomach, sensing some kind of safety there. The fear Clea felt—for how would she protect her daughter? For so long all of her memories of the Coast were of Alice's deterioration, her slow death. She had forgotten the happiness. They made their own lives, despite being locked away. The rest of the world rejected them, but they continued to live.

Clea opens her eyes to shouts and whistles. Someone has lit the trails of fuel. The place goes up with a *whoomph* and a vast crackling. When fire destroys it does so from the outside in. Only when the wind has fanned the flames does it eat the heart. The heat makes them all squint, their faces glow. Clea is in her small bed, cradling Alice's ruined head in her arms as her daughter takes her last breath.

How it still aches.

Clea knows that she killed Elma—all her life she has only caused harm. And yet Alice needed her. They came to need one another. Alice forgave her for leaving. Alice taught her to love. The years have not softened the loss, but she would rather the grief than nothing. Pain is preferable to nothing.

The buildings collapse one by one in the blue-orange haze of heat and the firefighters begin to hose the perimeter. There is wet white ash and black char now. Her father's hut. The crowd that came to watch. Standing in the smoke and shame. Twice now others have burned her history. The proof her family existed once, as prisoners of their own disease. They have rid themselves of the evidence of their own cruelty.

She covers her mouth, holding the past in her lungs.

Alice is curled inside her, a coil of smoke; smouldering.

The Lazaret compound had an air of mystery, a tiny village nestling in a hidden gully by the sea. We never went into the Lazaret but would pass it when climbing around the rocks. I was not at the hospital the day it was put to the torch, I only saw the charred ruins before they were bulldozed flat. There was a feeling of loss, the Lazaret had always been part of the hospital but the bright side was that Hansen's Disease sufferers did not need to be isolated from the community any more.

DEANNE LESLEY CHAD (MRS NEVILLE), *NURSES AT LITTLE BAY*

# Acknowledgements and Sources

This book was written and set on the country of the Gadigal and Bidjigal people who traditionally occupied the Sydney coast. In Angledool, it is set on the country of the Yuwaalaraay and Gamilaraay people. I pay my respects to their elders and storytellers past and present and I am grateful for their continuing custodianship of the land and water.

The idea for *The Coast* came when I was researching my second novel, *Long Bay*, and visited the Prince Henry Hospital Museum. This small museum is run by volunteers from the Prince Henry Hospital Trained Nurses Association, including the very helpful Lyn Smith OAM, and in one exhibit I came across photographs of the lazarets at Little Bay. That this quiet, idyllic suburb to the south of Sydney was a leprosy colony at the turn of the twentieth century came as a shock, and I began to wonder how the people trapped with this highly stigmatised disease lived in isolation. I finished writing *The Coast* during the COVID-19 pandemic, and that certainly helped me consider the continuing repercussions of stigmatising illness and the long-term effects of isolation.

I never would have been able to write this book without the advice and feedback from Yuwaalaraay reader Nardi Simpson and Gamilaraay and Yuwaalaraay reader Frances Peters-Little. Their connections to Angledool and their interrogations into Jack's character helped me a great deal. I'm immensely grateful for their insight.

Visiting Angledool was possible because of the kindness of Helen Williams and Aunty Brenda McBride. Their generosity and tour-guiding skills were legendary and I'm forever grateful to Sharon Quill for making the connections. In Lightning Ridge my thanks go to Cindy Brown Schuler for showing me around the Goondee Keeping Place. Her parents, Uncle Roy and Aunty June Barker, curated an amazing collection of artefacts and photographs of local Indigenous history.

My thanks also to the Gujaga Foundation in association with the La Perouse Aboriginal Land Council for reading this manuscript. La Perouse, home of the original inhabitants of the Coastal Sydney region, is just down the road from the former Coast Hospital at Little Bay.

Researching Hansen's Disease took me many places, but early on it was the assistance of David Russell, librarian at the History of Medicine Library at the Royal Australasian College of Physicians, which led me to the records that inspired this story.

Visiting Peel Island in Moreton Bay was another crucial part of my research and I would like to thank Dr Hugo Rée, the Friends of Peel Island, and Queensland Parks and Wildlife Service Ranger Dan Crouch (along with Jimmy and Mick) for their assistance and information. My tour of Peel Island was a remarkable experience and convinced me I had to include its history in my novel. The Neilma Sidney Literary Travel Grant from Writers Victoria allowed my trip to Peel Island to proceed and I'm grateful for the opportunity. Peter Ludlow's histories of Peel Island were helpful in my research and it was Kate Evans who first told me of the island's existence.

The Richmond River Historical Society in Lismore was a wonderful repository of Northern Rivers history. Jarrah Dundler shared some of his local knowledge.

In Carville, Louisiana, I had the luck of encountering Elizabeth Schexnyder, curator of the National Hansen's Disease Museum. Her insight into the history of Carville was so helpful, as were the museum's archives on the history of Hansen's Disease. Elizabeth also read a draft of this manuscript.

Completing this book was possible because of the Blake-Beckett Trust Scholarship from the Australian Society of Authors. I'm incredibly grateful to Wendy Beckett for her generous gift of this scholarship. My writing and editing gained focus from two alumni residencies at Varuna the Writers House and I was buoyed by the other writers there, the wonderful people who run Varuna, and the family of Eleanor Dark.

Early readers Poppy Gee (who also gave me this title), Ashleigh Synnott and Dr Henry Paolini (who worked at Prince

Henry Hospital in the 1960s) were so important. Thank you Celia Paolini for roping your father in.

My mother, Nancy Limprecht, and sister, Alma Klein also read drafts—I'm glad to have such eagle-eyed readers in my family. My workshop group and author Bret Anthony Johnston at the VQR Summer Conference in 2019 helped me in the early stages of this novel. My own writing students and colleagues at UTS inspire me constantly with their creativity, clever conversation and willingness to try new things.

Thank you to my publisher, Jane Palfreyman, and my agent, Grace Heifetz, for believing in me and indulging my unusual obsessions. Ali Lavau is the world's best structural and copy editor. Tom Bailey-Smith was instrumental in making this book the best it could be. Pam Dunne did an excellent proofread and Nada Bakovic designed a stunning cover. I'm overwhelmed by the kindness of Mirandi Riwoe, Suzanne Leal and Meg Keneally for reading *The Coast* and for their thoughtful words.

Finally, my family: Jupiter for taking me on walks; Eliza and Sam are too old to be excuses not to write, now they inspire me with their sharp wit and adolescent angst. They've taught me that it is worse to witness your children in pain than to suffer your own. Simon, thank you for reading, listening, supporting and giving (even building) me space to write. I could not have asked for a better life companion.

•

'Heritage of Woe: Lismore's Record in Leprosy Cases' from the *Mullumbimby Star*, 16 April 1925, p. 6 [p. 62]

Carroll, Lewis. *Alice's Adventures in Wonderland,* Macmillan, London, 1865, pp. 1–2, 8 [p. 87]

Rée, Gerald Hugo, *Loathsome no Longer*, Historical Society of the Northern Territory Darwin, 2015, pp. 116–117 [p. 161]

Cordia, Maylean, *Nurses at Little Bay*, Prince Henry Hospital Trained Nurses Association, Sydney, 1990, pp. 19–20 [p. 179–180]

Keats, John, 'The day is gone, and all its sweets are gone!', 'Ode To Psyche' in *Poetical Works of John Keats*, Cromwell, London, 1895 [pp. 182, 226]

Cook, Cecil, 'Leprosy in Australia', *Medical Journal of Australia*, 27 September 1924, pp. 336–337 [p. 287–288]

Molesworth, E.H., 'The Leprosy Problem', *Medical Journal of Australia*, 18 September 1926, pp. 365–381 [p. 289]

The letter from Dr Stenger to the *MJA* and his attitude of care for the patients is based in part on that of Dr E.H. Molesworth, who was the medical officer in charge of the lazaret at Little Bay for twenty-five years.